MALINCHE

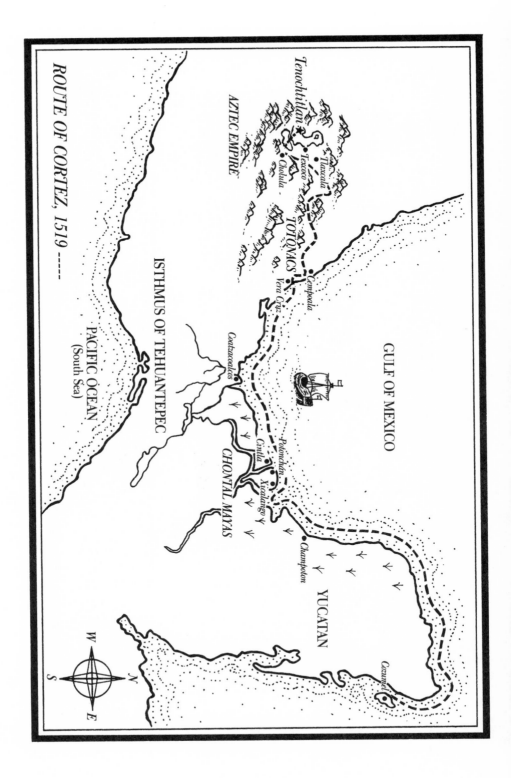

ROUTE OF CORTEZ, 1519 ‒‒‒‒

Tenochtitlan

AZTEC EMPIRE

Tlaxcala

Texcoco

Cholula

TOTONACS

Cempoala

Vera Cruz

GULF OF MEXICO

ISTHMUS OF TEHUANTEPEC

Coatzacoalcos

PACIFIC OCEAN
(South Sea)

CHONTAL MAYAS

Cintla

Potonchan

Xicalango

Champoton

YUCATAN

Cozumel

W N
S E

MALINCHE

Slave Princess of Cortez

by Gloria Durán

LINNET BOOKS 1993

First published 1993 as a Linnet Book, an imprint of
The Shoe String Press, Inc.,
Hamden, Connecticut 06514.

Library of Congress Cataloging-in-Publication Data

Durán, Gloria
Malinche, slave princess of Cortez / by Gloria Durán.
p.   cm.
Summary: A biography of La Malinche, the Aztec noblewoman
who served as translator, interpreter, and mistress
to Cortez during the Spanish conquest of Mexico in 1520.
1. Marina, ca. 1505-ca. 1530—Juvenile literature.
2. Mexico—History—Conquest, 1519–1540—Juvenile literature.
3. Indians of Mexico—Biography—Juvenile literature.
4. Cortés, Hernán, 1485–1547—Juvenile literature.
[1. Marina, ca. 1505-ca. 1530. 2. Aztecs—Biography.
3. Indians of Mexico—Biography.
4. Cortés, Hernán, 1485–1547.] I. Title.
F1230.M373D87   1993   92-31776
ISBN 0-208-02343-7 (alk. paper)

The paper used in this publication meets the
minimum requirements of American National Standard
for Information Science—Permanence of Paper
for Printed Library Materials,
ANSI Z39.48—1984. ⊗

Printed in the United States of America

This book is dedicated
to my granddaughter, Leah Durán,
my husband, Manolo Durán,
and my editor, Diantha Thorpe.

Contents

To the Reader

I wrote *Malinche, Slave Princess of Cortez* because for my students the story of Malinche has always been the most exciting part of Latin American history. For Mexican students, however, Malinche, the Aztec woman who made the conquest of Mexico possible, has long been considered a traitor. Did she betray her people or did they betray her? This is the question I deal with in the second part of this book. I base it in part on native sources, but largely on the documentation provided by Bernal Díaz del Castillo's *True History of the Conquest of New Spain*. This fascinating work by one of the conquistadors covers the seven years that the Indian chieftain's daughter spent as mistress and interpreter of Cortez. Very few changes have been made here from the historical record as Díaz presents it, although events are related from La Malinche's viewpoint, rather than the Spaniards'.

Since Bernal Díaz deals with Malinche's early life—before she was given to Cortez—in only a few paragraphs, the first section of the book relating her childhood and adolescence necessarily falls within the realm of fiction. But it is fiction informed by historical and anthropological sources. There is also heavy deduction from the few hints given us by Bernal. Apart from some memorable quotations preserved by historians, the dialogues throughout the book are, of course, invented.

For historical details where there is disagreement among authorities, I have chosen the version of her life that fits more closely my own understanding of her personality and her situation. For example, with respect to the question of whether Malinche had one or two children by Cortez, or the age at which she died, I have accepted the position of Henry Wagner in his *The Rise of Fernando Cortez.*

I suspect that my own view of Malinche has been shaped by the ideas of both Carlos Fuentes and Octavio Paz, who are far more charitable to her than the majority of their countrymen. Many years ago the recent Nobel Prize winner, Paz, said it was time for a reappraisal of the role of La Malinche. I can only hope that this book makes a small contribution in that direction.

I wish to acknowledge my thanks for the help provided by Dr. Michael Coe of the Departments of Anthropology and Archeology at Yale University and by Dr. George Whitney, veterinarian in Orange, Connecticut.

Malinali

ONE

The Birth of a Princess

*T*eteotcingo, *a royal and learned prince of Aztec society,* had consulted many astrologers about the future of his heir-to-be. Most of the soothsayers foretold that the child would become a brave and handsome prince who would someday live in the great citadel of Tenochtitlan and rule the entire Aztec empire. He had sacrificed to all the gods for nine moons that this should come to pass. But perhaps he had forgotten one of the idols. Or perhaps his sacrifices had displeased them. He had not ordered the death of any slaves. He had offered them only a deer he had himself killed in the hunt, an iguana, and rabbits and quails for the lesser idols. Perhaps this was why his long awaited first born turned out to be a girl!

At first he could not believe it. Cimatl, his wife, could hardly look at him. She lowered her eyes and wept. Teteotcingo comforted her as best he could. "Do not turn pearls to ashes, my love. She is only the first. Another day a son will come."

But the celebration had been planned. He could not cancel it and disappoint his many loyal subjects who had come from the surrounding villages. So his warriors continued to beat the kettle drums that boomed for miles away in the jungle, and the musicians piped shrilly on their bone and wooden flutes. The men, painted in many colors and adorned with green quetzal feathers, began their dance of celebration, circling around the shame-faced mother and child. Great bonfires were lighted and whole deer put to roast on spits. The sisters and relatives of Cimatl brought out enormous earthen jars of *pulque*, a beer-like fermentation made of maguey, so that in short order the dancers became very tipsy. Some of them leapt over the fire, singeing their feathers, but seemed to feel no pain. As the night wore on they consumed hundreds of tortillas filled with succulent meat of the wild pig, drank more pulque from the gourd ladle, and chanted praises to the baby princess.

The celebration continued until dawn, but not all those present were equally joyful. When the sun rose like a red ball in the eastern sky, the priests of Huitzilopochtli and of Tezcatlipoca appeared. They wore black garments stained with dried blood and their uncombed hair nearly covered their eyes. They walked in stiff military fashion up to Teteotcingo and thundered at him with their foul breath.

"How do you dare insult our great sun god and our god of night by celebrating the birth of a daughter? Do you think that they will permit a woman to rule over warriors? Rest assured that our lord at Tenochtitlan, the great Moctezuma, will hear of this. He will never allow this woman-child to wear your crown of feathers. You have brought this disgrace upon yourself by your impious behavior. Why did you not sacrifice slaves as we instructed?"

Yet before the unhappy Teteotcingo could find the words to reply, he felt the familiar touch on his shoulder of another priest, the fat little man from the temple of Quetzalcoatl, the god of the morning star and of the wind. Teteotcingo now realized that he had been there in the crowd ever since the morning star had announced the new day. Although the priest was wearing his red and white wind mask, Teteotcingo recognized his little voice, so feeble for the messenger of a wind god.

"Do not listen to these enemies, mighty prince. Be content with the blessing that Quetzalcoatl has given you. Your child will be greater than Moctezuma. Do not fear him. But take care that she serves Quetzalcoatl according to his laws. Although a ruler, she must not forget how to weave fine cloths and feathers. She must have both the virtues of woman and man, piety and courage, humility and strength. Then will Quetzalcoatl, the morning star, guide her through her journey on earth and give her a place beside him in the heavens."

The high priests in black made no attempt to control their indignation as they listened in shocked disbelief to these words. One of them snarled like the jaguar god Tezcatlipoca. Another raised his arms like a vulture about to take flight, and spat at the ground beside the helpless infant.

The fat priest of Quetzalcoatl, however, did not even look at them. Instead he consulted his soothsaying calendar again and decreed that the little princess was to be called Malinali, "dead grass," for the month of her arrival, and Tecpatl, or "flint," the name of the twelfth day of the month when she was born. "She has come at an excellent moment," he said to her father, Teteotcingo, "and now you must greet her with your song of praise." This was necessary since Quetzalcoatl was also the god of music and poetry, and those who worshipped him were bound to do his bidding.

For Teteotcingo this was not difficult. Although he was not a poet of the caliber of the great poet-king of Texcoco, like most Aztec chieftains, or *tecuhtlis,* he composed poetry on special occasions. He had been trained to do this when he was very young, just as he was trained to shoot an arrow or string a bow. Now, though the heir was a girl, he determined to call forth his best efforts. And the poem that he found himself chanting to the infant was something like this:

"You are my creation, my pearl, my jewel,
  My flower of feathers,
  Blown by Quetzalcoatl, born to light my days.
  Yet know, Malinali, that the flower withers,
  The grasses die, the sunset greys.

"You are dropped by the Giver of Life, oh my daughter,
  As a seed in the forest, a season to grow.
  Your eyes will seek sunlight, your roots will seek water,
  And you, Malinali, all this you must know.

"Think you not, as you listen to music and laughter,
  As your mother, Cimatl, holds you to her breast,
  That the flute that you hear will sing in the hereafter,
  That this land is a garden of pleasure or rest.

"I die, you die, earth dies each season.
  We are moments, and the earth is only a year,
  And the fog in the forest, it too has its reason:
  It is born from the well of century's tears.

"Yet still must we live, my flower, my essence,
  You must learn of your tasks in the years to come—
  For the will of the gods is made known in your presence
  And the will of the gods must always be done."

Teteotcingo might have gone on with this poem, but his words froze on his lips as he saw the tallest of the three angry priests fixing his evil eye on the princess. That piercing black eye was all that could be seen of the priest's features, covered as they were by his blood-clotted hair. As if to protect his daughter from any evil spell, he snatched her from Cimatl's arms and wrapped his warrior's cape around her.

Teteotcingo knew that he must prepare her for life now in earnest; the time for poetry had passed. Perhaps it would return again some day. But from this minute forth she must be strong and brave as a man, since she would have many enemies. Yet to honor Quetzalcoatl, she would also have to learn the arts of weaving, cooking, and all the skills required of women. In return for the god's protection, she must serve Quetzalcoatl all her life. Like any noble Aztec, she must never be proud, never slothful. All this he whispered to the infant whom he still cradled lovingly in his cloak, even after her sworn enemies had stomped away, angrier than when they arrived.

"You must learn to take up your broom and sweep by the light of the moon, Malinali. You must never succumb to slumber," Teteotcingo gently warned the little princess, whose eyes were already trying to close. "Little Malinali, my quetzal feather, you must never fear the jaguar of night for you will have the morning star as your guide. Remember this and you will pass through the forest of life without fear or terror."

Did she understand her father's words? Teteotcingo was sure that she had understood. And so the education of Malinali began, though she was still less than a day old.

TWO

Children and Gods

*T**he town of Painala, where Malinali was born, was eight* leagues or some twenty-four miles from the city on the gulf of Mexico known as Coatzacoalcos. Painala was one of the new Aztec outposts in the Isthmus of Tehuantepec, which separated Mexico from Central America. The town was a bustling center of commerce for it stood at the meeting point of two branches of the sinuous river, which was also called Coatzacoalcos, which means in the Aztec language "the sanctuary of the serpent."

Malinali was to remember how the canoes laden with beads of copal had their precious burdens transferred to the porters of her village, who in turn bore them part of the way to distant Tenochtitlan. There they would be burned as incense for the gods. Many of the canoes held tribute which her father Teteotcingo was required to inspect and record on a long scroll which he could later show to Moctezuma's overseers. Even rulers like Teteotcingo were required to do service to the distant crown, or the tribute that they themselves received could be taken away.

Besides copal, the canoes carried sea shells, jaguar skins, deer skins, peppercorns in sturdy baskets, bundles of brilliant feathers of the parrot and the quetzal bird, cacao beans to make frothy chocolate drinks, ladles made of tortoise shells to stir the chocolate, balls of rubber, quills filled with gold dust, pottery, and *quachtli*, beautifully woven cotten cloths which the women of each village embroidered according to patterns handed down through the ages. These were the canoes Malinali saw most often. But every eighty days there were special shipments; at these times the artisans sent their assigned tribute of precious jewelry worked in gold with incrustations of jade, amber, and turquoise, and beautiful feather mosaics to adorn the emperor and his most important warriors. Sometimes there were also shipments of slaves.

Every man, woman and animal—even the insect world of the Aztec empire—worked for the great master who dwelt beyond the volcanoes. It was to the capital of Tenochtitlan city that the porters brought their calabashes full of red dye from the cochineal bug. The scarlet cloaks worn at court, even the red dyed teeth of the prostitutes in Tenochtitlan, were all made possible by the busy little insect in the nopal tree.

But Malinali could not imagine when she was only three or four years old where all these precious gifts were going. All she knew then was that they seemed to be the property of her father and that all the people in the canoes treated him with the greatest of respect. She saw them bow low when they addressed her father and never look at his face. This was the proper attitude for subject peoples. Yet she did not understand the words they were saying. She had no idea that they were speaking another language, that of the Tabascans and the Mayas, very different from her own Nahuatl tongue.

They all wore only the *maxtlatl*, the loin cloth, to cover their sinewy bodies. There was no one with a *tilmatli*, or cloak, such as her father's. Even the other Aztec lords did not possess such a splendid garment. Teteotcingo's cloak was of two shades of blue, with silver circles, and had a fringe of dyed red rabbit hair. The softness of the fringe seemed wonderful to her touch.

Malinali was not permitted to go with her father down to the riverside except on special holidays. Then, her little hand in his, the tall, smiling child with red ribbons entwined in her shining black braids, and the elegant warrior in his blue cloak would make their way through narrow, winding paths, under a canopy of trees that almost excluded the sun. They would pass stocky old women, some of them in their doorways, grinding corn on their three-legged stones called *metates*. Younger women would pass them balancing on their heads the heavy jugs of water that they had fetched from the river. There would also be other, darker, children running beside them, playing or trying to be helpful. But Malinali, as the daughter of Teteotcingo, the lord, was never allowed to join them.

Most of her early childhood she spent indoors with her mother, Cimatl, in their house at the village center. The house was made of a pinkish-orange clay with a high gabled thatched roof, like all the other houses, except that it was much larger and included servants' quarters. Ventilation was provided by doors and windows facing each other. There was a central courtyard, or patio, where the meals were prepared, and bedrooms and workrooms around it.

In a sunny room at the back of the house Cimatl spun her cotton into thread, using a spindle and a clay whorl that turned on a half-gourd. On her simple loom, which was attached to a beam of the doorway, she also wove the lengths of cloth to be sent as gifts to Moctezuma. All the while Malinali squatted silently and watched her mother at work. Someday she would be just as skillful at the loom and the spindle. There was no thought of play. The closest she came to a toy was the small broom of reeds that she used to sweep the dirt floor of her bedroom every night.

At first there were no other children in that sprawling house, which could never throw off the moist embrace of the rain forest close by. Malinali's only companion was a pet monkey, Chitl, an orphan whom Teteotcingo had found in the jungle crying beside the dead body of his mother. Against his own better judgment, Teteotcingo had brought the animal home, and Malinali immediately began to mother it. She shared her ration of a single maize cake — which was all children of her age were permitted to eat — with Chitl, until Teteotcingo saw fit to provide the hairy little creature with a daily banana. Her mother insisted that Chitl be tied to a large coconut palm so that he would not get into the kitchen and help himself to tortillas, turkey eggs, or any of the fruit he could find there. But at night Malinali untied the animal, and he slept beside her on the little *petatl*, the straw mat which she spread on the floor of her room. Cimatl did not approve. She often complained to her husband that it was unsafe to keep the animal, that he was growing too large, and that he was certain to bite someone someday. But Teteotcingo could not bear to take the pet creature away from his daughter.

When Malinali was about seven, a distant cousin of her father's came to visit from the great capital city of Tenochtitlan and brought with him a little daughter. Although this man, Atlaua, was still young—in fact, several years younger than Teteotcingo—his wife had died, and their child, Metzli, was now motherless. Atlaua proposed that Metzli move into the home of the chieftain and be a companion for Malinali. He pointed out that Malinali seemed awkward with other children, that she appeared happy only with the monkey, and that no Aztec maiden should grow up without knowing the friendship of her peers.

Metzli was much shorter than Malinali even though she was a year older than her cousin, but she was very sophisticated. She had already been to the Telpochcalli, which was one of the two leading schools in Tenochtitlan. There she had been taught to serve and fear the gods, especially Tezcatlipoca, in whose honor the school had been founded. As a girl, she was also taught to spin, to weave, and to obey without question the warrior who would someday be her husband. In addition, she had learned much history and theology, and these she communicated with great authority to Malinali.

Although Malinali knew in a general way that there had been four different worlds and four different suns before the one that now lit the sky, her idea of the world corresponded largely to what she had been told by the priests of Quetzalcoatl. According to them, the Plumed Serpent, as the god was often called, went down to the land of the dead to gather the bones of long past generations, watered them with his own blood, and so created the present world. But Metzli asserted that this was not so and that she, as a learned person, could explain what really happened.

"If your priests had taught you any history of our people, Malinali, you would know that Tezcatlipoca, the lord of death, who is also the Great Bear of the night sky, made the first sun and the first world and that the men in it were giants. But silly Quetzalcoatl was jealous of this wonderful world and struck Tezcatlipoca a blow with his walking stick, so that Tezcatlipoca fell into the water and became a jaguar."

"Don't you insult Quetzalcoatl or I won't listen," said Malinali, suddenly remembering one of her mother's stories. She hastened to show Metzli that she was also familiar with Aztec theology. "Then your Tezcatlipoca in revenge ate up all his own giants, and there was no one left on earth. After this Quetzalcoatl became the new sun and made brand new people. You see, I knew it all already."

"That may be true, but Tezcatlipoca finished the new

people off with a blow of his claws. He was always the stronger."

"Well, then Quetzalcoatl raised up a great wind and blew down all the trees and . . . and though Tezcatlipoca had made some more new people, the wind blew them away."

"But a few were left, and they turned into monkeys. Maybe your Chitl is one of them. Small men without much brain," smirked Metzli.

"Don't you dare insult my Chitl!" Malinali cried. "You are only jealous that he spends all his time with me!"

"Cousin, you keep interrupting me. How are you ever going to learn? Do you wish to hear about these important matters or do you not?"

Chastened, Malinali nodded. Metzli continued. "Well then, the gods of creation let Tlaloc, the rain god, set up a new world, but again Quetzalcoatl spoiled it all by raining fire on it, and once more the creatures there perished or were changed into birds. Then they let Tlaloc's sister try to make the world all over again, but now Tezcatlipoca caused it to rain so hard that again everyone was killed or turned into fishes. The sky, which is water, fell down upon the earth and so both Tezcatlipoca and Quetzalcoatl had to agree to lift it up again."

"Well, I am very glad of that," said Malinali, "that Tezcatlipoca is not always so unpleasant."

"But wait. Even with the sky back in place, there was no sun. It had gotten lost. There was no one to light the earth. So all the gods came together to see who would make the sacrifice of turning himself into a new sun. And many gods offered themselves. And then, one by one, they leapt into a sacred fire to get the sun to appear. But when he came out, can you imagine what happened? I'll bet you can't! Well, I'll tell you. The moon also appeared, and she was just as bright as the sun! The gods were furious that she was so haughty, so they struck her a blow on the face with a rabbit. And if you look at her even now, you can still see the scar that the rabbit left."

"Yes," admitted Malinali. "That is true. I do see something like a shadow on her face even now. Then tell me, what happened next?"

"Well, the sun was out, but he refused to move," said Metzli with greater authority than before. "He was hungry for more blood. So more of the gods had to sacrifice themselves on the sacred brazier. And finally he began to rise in the heavens. But the priests of Tezcatlipoca and the sun god Huitzilopochtli know that he is *still* hungry for more blood. That is why men must take the place of the gods and provide the food to keep him going."

"You mean the human hearts that they feed him?" Malinali shuddered.

"That is what he likes best. But after all, they are only hearts of slaves or captives. You should waste no pity on them. Besides, what does it matter? Soon all of us will die anyway. Remember we are living in the fifth world since time began, the World of Movement, which will come to an end in movement . . . in a giant earthquake. So we may as well enjoy our life while it lasts."

In weeks to come Malinali was often troubled by these words of Metzli, which were so different from those of the gentle priest of Quetzalcoatl. According to him, blood sacrifice of human beings was forbidden. Only self-discipline, fasting, and application to duty were necessary to attain the paradise presided over by Quetzalcoatl, who was the morning star and—in the form of his twin—the evening star. Known as the Plumed Serpent, he was also the wind god, the god of writing and of all craftsmen. Because of Quetzalcoatl it was a duty to weave the most perfect cloths, to cut the most perfect stones, to fashion and hammer out the most perfect gold that could be created. All this, even

Malinali's sweeping, was to prepare for the day when Quet-zalcoatl would return to this world. And according to the god's own prediction this day was almost at hand. The 500 years since his departure were almost over. Malinali had listened carefully to the priest and waited anxiously for the return of Quetzalcoatl. But her cousin made fun of her.

"You are only a baby, just wait until you grow up. I bet you don't know what happened to Quetzalcoatl! No, they didn't tell you that, did they?"

"They told me that when Quetzalcoatl lived, even the cotton grew in many colors—pink, blue, red. His magic could do anything!"

"Then have them tell you how he let himself be fooled by the priests of Tezcatlipoca! " Metzli was triumphant.

"A god cannot be fooled! I don't believe you."

"Well, just listen. It was really very easy to deceive him because their magic was stronger than his. They gave him some wine that made him so drunk that he lay with his sister! Can you imagine what a disgrace for a god! And when everyone knew what he had done, he was so ashamed that he had to leave the great city of Tula. That was hundreds of years ago. Of course he threatened to come back and punish the priests of Tezcatlipoca. But he never did return. His magic was too weak. He only sacri-ficed snakes and birds and little butterflies, so he had no power. You better not count on him, cousin."

Malinali was so upset by Metzli's words that she stopped sweeping and ran to her father to ask him if this was true. Although he was busy fashioning a new bow for himself for the next hunt, he put aside his tools and spoke to her as seriously as if she were a grown person.

"Malinali, my little jewel. You must not listen to the tales of ignorant or wicked people. Your cousin only repeats what she has heard from the priests of Tezcatlipoca. If you want to know if the Great One watches over you, you have only to look up each morning when you finish your chores. Then you will find him who is the morning star looking down on you."

Malinali did not wish to interrupt her father, as she knew this to be rude. Still she felt she must know enough to reply to her cousin's attacks. "But tell me, father, is the story Metzli tells me true? Did Quetzalcoatl really do a wicked deed and have to go away?"

Teteotcingo searched his mind for the proper way to explain very complicated ideas to a child of Malinali's age. He did not wish to lie to her, for an Aztec prince should always speak the truth. He lit up his pipe and leaned back on his stool.

"The story that your cousin has told you happened so long ago that no one knows whether it is true or not. But this is not important since the Quetzalcoatl of whom she speaks was a man, a king of Tula, which was our greatest city before they built Tenochtitlan. Ignorant people who believe that Quetzalcoatl lived only as a man think that he was weak, but they still fear his revenge. They say that he sailed off into the great sea to the east, promising that when he had cleansed his soul he would come back. So this is why we must report to the emperor's palace in Tenochtitlan any sign from the heavens that he may be approaching—especially now, since it is almost the year for his promised return."

"But father, which is the real Quetzalcoatl? Is he the man-king or the god?"

"You say *real*, my child. How do you know if something is real? If you can see it?"

"Yes, if I can see it."

"Malinali, can you see the air?"

She looked around the courtyard and felt the warm, damp air on her cheek. "No, father."

"Yet you know it is there. Do you not? It touches you.

You feel it on your skin. Quetzalcoatl is the air, the wind. When we offend him by our sloth or our cruelty, he makes us feel his displeasure. In the hurricane he lashes our bodies and topples our homes and temples. Is this not power that can be felt?"

"Yes, father. But is so great a being also a man? Can he be both a god and a man? I do not understand. What can I say to Metzli?"

Teteotcingo pulled thoughtfully on his pipe, sending rings of yellow smoke upward. "You should not talk to her of these matters because *she* will never understand. A god can be both man and god, present and absent, wind and fire. Since he is also a man, he can understand our pain and suffering. He has also suffered. He is the only god who has dared to become a man. That is why Quetzalcoatl is greater than any of the other gods. But who knows if he will return again as a man! I do not know enough to tell you."

Malinali walked away sadly, not sure of what she could possibly say to Metzli. Teteotcingo was even more deeply troubled. He did not go back to carving his bow, but paced back and forth in the courtyard, thinking about what would become of his little daughter. He also thought about Cimatl, his wife. After seven years, it was clear, Cimatl was not going to give him a son, or any other child for that matter. Cimatl had become very distant to him, always busy with her weaving or embroidery.

Although he did not expect love from her, he saw clearly that she did not even enjoy his company. How different was her attitude to his cousin, Atlaua . . . . She always listened with an expression of rapt attention to the man's stories of life in the great metropolis, to the news of the last flower wars and the number of prisoners taken in them who would be sacrificed to the sun god—the very sort of news that made Teteotcingo sick at heart.

He knew that he could take another wife, since Cimatl would not give him a son. Many rulers had numerous wives. But such a course of action would not be easy. Cimatl would be furious if she were asked to share her home with another woman. And her family was powerful in Tenochtitlan. It would not be difficult for them to have him removed as ruler of Painala. It was much better, he decided, to prepare Malinali to succeed him, just as the priest of Quetzalcoatl had predicted.

Of course it might not be easy to persuade all the priests and noblemen that she should rule. There had not been a powerful female in the Aztec empire for many years. Yet in former times, Teteotcingo knew, both nobility and power were inherited through women. With the priests of Quetzalcoatl as his allies, he could make the others accept her as his heir. First, however, she must leave the spinning room of her mother. She must also be taken away from her cousin, who was causing such confusion, such doubt and grief. It was time for her to learn the duties of being a leader, a man as well as a woman.

So Malinali soon went down to the river every day with her father. Sometimes she took her monkey with her. Chitl was so much happier free of his palm tree prison. They would watch the canoes come up to the landing, see them unload their precious cargoes. Then her father explained to her the pictogram notations on his *amatl* scroll of cooked and pressed bark. These were how he kept count of each item that would be sent on the long way over the mountains to the capital city of Tenochtitlan. It was important to note everything carefully because if anything should be lost, Teteotcingo would need to prove that the loss occurred outside his jurisdiction. Even though he was ruler, any errors of accounting could have very serious consequences. So Malinali was trained to have a sharp eye and make sure that everything, down to the last gold-filled quill, was accounted for.

It was not all work down by the river. In a short time she began to understand some of the strange-speaking oarsmen from Tabasco, and sometimes they even brought gifts just for her, gifts that did not have to be sent away to Tenochtitlan. Her favorite canoes belonged to the two merchants from Xicalango who were good friends of her father. Chac and Xul would bring up fresh *huachinango* fish from the ocean. They also presented her one day with little clay figurines which had smiling, painted faces, unlike anything she had ever seen.

"What shall I do with these?" she inquired politely. "What purpose do they serve?"

Chac and Xul laughed and mumbled something to each other. Then Chac spoke. "They are to dwell in your house, Malinali. They are a gift from the gods."

"The gods?" asked Malinali. "Which gods? Are they from Quetzalcoatl?"

She looked at both traders, but Xul did not seem to understand. Although she was only seven years old, Malinali could see that Xul was very shy. He would smile kindly, but it was always Chac who spoke.

"Little princess," Chac replied, "in our country we know Quetzalcoatl by the name of Kukulcán. But of course our Kukulcán is even older than your Quetzalcoatl. We were the first to worship him."

"But how is that possible?" she demanded. "Quetzalcoatl is our oldest god."

"Perhaps. But that does not mean very much. You are a new people here. You have only been among us since your own father came just a few years before you were born. We Mayas have been in this land from the beginning of time. Our ancestors built statues of such size that the very gods themselves must have helped them. There is no one today who could move these stones. They are like mountains. And there is no one alive who is as magnificent as those god figures."

"Then I must know what they look like. You must take me to see them!" the girl commanded.

"And carry off the princess of Painala? Do you want your father to flay us alive? No, I will tell you how they are. They have slanted eyes like the jaguar, very thick lips, and short noses; they are part man and part beast."

"Then they are not Quetzalcoatl," Malinali said wistfully. "Quetzalcoatl is beautiful, and not at all like that. Quetzalcoatl looks only like a man. I do not care to see your statues."

In days to come she would always ask Chac about their gods and thank both merchants for the little figures they continued to bring. But more exciting, she began to understand the language they spoke to each other and proudly repeated many of their words. Soon Malinali began to communicate even with Xul, who was less shy in his own tongue.

Sometimes Teteotcingo would overhear his daughter chattering in the Chontal Maya language with the two merchants and wonder at her accomplishment. The Chontal Maya tongue was so unlike their own. It was full of little "plup-plups" like a pot of chili and beans boiling on the fire, so that words were lost in the tiny explosions of breath needed to pronounce them. It was so different from the bird-like "tla-tla" sounds of the the smooth, clear Nahuatl speech of his own people and of other civilized nations. That was why they called the Maya tongue Chontal—barbarian. He could hardly understand it, much less speak it with the ease of his daughter. Then he would remember the words of the priest: Malinali had been chosen by the Plumed Serpent to rule some day over the entire empire. As he thought more and more about his child's destiny,

Teteotcingo began to question his own ability to train her for such a task.

Malinali knew nothing of her father's worries. For her, the sounds and people of the busy river were so much more fun than the the the monotonous clicking of the loom and the drone of the spindle in the little room where Cimatl and Metzli silently labored. It was so much more interesting to be treated as a man and a prince than as a little girl!

Yet the river life lasted little more than a year. By the time she was eight, Malinali had grown so bronzed and tall, so strong and agile that if not for her braids, her white, sleeveless blouse, and her brightly colored skirts, she might have been confused with a youth of her age. Accustomed to calling out to traders above the din of the river, her voice had become far louder and more assertive than what was considered seemly in a young lady. She had begun to look at people, even at men, directly, her black eyes shining like embers, instead of casting her gaze downwards as befitted a maiden. At first Teteotcingo, accustomed as he was to seeing his daughter every day by the river, took no notice of the changes. But Cimatl, deeply disturbed by the strange, outspoken behavior of her daughter, repeatedly called it to his attention. Their daughter was losing all modesty. She was forgetting how to spin and weave. Her skin was becoming as dark as that of the common people. She might never be a ruler, but she should certainly plan to marry, and who would want such a shameless wife! Reluctantly, Teteotcingo agreed that Malinali should end her apprenticeship as a trade overseer. But he would not agree that she should return to the spinning room. He vowed instead to send her to a prestigious school for children of the nobility.

Malinali remembered the moment clearly. It was a rainy day in late summer with howling winds and palm trees lashing against the roof. It was hurricane season. Teteotcingo cleared his throat, tapped his pipe on the floor so that it sounded like the *besuconas*, the little brown lizards who make the same dull thud when they beat their tails on the wall. Then he called her to him and said that he had something very important to tell her. She already feared what was coming.

"Malinali, little quetzal feather," he began. "I have taught you all I am able to here in Painala. Yet a prince of even a small village such as this must be very wise and very learned. We have many subjects, and they will need your guidance. The soothsayers tell me that the stars will soon be favorable for your travel, so you must make the journey to Tenochtitlan."

"Tenochtitlan!" Her head swam in surprise. She could make no comment. She knew that her father did not wish to be interrupted, but she did not yet understand what was in store for her. Teteotcingo's voice had become stern and commanding.

"Once you are in Tenochtitlan, you will go directly to school, to the great Calmecac of Quetzalcoatl. There the high priestess, Ciuacoatl, will take charge of you. I have already sent her a message and she knows you are coming. You must prepare to remain there until you complete your studies."

Malinali's unspoken questions chased each other in her brain. "How long am I to stay there? Can I take Chitl with me? Will you come too? Will I go alone . . . ?"

She heard her father's voice rising above the storm outside and the occasional claps of thunder. His heart did not seem to be in his words. He was speaking to her as if she were a soldier, or his subject, rather than his daughter. "The trip will be a long one of many moons, of steep climbs along perilous paths. That, too, will be part of your preparation for ruling in my stead. You will cross mountains covered with a white mantle of what they call snow and wade through streams that will chill your bones. But I know you do not fear this. A woman of the land of the serpent who is worthy to lead her people will not complain of physical discomfort. You will depart with the next portage of tribute to the capital."

Malinali continued to listen to her father impassively, but her heart was sinking. She did not want to leave the hot lowland for the unknown cold of a faraway land. She did not want to be banished away from her home and from Chitl, whom she already knew would not be permitted to go with her. There was nothing to be done. She saw her mother, now standing in the doorway.

Cimatl seemed to guess the unspoken question in Malinali's eyes. "Chitl will be returned to the forest he has come from and will be far happier there," Cimatl said with a smile, as if she believed that this was so.

Chitl did not *look* happy when Malinali told him. He threw his hairy arms around Malinali's neck almost as if he understood. She knew he would not want to go back to the jungle, to flee from jaguars or the arrows of human hunters. His only family was here in Painala. But Malinali understood that pleading with her parents was out of the question.

THREE

The High Priestess

*J*ust as her father had fore-warned her, the voyage to Ten-ochtitlan was long and arduous. The little caravan in which Malinali traveled crossed marshes and swamps infested with alligators and water serpents, dense rain forests inhabited by pumas and jaguars, and large, sun-baked plains where there was often not a single palm tree for shade. Unmerciful mosquitoes seemed to follow them everywhere. But these hardships were left behind when they reached the snow-capped mountains of the sierra that rise up like fortresses to guard the central plateau of Mexico. Now the only enemy was cold, something totally new for a young girl who had known only the intense heat of the tropical lowland.

Throughout the voyage Malinali did not fear the dangers or complain about the hardships. Every member of the company suffered them in silence, and the porters had the additional burden of the heavy loads that they carried. It was because of this treasure that the caravan was also provided with many warriors to protect them from attack by evil magicians or thieves. For this reason Malinali felt very safe. Besides, one of her father's most trusted lieutenants, the eagle warrior Tlazolteotl, went with her, to make sure that no harm came to the young princess.

When they arrived at villages along the way, a fine meal of tortillas, eggs, or roasted game was prepared for them, and she was given several cakes of sweet maize. And when they reached the mountain passes, Captain Tlazolteotl brought her a blanket of rabbit fur to throw over her thin cotton blouse. The snow on the peak of Mount Citlatepetl was so dazzling that it almost blinded her, and her feet in thin sandals of deerskin and henequen fiber felt numb and painful.

Sometimes Malinali thought of her cousin Metzli, who had made this voyage and who so often boasted of her adventures. Now Metzli would hold her peace. Neither would she lecture so brazenly about all she had heard at her school. The Calmecac that she, Malinali, was to attend was by far the best school in the world. Soon it would be Metzli who would have to listen to her. The assurance she began to feel now about her future rule of Painala made any hardship worthwhile. She tried not to think of Chitl. When she got back, she would send Captain Tlazolteotl to find him in the jungle and the little spider monkey would have an honored position in the village.

In all, the voyage to Tenochtitlan lasted one and one-half months, or thirty days, for in the Aztec calendar each of the eighteen months was twenty days long. No one died on the voyage, or had broken limbs or had been bitten by scorpions or poisonous serpents. As the soothsayers had predicted, it was an auspicious journey.

They reached the outskirts of Tenochtitlan on the day of one acatl, the sign of Quetzalcoatl himself, who appeared at dusk brightly above their heads as the evening star, the planet Venus. It was almost night by the time they came to the stone causeway joining the land to the fortress-city surrounded by lakes. This was the smallest of the three causeways, or bridges, which offered the only land approach to the capital. It was wide enough to provide room for at least ten warriors to march abreast. Now, many other people, including laborers on their way home to villages on the lake shores, pressed against the porters of their party, forcing them to march by twos or risk being pushed from the raised highway into the dark waters on either side. Captain Tlazolteotl, to protect the child from being crushed, carried her on his shoulders.

What Malinali failed to see in the darkness and confusion of the multitude she sensed in other ways. The splashing sounds of the oars of many canoes, the shouting of rowers and the greetings to them by the warriors in her party. There was a sweet, smoky smell of tortillas being turned on braziers in the guardhouse where they stopped and saw the wives of soldiers preparing their evening meal.

They walked on for at least another hour, crossing a great stone dike which separated the sweet water of Lake Xochimilco from the salt lake of Texcoco to the north. The crowd thinned out when the causeway ended, and they reached a wide avenue leading into the center of the city. Then the Captain, himself tired, put Malinali down again. Still she could hear the canoes from the lake now paddling beside them. The Captain patiently explained that a canal paralleled the highway so that goods could reach the palaces of the city's central square by land or by water. In the misty darkness filled with vapors from the lake, Malinali began to feel the more dense and heavy darkness of the pyramids and temples that now loomed on all sides.

From what she remembered of the descriptions given by Metzli, she could distinguish the shrine, the *teocalli*, of Tlaloc the rain god and that of fearful Huitzilipochtli the war god, atop the main pyramid, for their fire blazed in the sky, and the smoke from their incense now blurred the evening star. The smells of tortillas and tobacco gradually faded and were replaced with a bitter, acrid stench like that of butchered animals. She grasped the Captain's hand more tightly when she thought she heard the muffled cry of a human victim being sacrificed. But she was not sure. Perhaps the sound came from a wild beast in Moctezuma's zoo, howling to be fed the body of a slave. She shuddered with both cold and fear. Everything now was so dark, so menacing.

At last Malinali could make out the round shape of the temple consecrated to Quetzalcoatl, the only one of its kind. She wished she could kiss the smooth, polished stones of that temple, but she dared not stop. She did not breathe easily until a person with a torch appeared in a doorway beside them and the Captain announced that they had arrived at last. This windowless building adjoining the temple was the Calmecac, and the person holding the torch was none other than the High Priestess, Ciuacoatl herself.

Malinali prostrated herself before the half-seen figure of the woman and wondered if she would be able to rise, so tired were her limbs from the countless leagues she had traveled that day. She heard the Captain's words as if they were part of a dream.

"Mother Ciuacoatl, daughter of the great Serpent Goddess, priestess of our lord Quetzalcoatl, I bring you Teteotcingo's child, as he has promised. I know you will guard her well. I leave you now as I must return to my company."

Malinali heard the answering voice, soft and rhythmic like the little waves of the lake. "May the Feathered Serpent protect you on your return journey. Tell Teteotcingo that all will go well with the little princess. The prophecy will come to pass."

Then Malinali felt a small, bony hand in her own and heard the voice telling her to arise. She followed the torchbearing figure down a long, dark corridor until they reached a small room barely light enough for her to see her guide. There at last Ciuacoatl stood in front of Malinali smiling, an ancient woman, with long silvery braids, not tall but still straight and slender as a corn stalk. Her withered face preserved the clear stamp of nobility with its prominent, high-bridged nose and small, well-shaped mouth. Only when she spoke was Malinali aware that most of her teeth were missing. In the penumbra of the room her eyes were almost invisible, but Ciuacoatl's gaze was so strongly fixed on Malinali that she could almost feel it as a tangible force. It was as sharp as an obsidian blade, but it penetrated without cutting. She motioned Malinali to sit beside her on a hard wooden bench which was the only furniture visible. Then she spoke.

"This is your home now, Malinali, my little one. I have been expecting you for many moons. As you know, I shall be your teacher from this time forth, for you must learn much before you are fit to rule your people. But now I can see that you are captive of the god of sleep. So we will talk more about all this tomorrow."

Malinali mumbled the required words of gratitude. Then the gentle woman took up her torch again and led the child down a narrower stone passageway to a small cell with a window facing an interior court. As far as Malinali could tell, there was nothing in the room, only a small petatl on the floor, much like her bedroom at home. On the petatl she spied a maize cake and a cup of water. Malinali pretended not to notice these, although she suddenly realized her own hunger and thirst, which she had forgotten in her weariness. She concentrated on listening silently to her new mentor.

"You see, we of the school of Quetzalcoatl do not boast luxuries or pleasures of the flesh. We make do with very little. For this reason he who is the Plumed Serpent loves us. You may have dreams of the highest heaven while sleeping on a floor of earth. And you will wake up more refreshed than she who lies down on feathers. So now you

may sleep, Malinali. Your broom is in the corner. You will
see it with the first finger of dawn. The morning star will
be your guide."

The morning star had scarcely appeared before Ciuacoatl was back again, bearing another cake of maize and
a cup of frothy chocolate. She told Malinali that she could
have breakfast; afterward they would discuss the program
of studies at the Calmecac. But Malinali, shocked at the
idea that she should eat in the presence of her teacher,
resolutely put the food aside and begged to be told all that
was expected of her. Ciuacoatl then quickly explained that
Malinali would pursue her knowledge of the household
arts, weaving, spinning, and religious devotions, in classes
with young maidens of her age. Because she was heir to a
throne, however, private lessons in the history of her people would be taught by the High Priestess herself. Malinali
would also be taught to read and write, to understand and
to draw the pictograms used for official matters.

Years later when Malinali was to think of her days at
the Calmecac, she had difficulty recalling the names of the
other children who were her classmates. The young boys
lived and studied in a different section of the complex so
she hardly knew they were there. The girl students, however, seemed in no hurry to befriend her. They spun silently, casting her not even a glance. At the hour of their
meal, they sat together with their special friends and chat-
ted confidentially while they nibbled on their cakes of
maize. Sometimes one would steal a glance in her direction. Malinali wondered why they seemed to find her so
different from themselves. They all wore the same white
cotton blouses and long ankle-length skirts decorated with
only simple white embroidery. Their straight black hair
was also braided with white ribbons. Although they were
children of noblemen, they could make no display of

wealth. On this point, as in all other matters, the Calmecac was very severe.

All, too, were subject to the same rigorous rule of penances, although perhaps the girls' were not so painful as those of the boys. "You are privileged, Malinali," Ciuacoatl told her one day. "You have only to sweep during the night, and to offer incense to the gods. And of course you must fast, and bathe in very cold water. But the boys are obliged to arise in the darkness and go into the mountains, each by himself. There they draw blood from their ears and legs with agave thorns just as Quetzalcoatl did."

"I do not complain about the penances, nor the sweeping nor the cold baths, mother," Malinali replied. "I have long been accustomed to these things. But why do the others not speak to me or invite me to join them when they eat together? Is it the way I speak that they dislike? I know I have an accent of the south."

The old woman almost smiled. "It is that you seem foreign to the other students, Malinali. Since you have lived surrounded by subject races, you almost sound like one of them. All this will change. Every student of the Calmecac must learn the arts of elocution and of rhetoric, of how to address each official at the court, the priests, and even people of lesser rank. Have patience, my child. We people of the plains do not have the easy ways of the coastal tribes. In time the other girls will befriend you."

Much later, Ciuacoatl's promise was realized, and Malinali was finally invited to join the others for their daily meal. It was then that she learned that she had first looked like a peasant, or almost like a slave, to them. Her year by the river with Teteotcingo and the thirty days of her journey to Tenochtitlan had turned her pale skin very brown. Her sun-baked look suggested to these children of nobility, who spent their days in cloistered rooms, that this was a person of another race, or at least of a different class in society. Now that life at the Calmecac had robbed her of a bronzed appearance, the other young ladies could see that Malinali was one of their own race and class. They begged pardon for their mistake.

In spite of this, Malinali never felt that she really belonged among them. What she later remembered best about her student days were the stories that Ciuacoatl told her when they worked together in the herbal garden of the central patio, tending the cayenne pepper, the *cihuapatli,* the dwarf agave and many other plants. Ciuacoatl would patiently explain the medicinal qualities of each, and Malinali would rush to draw water from an irrigation ditch so that the fierce mid-day sun would not burn them. As they gently lifted roots and pruned away withered stems and leaves, she would ply Ciuacoatl with hundreds of questions about their people, the Aztecs. She had never forgotten how the river merchant Chac had considered them almost barbarians. Only the wise old Ciuacoatl would know the truth.

It was Ciuacoatl who told her that her ancestors had come from an unknown, legendary land of seven caves which they called Aztlán, Place of the Herons. They had arrived in central Mexico only some two hundred years before and had fought constant wars with other tribes, vanquishing all who opposed them. At first their only god was Huitzilopochtli, the sun and war god, who was always hungry for blood. He was also a jealous god who had battled with his sister, the moon, and his brothers, the other stars, so that each day's rising sun represented his victory over these other gods of the universe. In like fashion he required constant sacrifice and struggle from his subjects.

In the city of Tula, Ciuacoatl said, the Aztecs discovered the advanced civilization of the Toltecs, their distant cousins, who had created an empire extending to both oceans while the Aztecs themselves were still savage tribes

wandering in the plains. In Tula they also discovered Quetzalcoatl, who was an older and kinder god than their own,
and under him the Toltec civilization had flourished. Since
the Aztecs were greatly impressed with all that they saw,
they adopted this Toltec god, thus enraging Huitzilopochtli. "And this struggle between the two gods has been
carried on by their priests ever since," Ciuacoatl concluded.

"Yes," Malinali then said, while the good woman rested
to catch her breath. "I have seen this in my own village.
But there it is Tezcatlipoca who is the great enemy of the
Plumed Serpent."

"Of course," the High Priestess replied, "that is as it has
always been. Tezcatlipoca is older than Huitzilopochtli.
Tezcatlipoca had his temple, even in Tula. But they are
both enemies of Quetzalcoatl since the god of death and
the god of war are always allies." She paused a moment,
reflecting on her own words. "But you should know, my
dear, that I do not condemn Tezcatlipoca. Death is not to
be feared; it is the common destiny of us all. But war and
human sacrifice? This is Huitzilopochtli's curse on the Aztec people! I remember at the coronation ceremony of the
first Moctezuma that sixty thousand prisoners had their
hearts wrenched from their living bodies to appease this
god! Though I was only a child, I shall never forget the
endless screams. The whole city reeked of blood. . . . Well,
it is not much different under the present Moctezuma!"
Ciuacoatl sighed as a cactus thorn pricked her finger.

Malinali often thought about these conversations and
many others like them and wondered why Ciuacoatl told
her such terrible facts only when no one else was around.
Also, she observed that although Ciuacoatl frequently referred to Moctezuma, calling him *tlatoani*, emperor or
great speaker, she displayed none of the fear that his name
inspired in most of his other subjects. After many months

of steadily growing friendship between mentor and pupil, Ciuacoatl had become closer to her than even her own father, who now seemed so far away. And, there was no one else at the Calmecac with whom she could forget her occasional spells of loneliness.

One day, after Ciuacoatl had told her about the rulers of Tenochtitlan reducing their kinsmen and allies in neighboring Texcoco almost to vassals, she broached some of her questions aloud.

"Mother Ciuacoatl," she began. "How is it that when you talk about the people of Tenochtitlan, you never say *we*? It is as if you did not consider yourself one of them."

They were in the priestess's own quarters with the open doorway leading to the main corridor. Ciuacoatl walked outside the room and peered in both directions to make sure no one was within earshot. All the other students were in their classroom; she could hear the purr of their spindles. Turning to Malinali, she smiled faintly. "I see, little flint, that you have almost pierced my secret. Well, no matter. I have always intended to reveal it to you. So, as you have observed, I can tell you that I am not *one of them*. My secret is that I am also a princess. I am the daughter of Nezahualcoyotl, the great king of Texcoco. You have heard of him of course?"

"Have I heard of him! Dear mother, I am not so ignorant! Who has not heard of the philosopher king? And you are really his daughter? But I thought that he had died many many years ago."

"That is true, Malinali, but don't forget that I am a very old woman, and I was his youngest child. Did you know that the first Moctezuma called him in to build the stone dike that separates the sweet from the salt water of Tenochtitlan? There was no one in this city of warriors who could do it. Texcoco was then far grander than Tenochtitlan. My brother and I grew up surrounded by men almost

as great as Quetzalcoatl. . . ." Then she smiled again at
Malinali. "Have you also heard of my brother, King Nezahualpilli?"

"Yes, mother. My father often spoke of him."

"Well then, when I was still a very young girl my father
gave me in marriage to one of the sons of the old Moctezuma. My husband was not a favorite son. He would have
preferred to be a judge or a priest of Quetzalcoatl, but
Moctezuma determined that he should be a warrior like
his many brothers. So he sent my husband off to one of
the flower wars. Malinali, shall I tell you about the flower
wars?"

"I already know, mother. I have heard Metzli's father,
Atlaua, speak of them. These are the yearly wars we wage
to take prisoners for Huitzilopochtli; we do not fight for
territory or tribute, only for prisoners to sacrifice."

"I see, my child, that you have been well informed.
Now, although it was not supposed to be, my husband was
killed in this war for the terrible Huitzilopochtli."

Then the woman fell silent. Her breast heaved slightly.
Malinali waited, not daring to speak, and in a moment Ciuacoatl continued. "Moctezuma soon wished to marry me
again to another son, because it was a great honor for him
to have a daughter of Nezahualcoyotl of Texcoco in his
family. But I appealed to my father to let me become a
priestess here instead. Even the great Moctezuma could
not refuse my dying father his request—not after all he
had done to help this city! So I was made High Priestess of
the Calmecac. . . . But I have told my story to none of the
other students."

"Then it will rest with me, my honored mother, Princess of Texcoco. Does my father also know your story? May
I tell it to him?"

Again Ciuacoatl arose from her bench and walked

toward the door as if detecting some danger. When none appeared, she returned and embraced Malinali.

"My child, there is no need to tell this to Teteotcingo. He already knows. You see, we are kin, Malinali. Your grandmother was a noblewoman at my father's court. We were cousins. When she lay dying at childbirth, I promised her that I would protect her little son, your father. And so I did. I arranged for him to be sent to the Calmecac, and it was my brother, Nezahualpilli, who urged the next tla-toani to appoint your father as ruler of Painala, which had just then been conquered. I am almost your real grand-mother, Malinali, and I shall always protect you, as I have your father, as long as I live."

This time it was Malinali who threw her arms around the old Ciuacoatl. She had no words to express her great joy at so suddenly finding a grandmother when she had thought herself so alone and friendless.

Time flowed quickly now, and Malinali learned many secrets from Ciuacoatl. She learned how to cast horoscopes and to tell the future in the stars, to foretell the outcome of illness, to see the omens in the flight of birds. Ciuacoatl also reported to her all the rumors being spread about the land concerning an impending catastrophe, and omens that the new emperor Moctezuma himself listened to and feared.

It was her own brother, Nezahualpilli, almost on his death bed, who had told the second Moctezuma of the ter-rible times to come. In a few years his cities would be rav-aged and his children killed. Even the priests of Huitzilo-pochtli had seen the shooting star, like a flaming ear of corn, rise into the eastern sky and fall again. But when the soothsayers said that the star was Moctezuma himself, he had them imprisoned or sacrificed.

"But what is it that he fears so much, mother?" Malinali

interrupted Ciuacoatl's whispered confidences. "There is no one who would dare to harm so powerful a king."

"He is smitten by his own guilt, little one. He claims that he is heir to the empire of the Toltecs, but he knows that the true heir is King Quetzalcoatl, who exiled himself because of the treachery of the priests of Tezcatlipoca. And now, according to Quetzalcoatl's very own words, recorded by the scribes so many years ago, our departed king is to return. We expect him very soon. So even the great Moctezuma must tremble for his fate."

So that was it! Malinali remembered now that her father too had been ordered to report any signs of the god-king, should he appear from the great Eastern Sea. Even her father did not know that it was fear, not devotion, that inspired Moctezuma's vigilance.

Often Malinali thought about her father in the cold nights when she shivered too much to sleep. She thought about Chitl too. How warm he would have felt beside her on the petatl! In the first year of her stay at the Calmecac her father would send her news from home by messenger. There was no news about Chitl, and so she worried. Then, after three years, there was no news at all, not even that all was well in that distant outpost of empire. Finally she confessed her worries to Ciuacoatl, who promised to send a messenger of her own to Painala. The old woman assured her, however, that the city had suffered no attack from unfriendly tribes, since the tribute continued to arrive on time. If it had not, the officials at Moctezuma's court would have made public complaints. Three months passed before the messenger returned.

Ciuacoatl had also become alarmed at the silence from Painala and had taken the precaution of sending a spy, rather than an ordinary messenger, to find out what was happening. On the day her spy returned, Ciuacoatl called her pupil away from the spinning room to her chamber.

Scanning the old woman's somber face, Malinali needed no knowledge of omens to understand that something dreadful had happened.

Beside Ciuacoatl stood the messenger, Xochi, one of the oldest students of the Calmecac disguised as a *pochteca,* or trader, with bundles of cotton protruding from the sack at his feet. This, said Ciuacoatl, was the disguise he had used to enter Painala safely without arousing suspicion.

Xochi did not look at Malinali, but spoke to her with eyes averted, staring at his henequen sandals which were in shreds.

"Malinali, I bear you sad tidings. Prepare yourself. Someone you love has departed to a better world."

"I know, I know, Chitl is dead. I have long feared this," she said, trying to sound as brave as possible.

"Malinali, I know nothing of Chitl. I spoke to no one who mentioned this name. It is your father, Teteotcingo, I speak of. He is with us no more."

She looked at Ciuacoatl, who was also staring down, her eyes glistening. So Xochi's words must be true. But her father! How could this be? Her father was still young and healthy. He was no more than forty years. She was twelve years old, and forty years may have seemed ancient to her classmates, but for her Teteotcingo was still a young man. He was a child compared to Ciuacoatl! How could a young man die so suddenly, without giving her any warning? A hard knot formed in her throat. It was not easy for her to speak, but she had to know many things. She threw herself at Xochi's feet.

"Was this a flower war? Did some enemy slay him?" she cried out. "Tell me everything! I want to know it all! I must know. . . Oh my father, my poor father!"

Xochi tried to raise her up, but she would not let him. So he bent down to whisper to her. "Princess, I know little. People did not wish to talk. They seemed to be fearful.

Perhaps it was an evil insect, or some food that he ate. Your mother did not speak to me for I was only a trader."

Malinali looked up at him searchingly, finding eyes that were also brimming with unshed tears. "Then tell me, what did the people say? Is my mother deeply grieved? Has she covered herself with ashes? Yes, of course she has. She is helpless now. She will need me at once to rule our city. That is what I have been trained for. That is why he sent me here. Now I see that I must return."

At this point Ciuacoatl intervened, also kneeling on the floor and embracing the bereaved princess. "No, Malinali, you must not go. I am your mother now; I am your only mother. Cimatl has remarried. Your father died more than a year ago. She has wed Atlaua, Metzli's young father, and is expecting a new child. You will not be welcomed in Painala now. You must stay here with me and become a priestess of Quetzalcoatl."

Malinali hugged the old woman, while both of them held back the tears they had been trained to imprison. She loved Ciuacoatl with all her heart, but she knew that she must go back. Was it not foretold that she would rule in Painala? Had Ciuacoatl not proclaimed this herself? Certainly the priests and followers of Quetzalcoatl would protect her! Even the dangers of returning alone did not dissuade her. Her father would have expected this of her.

Against Malinali's steadfastness of purpose the Priestess was powerless. She could see that her student was determined to go. Sadly, Ciuacoatl agreed. With Malinali gone she would be losing her last of kin. She insisted that Xochi accompany the girl. He was also from Texcoco and could be trusted. He had already made the journey; he knew the route and could protect her. Ciuacoatl found him new sandals, decreed that they should rest one day and give prayers and sacrifices of birds and snakes to Quetzalcoatl. Then, two days after he had returned, the false trader set forth again at night. This time he was accompanied by another whose face was hidden.

FOUR

The Warrior Princess

*B*oth traders were dressed alike
in loincloth and cloak, and
carried hemp sacks of merchandise on their backs. Ciuacoatl decided that Malinali was safer dressed as a boy, and
this was still possible since her body had not yet fully taken
on the contours of a woman. If she felt the glance of a
passerby drop to her chest, she could always cover herself
discreetly with the ample cloak of a merchant. Her hair, of
course, was now cut short so that she seemed to be a
younger brother, and Xochi treated her, in fact, very
much in this fashion. They both carried the flint-tipped
spears they might need in case of attack by man or beast.
No one would notice them as they trudged silently along
the dark causeway over the waters of the lake and started
the long trek back to Painala.

Malinali clutched her spear proudly in the knowledge
that she was now also going to learn the skills of a warrior.
In the course of the voyage Xochi would train her in the
use of this deadly weapon, with its many blades of razor-
sharp flint embedded in the wooden shaft. And she would
become skillful enough in its use to spear large fish in the
lakes and rivers that they crossed.

All her training at the Calmecac was called upon by the
perils of the voyage. Like all traders, Malinali and Xochi

had to protect themselves against attack by thieves or sorcerers, and all the more so because they were traveling alone. Since they did not dare to spend the night in the towns and villages they crossed, preferring to take their chances in mountain caves or in whatever sheltered area nature provided, one of them always had to stand guard against wild beasts and other dangers. There were the jaguars which Malinali greatly feared, since these were the incarnations of the terrible god, Tezcatlipoca. There were also serpents, some evil, though Malinali was less afraid of them since Quetzalcoatl, the Plumed Serpent, would always protect her. What she feared most, however, were not the real animals, but the *nawales,* human beings who were said to transform themselves into beasts and suck the blood of sleeping persons, causing grave illnesses. She was thankful that she had been trained never to sleep through the night, but to arise and sweep or do penance. The discipline they had both learned at the Calmecac steeled them to stand guard over each other's slumber in the few hours they permitted for rest.

As the weeks of physical exhaustion and constant danger continued, a great bond developed between the two. Malinali counted on Xochi to protect her, and he too counted on the princess to do her share of providing them both with food. Ciuacoatl had instructed her in the properties of many of the plants in the jungle, plants that could be used for both food and healing. The hares and serpents that Xochi speared they cooked together at night. Malinali learned to use her flint to build a fire, and prepared whatever game Xochi found with herbs that she had gathered along the way.

She began to notice Xochi's physical appearance more than she had done with any other man, except her father. Xochi was very tall and thin, but exceedingly strong. His black eyes were also strong, and now they never looked downwards when he addressed her but met her own gaze without flinching. At these times she instinctively covered herself with the trader's cloak, but she did not fear Xochi's stare. She sensed his admiration and took satisfaction in it. At the same time she regretted her own appearance. Her pale skin, exposed to constant sun and wind, had taken on the earthen tones of her earlier voyage. And though she carried no obsidian mirror to examine her face, she could feel that her complexion had coarsened in spite of frequent washings in rivers and streams.

In the entire trip, the only city where they stopped to rest was Cholula, because this was the city devoted to Quetzalcoatl. Immediately upon entering it, they climbed up to the great round temple of the Plumed Serpent and laid upon the altar a quetzal feather with a vial of gold dust. A priestess came out from behind the altar and thanked them on behalf of the god. She asked them who they were, and when the two traders revealed to her their true identities, she blessed them again and sent greetings to the priests in Painala. She also warned them not to enter that city directly. It would be better, she said, for Malinali to wait outside in the forest while Xochi went to the temple and received instructions from the wise men there.

The advice of the priestess was very prudent, they decided, and probably dictated by the god himself. They remembered her words and did just as she had instructed. When at last they could hear the distant cries of children in the streets of Painala, they knew it was time to separate. Malinali chose a clearing in the jungle where she had been with her father and knew to be fairly safe. It was here that he had found Chitl so long ago. Xochi promised to return after he had taken counsel with the high priest. He regretted leaving her alone, but he knew now that Malinali could handle her spear and was not afraid.

Xochi remembered exactly where to go. Greeting

townspeople he had met before, he made his way to the house of Quetzaltotolin, the very same priest who had protected Malinali at her birth and who usually personified Quetzalcoatl as Lord of the Winds. He, too, lived in a round house, so that the god of the wind could blow in any direction and not be confined within the prison of a square structure. Although in public he always wore his bright red wind mask which looked like a cross between an alligator and a toad, he was now quite unimpressive. He wore a simple white robe with no adornment over his plump body and was bent over tending his garden. Xochi greeted Quetzaltotolin with all the ceremony due his rank, prostrating himself before the priest could even arise from his bending position.

"Oh great father and honored messenger of the Lord of the Winds, I have important news for your ears alone. Have I your leave to speak?"

The old man straightened himself up slowly and with difficulty, as his back pained him in the rainy season. "Yes, my son," he said. "Our lord Quetzalcoatl is listening. Speak!"

Xochi instinctively lowered his voice, then related all that had happened to him and Malinali and asked if it was safe for her now to proceed into the city.

Quetzaltotolin was overcome with joy upon learning that Malinali was still alive. At her father's death he had sent a temple attendant to Tenochtitlan to bring her the unhappy news and to request her return. "But the poor fellow never came back," Quetzaltotolin sighed. "Perhaps a jaguar or some other agent of Tezcatlipoca murdered him. I know not. But after this no one else wished to undertake such a dangerous errand.

"My own spies have told me that Malinali's mother herself instructed the porters and warriors who bring the tribute to Tenochtitlan to say nothing of her father's death.

Without Teteotcingo, Cimatl, as his widow, has no right to rule. If Moctezuma does not wish to confirm Malinali as the new tecuhtli, *he* must appoint someone else. But only Moctezuma can do this. You see, there are but three ways to rule throughout the empire. One can be elected, as Moctezuma himself was, or appointed, as was the case of Teteotcingo, or inherit the crown, as Malinali's father hoped she would. But no one under our law has ever appointed herself, as Cimatl has done. And this after not even observing a decent mourning period for her husband before remarrying! And then marrying his cousin Atlaua!"

"Then how did she dare do such a thing?" Xochi could not resist asking.

Quetzaltotolin patted the young man's lowered head, smiling. "I can only guess about this, my son, but I think that she and her new husband were waiting for the birth of a male child to inform Moctezuma. Perhaps they have already sent a messenger to bring him the news, although her infant is less than a week old. They hope that with the succession secured, Moctezuma will appoint Atlaua as the new tecuhtli of Painala. So it was well you did not go immediately to Malinali's old home. Who knows what would have happened!

"Send me Malinali at nightfall and then depart quickly for Tenochtitlan," he continued. "You must go directly to Ciuacoatl. She is the only one who can win Moctezuma to our side. As the daughter of Nezahualcoyotl, she still has great influence at court. Cimatl and Atlaua have trampled on our people's laws and customs, which Moctezuma, as Tlatoani, is sworn to defend."

Xochi listened with sinking heart to the high priest's instructions. He would have liked to remain and to protect Malinali against the dangers she now faced. But he also understood that without him there could be no help from the capital. Then as he took his leave of Quetzaltotolin, an important question occurred to him. "Tell me, Father, do you know how Teteotcingo died? Malinali and Ciuacoatl would like to know this."

Quetzaltotolin shook his bald head sadly. "Alas, dear boy, I can tell you no more than the others. His death is very much a mystery. I did not even see him before he was burned, since they called in the priests of Tezcatlipoca instead. It was announced that he had been stung by a scorpion. And although this is possible, Teteotcingo was a strong man and should have recovered. Unless, unless. . . . But I do not know. It is better not to ponder this, since we can do no good. Better tell Malinali at least that it *was* a scorpion. And remember, flies do not enter a closed mouth. Say no more of this to anyone else." Then, putting his hand gently on Xochi's shoulder, he escorted him to the street entrance of the temple precinct.

Xochi found Malinali exactly where he had left her. She had not been alone in her waiting. A marvelous yellow hummingbird had appeared, and although it was busy emptying nectar from the orchids that sprouted everywhere, she was sure that it was also watching her.

"Perhaps it was the soul of your father welcoming you, Malinali," suggested Xochi, although he knew that this could not be true. Her father had not died a warrior's death. He could therefore never become an exalted hummingbird.

"Yes, perhaps," Malinali agreed to the pious lie. "Or perhaps there were other eyes watching me. Perhaps it was Chitl who did not recognize me the way I look now, with these clothes and this hair! Perhaps he observed me and did not dare approach."

Xochi laughed. "Let us hope that nobody recognizes you!" He then related Quetzaltotolin's words to Malinali, who listened but said nothing. No words could express her grief when she thought of all that had happened: her father's death, her mother's betrayal, and now the departure of Xochi, her friend and only protector. But no, there was still Quetzaltotolin, the servant of Quetzalcoatl, who watched over her. She accepted the wisdom of his command.

Darkness was already falling. At the edge of the clearing the two students embraced as comrades, holding each other at arms' length, touching each other with the greatest of tenderness and respect. Then Malinali walked swiftly toward the high priest's round house. And when she was hidden from Xochi by trees and twilight, he plunged again into the deep, black forest with clenched teeth and a heavy heart. There were no hummingbirds now.

Quetzaltotolin was waiting for Malinali. He recognized her immediately, in spite of her boy's attire. In his private chambers he spoke in the thin, old man's voice that she had not heard for more than three years.

"Malinali, my child, it is better that you stay here until we determine what fate your mother has planned for you. I myself shall go to see her in the morning. Until now she has said nothing official about you. This has not been required for you are still too young to rule. But we must determine whether she will honor your father's will. She knows that he wished you to be his heir. She knows that very well, but the priests of Tezcatlipoca have never accepted it—and her new husband is of their party. He has great influence over your mother and no doubt is determined that his own son should be the next tecuhtli. This is what I suspect. So you are safer in the protection of Quetzalcoatl. You may sleep here in my room. No one else must see you."

Malinali readily agreed and laid down her petatl in a

corner. She was too tired to desire food. Besides, she had found a ripe, fallen pineapple in the forest clearing, and it lay heavily now in her stomach.

Although her body wished to rest, Malinali slept little that night. It was not only that she felt she must get up to sweep in the honored sanctuary of the god. But even when she lay on her mat, her light slumber was disturbed by the high-pitched snoring of the priest. The shrill wind of Quetzalcoatl seemed to seek outlet in the old man's withered nostrils, which made a sound like the crying of a jungle bird. She found herself thinking of Xochi and worrying about harm befalling him. Perhaps the spies of Tezcatlipoca had seen him and pursued him as they had pursued the other messenger of Quetzaltotolin. Would the wind god protect him?

Then, to stop thinking about Xochi, she tried to imagine her mother. Would Cimatl welcome her back or plot against her with the new husband? Cimatl had never been very affectionate, but that was not unusual. Mothers were often very severe and critical of their daughters—perhaps, Malinali thought, for not being sons. Had she intended for Malinali to stay forever at the Calmecac and so leave the way open for the new heir? Perhaps that would have been better after all. Then she might have seen Xochi again. . . .

In her fleeting dreams Malinali saw herself tied with rope and in a canoe floating down a river, her mother laughing beside her. There were two warriors there who were not of their people. Then suddenly a house appeared, floating on the waters, and the warriors fled. A huge figure dressed in gleaming cloth like gold stepped out of the house and climbed into the canoe. He bent down and untied her ropes. She screamed, thinking he was going to sacrifice her, to cut out her heart. That was how she awakened.

When she looked around, there was no one else in the

room. The sun already had laid a shining yellow carpet in the doorway. It was very late. Quickly she grasped the broom in the corner to do penance for having overslept. She also refrained from eating the sweet maize cake left by the priest.

Malinali felt more and more hungry as the morning wore on, but she resolved to keep her fast until the priest returned. When the sun was directly overhead, she heard him shuffling along the muddy courtyard. When he entered, she bowed before him, not daring to ask for the news of his mission until he should deign to speak. He too was silent, and motioned her to don the woman's clothes he had brought from her mother. Then they both kneeled down, and together they prayed to Quetzalcoatl for guidance. At last the priest told her to eat the maize cake which she had left on her petatl.

"Now I shall tell you the words of your mother, Cimatl. You should know that she sounds very pleased that you have come back and demands to see you before the sun sets. I told her that I would not permit this unless she promises that the wish of Teteotcingo will be respected and that you will become the next tecuhtli. She replied that she could give no promise until she had spoken to her new husband, since this is a very serious matter of state. If he agrees, she will come here herself to fetch you this very afternoon. If he does not, she will send a messenger."

Malinali made herself useful to the old priest while she waited for the fateful news from her mother. She mended his cloak, which had many holes, and prepared some frogs for his dinner. All afternoon it blew and rained so savagely that it seemed as if both the wind god and the rain god were doing battle. When the rain tapered off, her mother appeared at the priest's gate.

When she saw Malinali, Cimatl rushed to her and embraced her in the folds of her wet cloak. Then she held her at arms' length and slid her fingers through the girl's short hair.

"How you have changed, little flint. How brown you are! I can hardly recognize you. But I do not understand why you did not come directly to your home. Why should you let the priests tell you what to do? Do you not know how well your mother loves you and wants only the best for you?"

"Yes, mother," said Malinali, suddenly ashamed of her precautions. "But this is what the priestess of Cholula instructed me to do."

"Well, I shall not blame you. I see you know nothing of priestly politics. Quetzaltotolin tells me that before you are allowed to return, I must swear that you will be the next tecuhtli. Do you really demand this as a condition for coming home?"

The priest himself replied to Cimatl, thus saving Malinali from further embarrassment. "We must insist upon this, my lady. Otherwise the child will be a ward of Quetzalcoatl and live at the temple."

Cimatl looked around at the empty quarters of the priest, made even less hospitable in the sudden gloom brought on by the torrential rains. "You cannot keep my daughter here away from her mother and her home," she said, with all the authority of a queen. "This is not a suitable place for a princess."

"Then you must swear on the altar of Quetzalcoatl that she will succeed Teteotcingo, that she will be the new tecuhtli," said the priest simply.

Cimatl replied with a laugh, not even looking at the earnest old man, and not ascending the altar. "Very well, I will promise this to the god of the winds. From the mother of a tecuhtli that is enough promise. Now, my dear sir, may we leave in peace?"

Malinali's house looked smaller than she had remembered. Everything looked small in Painala compared to the massive scale of buildings in Tenochtitlan. Yet she was almost happy to be home. She had so many fond memories of that house, of Chitl lying beside her in her little room where she prayed and swept, and of her father's tobacco smoke that faintly infused every corner.

But Cimatl did not lead Malinali to her old room. This was now being used by Metzli, Malinali's cousin and former companion and now Cimatl's stepdaughter. Her mother offered her instead an even smaller room at the end of a long corridor which had formerly been used for storage. The walls glistened with dampness. There were no windows.

"Since you have been leading such a monastic life, I am sure you will not object to these modest quarters while we are making other arrangements," said her mother.

Malinali agreed, after a moment's hesitation. She knew that when she was the tecuhtli she could choose whatever room she liked. Or even build herself a new house. But she said nothing about this to her mother. Their conversation was cut short by the shrill cries of her new stepbrother, demanding his mother's breast.

"Oh, my darling wants to be fed," laughed Cimatl by way of explanation. "Come with me and I shall introduce you."

Malinali followed her to the room that her mother had once shared with Teteotcingo. Here an unfamiliar servant handed Cimatl a little bundle of screaming flesh swathed in white cotton, which Cimatl immediately introduced into her ample blouse. While she nursed the infant, she smiled up at Malinali. "What a large family we shall have now: you, the baby, and Metzli. I'm sure Metzli has many things to tell you. You will have so much to talk about while you spin together."

"But Mother, I am to be the new tecuhtli. I shall not be spinning. I'll be attending to matters of state."

"Ah yes, I almost forgot. But you must wait many moons before that. Your stepfather and I have decided that you must marry first. You will need a brave warrior, because now we have many enemies, Malinali. Since your father's death, the subject peoples around us grumble and threaten to join Tuchintecla, who has rebelled against Moctezuma and threatens to take the city of Coatzacoalcos. You will need a strong warrior as husband to preserve your rule. Surely you understand this, do you not?"

Malinali could hardly speak. Why had her mother not mentioned this at the temple? she wondered. Finally she asked, "Does Father Quetzaltotolin know of your plan and approve?"

"Of course he must approve, my dear. I am your real mother, not a mere priestess, and as acting ruler I make all the important decisions. Do not worry, Malinali. You are almost twelve. In a very short time you will marry and take my place."

So this was why Cimatl had not actually sworn her promise on the altar of Quetzalcoatl! She had tricked them both. They had been too polite to insist that she mount the altar. And now Malinali saw that she was trapped. She would have to marry in order to gain the power that her mother, in bad faith, had promised her. As she stared impassively at Cimatl, she began to consider the idea of marriage, which was totally new to her. Although as a little girl she supposed that someday she would have a husband, she had forgotten all about it at the Calmecac. Certainly she had no wish to repeat the High Priestess's unhappy experience. In a moment her thoughts returned to Xochi. She smiled.

"Very well, mother. Since I must marry, I shall choose a husband for myself."

Cimatl almost forgot the nursing infant at her breast, so great was her astonishment at Malinali's proposal. The girl had assumed she could choose her own husband as she might select a particular thread for her embroidery! Perhaps this is what came of her unnecessary training at the Calmecac! It was for her mother to undo the child's outrageous notions. "But, my darling, a princess cannot *choose* a husband. We have chosen one for you in order to make a good alliance for Painala. This is the way it is done, the way it has always been done."

Malinali saw clearly that there could be no truce between them, no compromise. She would be forced into marriage with some subservient prince of her mother's choosing so that Cimatl could continue to rule. Malinali would be tecuhtli in name only. The man she took to husband would be controlled by her mother. Quetzaltotolin had not even suspected this plot against her. He was too old, too trusting, just as she had been. So now she must defend herself. There was no one else she could count on. Here was a more dangerous jungle than the one she had just passed through. And the house that she had momentarily thought of almost as a refuge was only a trap.

Desperation gave her courage. She looked at Cimatl directly, as she had learned to do with traders by the river. "Why then, mother, did *you* choose Atlaua as a husband for yourself? What alliance does he bring to our city?"

Cimatl's expression of surprise hardened into displeasure. She called the servant to take away her screaming infant, and then addressed Malinali in a tone of offended authority. "We shall discuss this further at another time. Now you must go to your room and beg forgiveness of the gods for your arrogant behavior. The guard who stands in the doorway will escort you. I regret that the Calmecac did nothing to quell the pride and temper that you seem to have inherited from Teteotcingo."

At a signal from Cimatl the guard approached and took Malinali roughly by the arm. As she was forced from the room, she could only whisper to Cimatl, "How dare you breathe my father's name!"

The next day a servant brought her a broom, a maize cake, water, and her spindle and clay whorl, along with the cotton and half-gourd that she would need for her spinning. As punishment she was not allowed to see Metzli. She was left totally alone. In the little back room she did not hear even the noises of the courtyard. Of course she should not have reprimanded her own mother, she thought with regret. Cimatl deserved reproach for not mourning her father, but since she was not heir to the throne, at least not legally, she could marry whom she liked. Malinali wondered what evil spirit had made her speak up in that way. Depressed by her isolation, unable to communicate with her friend, Quetzaltotolin, Malinali began to question her own judgment and the wisdom of her attitude toward her mother.

After two days Malinali had a visitor. It was Metzli who tiptoed into her room as if afraid of discovery. There was great embracing, and also sorrow that she found Malinali in such disfavor. She told Malinali about her own regret at the appearance of the new little brother. "All he does is cry and suck at your mother's breast," she complained, "and yet my father finds him so charming. It is quite disgusting!"

Malinali took some satisfaction in realizing that she now had a possible ally in Metzli, who might be persuaded to help her. But first she inquired if there was any news about Chitl. No one had been willing to tell her anything about her pet monkey.

Metzli hesitated, as if preparing to deliver unhappy news—or perhaps she was merely trying to whet Malinali's curiosity. "Well, I'm very sorry about your monkey," she said, finally. "The fact is that he came here very often after you left, looking for bits of food in the kitchen. He developed quite a taste for the maize cakes. And he was always chattering and moaning. Your mother complained about him, but while your father was around, nothing was done. Sometimes he would even take Chitl down to the river with him and feed him bananas. But after your father died, Cimatl asked my father to get rid of him. So he shot an arrow at the monkey's thieving hand, just as he was about to help himself to a turkey egg. I suppose Chitl finally got the idea that he was not welcome, because he departed in a hurry and we have not seen him since," Metzli laughed.

"Well, at least he may still be alive," Malinali sighed in relief. "When I am able, I shall go to look for him."

Metzli stared at Malinali in disbelief. "How can you still be so interested in a stupid spider monkey? I should think you would be asking me about the prince you are going to marry. Haven't they told you?"

"Why should I ask, since I shall not marry him, whoever he is. You can marry him instead if you like. Besides, you are a year older. They should marry you first."

"No thank you, little sister. He is all for you. All of him. Do you want to know how much he weighs?"

"Oh, so he is a fat prince? And what else do you know about him? But don't tell me. I really don't care."

"Yes, I can see that. Well, I shall tell you anyway," Metzli chuckled. "He is the youngest son of the Totonac prince, and they say he is just as fat as the old man. But my father says we need better relations with them so your mother is proposing the marriage. Watch out or he will crush you to death on your wedding night!"

"Watch out yourself," shouted Malinali as she threw her discarded trader's cloak at Metzli. "I shall never marry him. Never! You'll see."

Metzli left giggling, and Malinali was immediately sorry

that she had lost her temper again. She did not enjoy her solitary confinement, and Metzli was better company than no one at all.

A servant brought Malinali a daily allotment of food and water every morning with great punctuality, but she saw no one else. It was several more days before she again heard footsteps in the corridor. At first she thought it was Metzli, but the steps were heavier and hesitating. Then she saw Atlaua framed by the entrance to her room. Before he spoke he stared at her a long time as if he were studying a pig that he might decide to purchase. His eyes were small and narrow, invaded by flesh from his expansive cheeks. He rested against the wall, as if for support. His flushed face suggested that he had drunk a cup too many of pulque. He certainly did not look as handsome as he had been a few years before. His hissing voice and fleshy frame made her think of a boa constrictor she had once seen in the jungle.

"Many moons have passed since we last saw each other, little princess. You look just like your mother now, only of course younger and more beautiful. You have grown like a nardo lily, and I am sure you smell as sweet."

Malinali remembered how little she had liked Atlaua. She stood up from the bench where she had been spinning and addressed the man with great formality. "Thank you for your visit, stepfather. As you see, I am busy spinning. I should like to speak with my mother. May I know where she is?"

"She is down by the river, checking the tribute, a long way from here." Atlaua slid along the wall toward her.

"But why do you not do this instead? My mother has had no training for this work. Does it not better suit her husband?"

Atlaua frowned. "Be careful, Malinali. You are not te-cuhtli yet. Your mother enjoys this task. She has been doing it since your father's untimely death. But he certainly should have trained her, instead of you."

Malinali compressed her lips, deciding not to reply. "Then what do you do, Atlaua? Of what are you in charge in our city?"

He smiled broadly, showing his large white teeth. "I command the warriors and the guards; I advise your mother on matters of state."

"Like my marriage?"

"Exactly. I understand that you are not happy with her arrangement."

She returned Atlaua's stare, but she expected no help from this man.

"I have come here as a friend to you, Malinali. Since you seem to be opposed to this marriage, I may be able to persuade your mother to change her mind."

"I should be most grateful, stepfather."

"Would you indeed be grateful, Malinali? How grateful, little one? Are you prepared to show me?"

"What do you mean?" she asked him, but she had already sensed his intent in his greedy eyes. Like Tezcatlipoca whom he worshipped, he was a jaguar who would consume her: she was his prey. His mouth was open; his lips smiling, already savoring the kill. He was using words only as snares.

Atlaua did not realize that she had seen through his disguise. He continued casting his net of words before him as he moved closer to her. "I mean, little one, that I do not wish to give you to the Totonac princeling. He would not appreciate you, at least not as I do. Will you permit me to visit you tonight, Malinali? You know, I have long admired you, my dear. And now you are almost a grown woman." His outstretched arms were nearly around her waist.

Instinctively she reached into the corner, trying to grasp the broom to ward off Atlaua's embrace. Instead her hand found the razor-tipped spear, which had been overlooked in her hasty captivity. Malinali seized it with a new sense of confidence and rage.

"Do not come any closer," she said hoarsely, "or I shall pierce your heart. I have used this spear many times." Her eyes shone fiercely, like a warrior's in battle.

Atlaua stopped, realizing that he was unarmed. He had never expected such determined resistance. He retreated back into the corridor, perspiring and angry, but still facing her. His voice shook. "You shall regret this, Malinali. I warn you. Without me as your friend, things will go much worse for you. What a stupid girl you are!" Then he disappeared, almost at a run.

Malinali stood unflinching for several minutes. When she was sure he was gone, she put the spear down and took up her broom. She began to sweep with all the force of her indignation. With each stroke of the broom she tried to cleanse her room of Atlaua's presence. She could spin no more.

After the episode with Atlaua, Malinali suspected that Metzli would not be allowed to pay her further visits. This proved to be true. She spent her time trying to imagine a plan of action that would allow her to escape the house and seek refuge with Quetzaltotolin. At night her dreams were more feverish than ever. Usually she saw Atlaua pursuing her, armed with his own obsidian dagger. But when she turned at last to face him, brandishing her spear, she saw that she was not alone. A golden warrior stood beside her, and he rained fire upon Atlaua, who crumbled like a twig on the brazier. The dream gave her hope that her imprisonment would not last and that she should have her revenge against her stepfather. Confinement and silence were hardening her spirit in a way they had never done at the Calmecac. She felt not only alone, but surrounded by enemies. Cimatl seemed to have totally forgotten her.

Then, one night, her mother appeared. Cimatl was smiling as if all had been forgiven. She even apologized to her daughter.

"I am sorry to have neglected you so, my dear, but I have been very busy at the river inspecting all the new tribute to be sent up to the capital. There are problems with everything. The feathers are of poor quality, and the slaves they send are so thin and sickly-looking they will be regarded as an insult to Huitzilopochtli. I fear you will not enjoy being tecuhtli."

Malinali did not trust herself to reply.

"But I do have a surprise for you, little girl. Today one of the canoes that I inspected had a pet monkey on board. The Tabascans who own it, two merchants, say that they found the animal by the river bank and have offered to sell it to me. They want three quills of gold dust, far too expensive. But as you can guess, Malinali, I think this may be your dear Chitl again, although of course I am no authority on monkeys. They all look much the same to me. But if if will make you happier, I shall buy him for you."

Malinali almost threw herself into her mother's arms. She forgot everything at the prospect of recovering her pet. Even the back room would not be so lonely with Chitl there to make his funny faces and to sleep beside her on the petatl.

"Oh, mother, will you really buy him for me? I would do almost anything to have Chitl back!"

"Well, we shall see about that. But you must come with me now to make sure that it is really he. Otherwise I should be wasting my gold."

"Now, mother? It must be so dark by the river now! We might not see clearly what this monkey looks like. Can they not bring him here? We could tell immediately that it is Chitl if he knows his way around this house."

"But my little flint, they are returning home this very night. I thought that you would be pleased to leave your room on so cheerful a mission. Do not fear the dark, my dear. I have two strong guards to protect us. You will not need your spear. These Tabascans are peaceful enough; they are not warriors, only merchants."

Malinali now looked at her mother's companions, who remained half hidden in the doorway. She could see that they were tiger-knights, as Atlaua's warriors were called, with jaguar heads painted on their helmets. The idea of going down to the river with such warriors was far from appealing, but the prospect of recovering Chitl was worth any danger. Besides, these men were Aztecs, and she was their future tecuhtli. They could do her no harm.

Dismissing her somber thoughts, Malinali accepted Cimatl's outstretched hand and followed her mother and the two warriors out into the street. She had not seen this street at night for many years. Just as she remembered, there was a faint glow in the sky of pinkish smoke that rose up from each house above the courtyards. Women were preparing the evening meal. The air was filled with a pungent aroma of suckling pig and the heavy sweetness of fried maize cakes. But there was no one in the streets. There was no moon in the sky.

FIVE

A Mother's Betrayal

*Malinali had never been to the
river before at night. She*
imagined that it would be deathly silent once the hub-bub
of the daytime activity—the buying and selling, the hawk-
ing of merchandise—was over. In fact it was now full of
the sounds that before had gone unheard. Crickets and
dragonflies buzzed and hummed everywhere. The bull-
frogs croaked so loudly they seemed three times their size.
And then she heard the splashing approach of the canoe
of the Tabascan merchants, cutting the water swiftly from
somewhere out in the middle of the river.

She strained her eyes to distinguish the little crouched
shape of Chitl, but in spite of the torchlights on the pier,
it was much too dark. The guards stood beside her, as if to
prevent her from falling into the black waters below. Then
she thought she heard familiar voices as the Tabascans
muttered to each other. Their canoe was now directly before her, but she saw no sign of Chitl. At this moment Malinali's original suspicions returned as cold certainty. The
trip to the river was to remove her from any friend or protector who might hear her cries for help. She had fallen
into the final trap!

Instinctively she turned to take flight, to seek refuge in
the jungle, but the guards caught her. They held her very

tightly, and one of them fastened a hemp gag around her mouth. Then they bound her hands and feet with a coarse rope that cut into her skin. She looked so pathetically like a deer captured for sacrifice that Cimatl shuddered and told them to loosen her bonds. "There is no need to torture her, after all," she reprimanded them. "She is my daughter, not a warrior who is going to escape." Grumbling, the guards obeyed.

All was suddenly silent. The burly tiger-knights now held Malinali upright, facing her mother. Cimatl leaned against a pole on the landing to steady herself from the ordeal. Even in the dim light of the torch above her, Malinali could detect the sadness in her mother's face. Cimatl's voice was hardly more than a whisper.

"I regret that I was forced to deceive you in this way, Malinali. You should know that I did not wish to do this. I had intended that you stay at the Calmecac and not return to Painala. You would have been happy there. Why could you not let well enough alone? But perhaps the gods did not mean it to be. Your father had turned your head in making you believe that you should be the next tecuhtli, so you were consumed by ambition.

"When you were a child, you never spoke to me," Cimatl continued still in a whisper. "It was always your father whom you sought out. You would spend hours together, you two, and when I appeared your conversation would stop, as if I could not understand. But I understand now. After all, I was only a woman. You disdained me because I had no power." Suddenly her voice became shrill and accusing. "You have always lusted after power, almost like a man! And now I find you want something else as well. At last I understand your anger about my marriage to Atlaua. And I see why you refused to wed the Totonac prince.

"You wanted Atlaua for your own husband! You did not want me to have the only man I have ever loved. I could hardly believe it, that you would do this to me, your own mother! How *could* you have asked him to divorce me and marry you instead? Do you really find him so attractive? He may be younger than I am, but he is still more than twice your age. He was already fifteen when Metzli was born. Well, no matter. At least *he* is loyal to me. And how deeply it pained him to reveal your words. The poor man nearly cried! How shocking that a girl of twelve is so brazen. Although, in truth, I suspected this from the moment of your return."

Malinali's astonishment was such that she could not have replied, even if she had been able to speak. Still she squirmed desperately to loosen her gag. Without the use of her hands, the attempt was useless. There was nothing to be done but listen, horrified. What punishment did Cimatl have in store for her?

Her mother nodded towards the guards again. "I could easily ask these gentlemen to put an end to you, Malinali. They are expert in the use of the dagger or the club, and my better wisdom tells me that I should let them do their will. While you are alive, I fear that you will always be a menace to both me and my son.

"But I still have a mother's affection for you, in spite of all you have done. I am a pious woman. So the dagger will not be your fate. I have decided upon a different course. These merchants in the canoe will take you away from Painala. They will bring you to a different land very far from here. There, my daughter, you will also live in a fine home, but not as a princess—as a slave. You will have a kind master. This they have promised me. So you are luckier than you deserve. Let us hope that you learn from your mistakes, Malinali, and do not seek to escape. Painala controls the river routes. If you appear in this city ever again, I shall let my guards do their will with you. Since you are an intelligent girl, I am sure you understand."

Malinali shook her head furiously, sideways, in her futile attempt to deny Cimatl's accusations. But her mother did not seem to notice and motioned the guards to lower Malinali into the waiting canoe. The two merchants tied her to a seat between them, perhaps because they feared she might throw herself overboard. Then they paddled silently out into the center of the black river. Everything returned to normal: the heavy croaking of the frogs, the humming of the crickets, the splashing of the little waves against the canoe.

Malinali's heart pounded louder than the frogs or the crickets along the river. Could her captors hear it? What sort of men were they? Where were they bringing her? What would they do with her? Would they ever take off the gag that was cutting her face and permit her to speak?

Only about an hour had passed when one of the merchants bent over to her and whispered, "Do not fear, Malinali, you will be safe with us. We are your friends. Do you not recognize us?" Then he cut away her gag with a flick of his knife.

Malinali sucked in a lungful of sweet night air. She still could not see her captors, but the voice sounded familiar.

"Yes, I think . . . I have heard you speak before. . . Many years ago. . . . You have a strange accent. Who are you?"

"We are Xul and Chac. Don't you remember us? The ones who gave you little presents when you were a child? We even taught you to speak our language then. Have you forgotten?"

Yes, they were really her old friends! Hope flooded her heart for a moment, then stopped. "If you are my friends, why are you taking me away? Why do you plot to destroy me?"

"Little Malinali," said the same voice in the dark. It was Chac's. She remembered that Xul usually said nothing. "You are indeed fortunate that your mother selected us as her accomplices. With some other traders it would not have gone so well for you. Cimatl gave us instructions to sell you to some far away buyer in Xicalango, too far away for you to ever return."

"Then are you really going to sell me as a slave? Have you no loyalty to my father, Teteotcingo, who was also your friend? You know I should be the new tecuhtli, that it is my legal right!"

"Patience, little princess, and hear me out. It was your stepfather who urged your mother to do this. At first he wished to put you to death immediately, and he chided Cimatl for her softheartedness. But we persuaded him to accept our offer. We promised to sell you to a wealthy prince and to bring him the sale price. We said you would fetch a handsome sum because you are learned and beautiful. So this we must do, or he will put us to death when we return to Painala."

Malinali said nothing, but her silence was an accusation. Chac continued to plead with her.

"Please try to understand, Malinali. We *must* return to Painala. That is our livelihood, to trade and sell. We do not dare to undertake any other route. We cannot go to Cempoala. We have bad relations with the Totonacs. They, too, would kill us. We must return to Painala. And so we will sell you to a buyer who will treat you well."

"Then sell me to Ciuacoatl, the high priestess at the Calmecac. She will pay anything you ask."

"In Tenochtitlan, you mean? But that is impossible. If Atlaua found out, he would have Xul and me flayed alive immediately. For him and your mother, the worst possible outcome would be for news of this night to reach the capital."

"All right, then at least you can untie me. My bonds are cutting my flesh."

"Only if you promise not to escape, not to jump overboard. The river, as you know, is full of alligators."

"I promise," said Malinali. Knowing that she had been trained to keep her word, they untied her.

As dawn approached she began to make out the new world around the gently moving canoe. The river had become very wide now, even to the point of overflowing its banks, and trees appeared to grow directly out of the water. She was not surprised by the mangrove trees, which always create an impassable barrier between land and water, their roots forming a world that can be crossed neither by foot nor by canoe. But there were other trees also engulfed by the swollen river: giant silk-cotton trees, huge mangos, papaya, mamey and coconut palms. Just beyond them, partially in the water, were many huts, some on stilts, and smoke was beginning to rise from among them. The area was far more populous than the country around Painala.

By the time the fiery ball of the sun appeared on the eastern horizon, they had reached the sea. Now Chac and Xul transferred both Malinali and their small dugout canoe to a much larger oceangoing vessel, a pirogue. It too was a canoe, but it was also a public conveyance which had been carved out of a gigantic mahogany trunk and had many oarsmen lining its sides. Malinali paid it little attention. She sat fixed instead by the sight of the great ocean, which she had never seen before. The morning sunlight had given the sea a blinding corridor of gold. The spray cast by the waves into the canoe was light and airy as the sky and cool as mountain snow.

At first the river pursued them into the sea, bringing with it the silt that gave the water a dark honey tone. As they pulled farther away from the shore and down the coastline, the sea became turquoise, exactly the color of the stone which she had seen many times being carried as trib-

ute to Tenochtitlan. The waves seemed like chains of
mountains to her, and made her stomach churn and her
head feel dizzy.

The pirogue was of impressive size, but it could not
navigate waves of truly great dimensions. Still, they traveled far enough from shore to be accompanied by dol-
phins and manatees, sea creatures she had never before
seen or heard of and which caused her great wonder.
They seemed so much less fearsome than the alligators
and other denizens of the rivers.

For two days and two nights they sat and slept on the
hard wooden benches of the vessel. Each passenger supplied himself with food from his own provisions. Xul offered Malinali maize cakes, but the rolling and pitching of
the canoe robbed her of appetite. Only her eyes feasted on
the cornucopia of stars that glistened above them in the
darkness of night. In the jungle she had seldom seen stars,
for they were hidden by the trees. The spectacle of the
heavens was reserved for the priests and astronomers in
their pyramid-top observatories. Now, though about to become a slave, she saw a new world opening above her.

By the time the sun was directly overhead on the third
day of the voyage, the large boat entered a bay and approached the shore. The water had turned brownish once
more and Malinali could see that they were at the mouth
of another river. Chac told her it was controlled by Taabscoob, the ruler of Potonchán. Here Xul and Chac lifted
up the dugout, together with its merchandise, and lowered
it down into the water beside the oceangoing canoe. Then
Chac jumped into it, holding it close beside the larger craft
while Xul lowered Malinali down beside him. Then he
leapt into it himself. They paddled swiftly and silently, and
in a few minutes they reached the shore. Once they had
beached the canoe, Chac invited Malinali to sit down while
he explained the nature of their destination.

"Now I shall tell you, Malinali, why we do not go on to Xicalango. It is not the length of the voyage that deters us. Our city is not so very far from here. Only a day's journey more. But we are your friends, and we swear to protect you from harm. So we must tell you about our own problems. As merchants we do not engage in armed battle and so cannot take captives for sacrifice. We are therefore criticized by people of our village who are jealous and resentful of our wealth. They say that the rain god Tlaloc is angry with us now, because there have been so many floods and so much damage to houses and crops. They insist that we must do something to appease him.

"For this reason the members of our guild have been planning to buy a slave for sacrifice so that the others in our city will stop accusing us. If Xul and I return with a slave as desirable as you, an Aztec and a virgin besides, they would demand you for Tlaloc."

The sun was beating down upon her head, but Malinali felt intensely cold. Her hands nearly trembled. She sat on them to conceal her feelings from the traders. She did not wish them to see fear in an Aztec princess.

Chac was not easily deceived. The clever trader laughed to reassure her. "Have no fear, my young friend. I am telling you this so that you will understand we have nothing of this kind in store for you. We are taking you instead to the first wife of the prince of Potonchán. She lives in Cintla which is only a short walk from here. It is too far to carry the canoe, so Xul will guard it while we continue together on foot."

Xul sat down beside the canoe and silent still, waved her a sad farewell. Did Xul not bid her goodbye in his own tongue because he knew of even greater misfortunes in store for her? Or did he think she would not understand? Had he forgotten that time long ago when he had told her so many stories that she had listened to with such delight?

She would understand him still, she realized, for during the voyage she had been eavesdropping on the Maya oarsmen and had followed every one of their remarks, even those she would rather not have understood.

Chac walked beside her and held her hand so there was no possibility of escape. It would have been useless in any case. She was lost and not among her own people. She began to realize what it felt like to be a slave, even though Chac talked to her kindly about her new mistress. "She is an old woman, who comes from an important family in our land. We have known that she needs a helper such as you for a long time. Of course she does have another slave, though this girl is not very bright. But, I will not insult her. You will soon find out everything for yourself."

SIX

The Life of a Slave

*F*or a person who had lived in the majestic city of Tenochti-tlan, Cintla was a pathetic hamlet, a suburb of the town of Potonchán. Unlike Painala, which enjoyed some of the trib-ute that was sent up to the capital, Cintla was only a collec-tion of adobe huts, wandering turkeys, noisy parrots, screaming naked children and bare-breasted women.

Malinali was surprised that these women, matrons and young girls alike, went so shamelessly through the streets. It was true that some of the poorer women in Painala also wore a minimum of clothing. The climate was so unbear-ably hot and humid in both places that almost anything on neck or shoulders made the skin burn. But women of her class still affected the traditional Aztec *huipil*, a sleeveless embroidered blouse. Now as the trader led her through the village, young girls giggled and pointed at her. She could not hear what they were saying, but she knew they were making fun of her.

Mayab, the former first wife of the ruler of Potonchán, who was to be her mistress, also smiled at the cotton blouse that Malinali wore. She greeted the girl with good humor but a total lack of respect.

"I know that you come from the proper city of Tenoch-titlan, my princess, but here you will soon learn to live like the rest of us. With such finery as you now sport you will never be able to work." Mayab was extremely fat and old, and she did not bother to rise when the newcomers entered her patio. There she sat on a little wooden stool before a brazier, mixing a pot of *pozole,* with her huge breasts almost hanging into the corn soup.

How demeaning for a prince's wife, thought Malinali. But then she remembered what Chac had told her. Mayab was simply a first wife, long since replaced in her husband's affections by dozens of younger and more desirable companions. She was a retired wife, entitled to a home of her own in the town of her birth. So as not to incite the anger of her family, Mayab's husband Taabscoob also provided her with slaves.

Chana was the first slave. She had eyes with heavy lids, fat cheeks and a pouting mouth. She reminded Malinali of the jaguar baby dolls that Chac and Xul had given her long ago. Chana grinned broadly and with genuine friendliness to greet Malinali. She was happy to have a new slave to share her work and the chatter of the household.

Chana, Malinali now learned, planted corn, beans, and squash in the little garden near their hut. She also fished with a net in the river, and caught the plentiful turtles that she prepared over the charcoal brazier in their tiny courtyard. Besides this, she swept the dirt floor several times a day and did the spinning and weaving of the few clothes they needed. But Chana was a poor weaver, and the cloth she wove was of such poor quality that it could not be sold.

Mayab was the merchant of the family. Selling was what she liked best to do. Everyday, as Malinali was to see, she would slowly walk a league to market, rent an awning for the price of several cacao beans, and squat on her petatl while she gossiped with friends and awaited customers. She had purchased Malinali because Chac told her that the princess had spun cloth for the royal court. She assured him that Taabscoob would pay half the slave's price, as he expected to receive the same share of her work. Chac wisely decided not to mention anything of Malinali's beauty to Taabscoob. He promised this to Mayab.

Although the old woman seemed to be concentrating on her soup, she was observing Malinali from the corner of her eye. Immediately she realized what a bargain she had acquired in the Aztec princess. She would make certain to keep her prize. As Malinali stood over her, wondering what drudgery she would have to perform, Mayab gradually raised herself up. She patted her new slave on the hand.

"You are a little giant," she said, not unkindly. "And you look very strong. But all the same, I will not put you to work outside our home. I will not have the neighbors or any other busybodies staring at you. Here you will sit and spin and weave, since that is what you do best. Chana can continue with the planting and fishing. And your name is much too long for this climate. I shall shorten it to Mali."

Mayab handed a basket of cacao beans to Chac in payment for the princess. When he departed, Malinali felt her entire world vanish with him. Not sure of how much Chontal Maya the girl still understood, Chac had translated everything that Mayab said. Now Malinali would have to be born again, not as a princess, but as a slave, with a new name and a new language. But her Aztec pride remained. She would not succumb to these circumstances. She would play the role of slave; she would do what was expected of her, but the stars could not have lied. Somehow, she would still live to rule her people.

Mayab jerked her hand. "Take your straw mat to my room—there," she gestured cheerfully. "Since you also are a princess, I do not mind sharing my quarters with you."

Within a month, to all appearances the new slave Mali had adjusted to her condition. She dressed, or undressed, like the others. Here it did not matter. They were almost always alone. Besides the spinning and weaving which were expected of her, she ground the corn for their pozole, prepared the fish that Chana caught and learned to make fine, thin tortillas. She also prepared the pulque that Mayab liked to serve on the rare visits of Taabscoob or Halach, Mayab's eldest son. Someday Halach would be the new ruler, Chana whispered, and if Mayab lived long enough to see this, her own position, as mother of the ruler, would improve greatly. So Mayab was overjoyed whenever Halach came for a visit, but she always warned Malinali to hide in Chana's little, dark room.

Malinali understood the reasons for these precautions when it became obvious that Chana was pregnant. She told Malinali about her condition amidst great choking sobs.

"Don't think I didn't try to avoid this, Mali. I have to go out every day among these men. And they do what they want to me. Everyone knows I am only a slave. The old woman does not protect me, the way she does you. I wish I had been a princess. But my poor parents could not even feed me, so they sold me to Mayab. And now the same thing is going to happen to my child. Oh, I wish they had killed me instead!"

Malinali tried to hush Chana's wailing so that she would not awake Mayab and be punished. She had seen some cihuapatli on Mayab's shelf. Malinali remembered the High Priestess's instructions about this herb that they cultivated in the patio of the Calmecac. It was women's medicine for hastening childbirth, though Ciuacoatl said it could also combat nausea. Mayab had apparently bought it for her arthritis. Malinali took a little of the root and prepared it for Chana as a tea. The girl's sobbing stopped, and her nausea subsided, but Malinali was troubled by her own theft.

The next morning, though fearing a beating, she confessed to Mayab what she had done. Mayab only shrugged her shoulders. "Yes, I could tell she was with child. It shows on her face. Well, I suppose I must resign myself. She won't be so useful for a while. But if those herbs help, you might as well use them. They don't do a bit of good for my arthritis. It is the rain god's revenge on my poor bones."

Malinali continued to care for Chana during the months of her pregnancy, and Mayab was grateful that Chana could continue to work. When the girl finally went into labor, Malinali again gave her infusions of cihuapatli which did, indeed, hasten the infant's birth. Chana squatted on her petatl and the little boy was born much more quickly than Malinali expected. Mayab, who knew more about such matters than either of the girls, cut the umbilical cord with a flint cooking knife and buried the afterbirth under the hearth, as was her people's custom. But when the baby screamed during the night, Mayab could not sleep and told Chana she must sell him or give him away. Mayab would have liked to sell him herself, but this she could not do because he belonged to Chana.

Chana again clung to Malinali and wept. "What can I do? I cannot sell him into slavery. How can a mother do such a thing?"

Malinali was on the verge of tears herself. She thought of her own mother and grew bitter with anger and hurt. Yet for the downcast Chana she tried to make her tone confident and reassuring. "Then don't sell him. Give him away to some good people who have no children of their own. Do you know any?"

Chana shook her head, dazed, so Malinali went to Mayab for help. From her seat at the market, Mayab knew everyone not only in Cintla, but also in Potonchán and all the surrounding towns. Mayab readily agreed to inquire, and in a few days the right person was found. The infant was still unnamed because Chana had no cacao beans to pay for the naming ceremony. They called him simply *auahmuli*, "boy," but Chana loved him nonetheless. She kissed him goodbye tenderly and handed him over to a childless merchant woman from Xicalango. After this life returned to normal.

Each day Malinali spun and wove and saw no one but the other two women. On clear nights she slept in the patio between their two rooms, under the stars. Sometimes she prayed to Quetzalcoatl for deliverance from this empty life, but often she forgot to pray. And so six years passed.

Then one day life, which had been as plain and monotonous as the flat earth beyond their doorstep, was shaken by a tremendous event. Halach rushed into their hut unannounced with the terrible news. "Mother!" he cried. "Put your ears and mind to work. Consult the stars and search out the meaning of what I am about to relate! For this is surely something foretold by the heavens. Mother, listen! A huge house has appeared floating off the waters of Champoton. I did not see it myself, but a trustworthy warrior I know swears by it. He says that tall pale men with hair on their faces and shining silver swords came from this floating house and took water from the sacred wells of Champoton. He also told me that our brothers at Cape Catoche had seen the same house and given battle to these men last year so that they fled and disappeared into the eastern sea. All those who dwell between here and Champoton now seek our help to attack the strangers. Who are these men, mother, and what do the stars tell us to do?"

Excited at hearing Halach's words, Malinali forgot to flee into the safety of Chana's dark room. Surely this event was the prophecy of Nezahualpilli and all the wizards of Moctezuma who had predicted the return of Quetzalcoatl! Who could these strange pale men be but the warriors of the wind god? Malinali fairly burst with questions, but as a slave she dared not say a word. She stood near the window, straining to see beyond the plain, almost as if she hoped to catch sight of the mysterious vessel.

Mayab, however, was thinking not of prophecies but of immediate affairs of state. "There is no time to consult the stars, my son," she said. "We must join the others to give battle. We can do no less, or they will put us to shame. Besides, you will win great glory by conquering these intruders. They bode us no good."

Stirred by Mayab's call for battle, Halach dashed from the hut with a promise of news to come. He returned the next night, bloody and exhausted, but smiling triumphantly.

He told his mother in glowing terms how they had darkened the sky with their arrows and how hundreds of the strangers had been killed. "Did you not hear our drums and conches defying them to advance? They have metal sticks that breathe fire. But our courage is stronger than their black magic. Now the warriors of Catoche will not boast so much. Our victory was greater than theirs." Malinali could hardly believe him. If these had been the messengers of Quetzalcoatl, they could not be defeated. She must have been wrong. Life was to continue as before.

In fact, her fate took a turn for the worse. Halach had seen her. That was enough for him. Because he was now a hero in his mother's eyes, Halach demanded a reward in the person of the slave Mali. He wished to add her to his harem. But Mayab was a shrewd merchant who would not be done out of her prize so easily, even by her favorite son. "No, I can not give her to you, my son," she said after a moment's hesitation. "I am not a rich woman to make you such a gift. Besides, your father owns half of her. But out of my love for you, I shall lend her to you from time to time. Remember to treat her well, because she is still mine."

Malinali stiffened when she heard Mayab's words. She thought of Chana's helplessness, now so nearly her own. She should have suspected that sooner or later this would surely happen. Although she knew through Chana that Halach did not mean to kill and eat her, as she had feared with Atlaua, she could not be absolutely sure. Hadn't the Maya oarsmen referred to her as an *awah*, a pumpkin, and an *askulh*, a tortilla? Did they not think of her as food? She sensed that her body in some way would be consumed, that she would be used like any other object. Never had she felt her condition of servitude more keenly.

The next day Halach sent a male slave to fetch her. Mayab told her that she must go and that she should not fear her favorite son who was both generous and gentle.

"But you promised me that you would never permit this, mother Mayab," Malinali pleaded. "Remember, I was a princess and have served you well for six years."

"And remember, Mali, that you are still my slave and must do as I command."

Halach's beady-eyed emissary clenched her hand in his wet palm. Now she did not have a spear or even a broom to protect herself. Besides, she realized that Mayab was capable of cruel punishment to those who disobeyed. And if she escaped from Mayab, where could she go? Where could she hide? On one side of the plain was the swamp, infested with snakes and alligators; on the other, the ocean.

When she arrived at Halach's house, her hand red from his servant's tight grip, she was hardly able to breathe. To her relief, Halach was quite drunk on pulque. He staggered out to greet her, grunting, but soon fell flat and unconscious on his patio. She escaped in a few minutes with only a torn skirt. The next time he called for her she was not so lucky. He threw her onto a stone floor and handled her very roughly. Again he tore at her skirt and forced her to endure his clumsy embrace and the bitter stench of pulque on his breath. Like Atlaua, he was a boa constrictor, about to crush her to death. But her anger was greater than her fear. This was the true meaning of slavery: she no longer owned her own body. How could her mother have condemned her to this? Had she hated her so much? And now she had also been betrayed by Mayab. She was totally without friends, helpless and at the mercy of this intoxicated beast. He breathed heavily as she struggled to escape from under him. But Halach only laughed at her fearful eyes and told her to be grateful that she was his mother's property.

When Halach allowed her to return home, Mayab was again very kind and solicitous. She directed Chana to make poultices for Mali's bruises and gave her a gourd filled with frothy, freshly made chocolate. But Malinali did not drink it. After this and every other outrage at Halach's brutal hands, she swept and prayed constantly that she would not be with child.

The following year the floating houses returned. This time Mayab consulted the stars and also other wizards and priests of some importance in Potonchán. Malinali, made bold by months of despair, dared to suggest that before fighting again they should make sure that the strangers were not messengers from Kukulcán, which she remembered was the Maya name for Quetzalcoatl. Perhaps Mayab gave some thought to her words. Perhaps not. In any case, this time the stars told them not to fight but to trade. Like all the other merchants, Mayab was so curious about the strangers' shiny metal clothing and the white skin beneath it that she did not drive as hard a bargain as she might have. Still, she was thrilled with the beautiful green beads she had got from the strangers for some gold bracelets she never wore. But her husband, Lord Taabscoob, feared they had made a terrible mistake. Within a few weeks of the departure of the floating houses an ambassador arrived from the Aztec capital of Tenochtitlan.

The ambassador, Tletelpotomki, could not speak the Chontal Maya language and made no attempt to do so. But Taabscoob understood that Moctezuma was angry about the peaceful reception they had given the strangers. As he cast about for a way to protest his esteem for Moctezuma, he suddenly recalled that his first wife's slave spoke the Nahuatl language. He begged Tletelpotomki to wait until an interpreter could be brought. Messengers were dispatched to the little hut in Cintla and soon returned with Mayab and Malinali in tow. Both arrived with deep foreboding.

Malinali, walking in the wide shadow of Mayab, observed that the tecuhtli's house was far grander than that of his wife. In its spacious central courtyard Taabscoob awaited them with the skeptical Aztec ambassador. Remembering her lessons in court etiquette, Malinali kneeled and bowed her head to the ground before Tletelpotomki.

The ambassador looked surprised at seeing an Aztec woman as a slave, but was more concerned with other matters. "What has happened that the people of Potonchán allowed these intruders to land and even traded with them?"

"They captured two of our people last year who can now speak the strangers' tongue," she told the frowning Tletelpotomki. "These people explained to us that the visitors wish us no harm."

"And the ones from the floating houses did not command you to accept their lord as your master?"

She had heard Halach report this request to Mayab, but she said nothing. She cast her eyes to the ground. It would only do her and all the Maya people harm for her to confirm Tletelpotomki's suspicions. Surely Moctezuma would use Potonchán's friendship with the strangers as a pretext for conquering the city.

Tletelpotomki had little patience in waiting for her answer. "Your silence is useless, stupid girl," he snarled. "Our spies have already informed us of the matter. You are a slave here. You owe these people nothing. Remember that you are Aztec. Your loyalty is to us."

Malinali bristled at his arrogance. Did he expect truthfulness and loyalty to the Aztec empire from one who had been sold as a slave? Did he imagine he could frighten her into revealing matters that were in her interest to keep hidden? He was no better than Atlaua, no better than Halach. Now it was she who held power, she who had mastered two languages when he knew only one. Besides, it was she who knew the secret he wished to discover. She would lie to him.

She daringly raised her eyes to meet his. "No, the strangers did not demand allegiance to their emperor; they asked only for trade." Observing the frozen smile on the ambassador's face, Malinali knew he did not believe her. Immediately he left the courtyard, and his retinue of warriors with him.

The matter did not end so simply for Malinali, however. Now Taabscoob demanded that Mayab give him full interest in Mali; he promised to replace her with a slave even more dexterous at weaving. Mayab refused. She was very strongwilled, and her family was noble, so she had certain property rights. Although she had agreed to lend Malinali to her son, who would some day be ruler, she was determined, out of spite, to keep the girl away from her husband.

Now Malinali lived in fear of both Halach and his father. Because Taabscoob could not punish Mayab directly, she was afraid that he would vent his anger on her, perhaps have her thrown into a *cenote*, a sacred well, as a sacrifice to the god Tlaloc. But as it turned out, Taabscoob took his revenge on his rebellious wife in another way, in a way that could not have suited Malinali better.

It happened the following year at the time of the great battle of Cintla. There was so much excitment in the village that Mayab nearly forgot to eat. Everyone was now talking about the whole city which was floating on the waters; it was no longer a few houses as before. They all knew that Moctezuma would be furious if they did not resist the invaders, and the kinsmen of Taabscoob were calling him a coward for the gentle reception offered the year before. Taabscoob, in turn, blamed Mayab for her advice and its apparent consequences. This time, he decided, he would listen to no one's advice. He had his face and body painted in black and white stripes in preparation for hostilities, ordered the largest drums and gongs to sound, and full scale war to be announced to all the people in his realm.

Malinali did not witness the first battles on the banks of the river and in the central square of Potonchán because Mayab would not let her leave the house. With bands of warriors all over the town, it was much too dangerous to go outside. Mayab herself prayed and burned incense of copal in the little clay pots of the patio which were her private altars, each pot representing a god or some powerful ancestor. But Malinali could think of nothing now but the momentous struggle being waged between these whistling, painted men and the pale strangers from the sea, a struggle that reached its climax at her very doorstep.

Mayab's house was on the outskirts of the village. It stood like a sentinel next to the dreary, treeless plain where the final battle against these mysterious enemies took place. The three women, each with her own hopes and fears, crowded, spellbound, in the doorway. Malinali knew that somehow her fate was being decided there, right before her eyes. First she saw the Maya warriors as numerous as locusts, bristling with spears, slings, and stones, large bows, *macanas* or wooden swords edged with flint, and copper-tipped arrows. They looked invincible in their black and white war paint and their rainbow-colored feathers. Mayab laughed. She was sure that the ridiculously few invaders would not last more than a few minutes.

Then they heard a boom like thunder and saw clouds of smoke arising from the battlefield. Malinali guessed that this terrifying noise must have come from the strangers' fire sticks. She could observe little, since their own warriors were throwing up straw and earth to hide what harm had been done them. Secretly she rejoiced that the Mayas must be retreating toward the swamp, turning their backs to the enemy, or they would not have tried to conceal their actions.

Mayab, however, groaned, also guessing which way the battle was going. But worse was yet to come. Before their own retreating men knew what was happening, there was a trembling of the earth as what appeared to be enormous deer, with two heads, one human and one animal, came rushing from the sea onto the plain. They joined the attack of the foot soldiers, spearing the retreating Maya warriors as they fled. Now all three women realized that their side was fighting not men, but gods, a handful of gods who could be everywhere at once. The battlefield ran red with Maya blood. Mayab sank to her knees and wept. Chana cowered. But Malinali stood rooted to the spot.

Then she saw their leader separate himself from his deer body. Even though he wore cotton armor, she could see that he was lean and muscular and that he walked with

the grace of a deer. Apparently indifferent to all his ob-
servers, he removed the metal helmet he was wearing, un-
covering a mass of curly black hair, and bent down on one
knee. She could see that one of his sandals was missing,
lost in the battle. Malinali prayed she might find that san-
dal as she studied its owner. His skin was indeed whiter
than hers but nevertheless bronzed by exposure to the sun.
His features were strong and regular; except for the black
hair on his chin he might even have been a Toltec warrior.
Though he was scarcely taller than she was, there was an
air of great authority in his every motion. If not a god, she
thought, he was surely a king.

She remembered that she had never seen a likeness of
Quetzalcoatl. He was always shrouded in masks or other
disguises. Could he have looked like this man? She stood
breathless as he lowered his head, then traced his right
hand down in a vertical gesture and then in a horizontal
one. This could be nothing other than some form of devotion. But since there was no idol present, he must be his
own god, acknowledging his victory. But acknowledging it
to whom? To a god greater than himself? She did not care.
This was the closest to Quetzalcoatl she had ever been. *He*
would be the one she would worship. He was the one who
had heard her prayers. A great feeling of warmth and
happiness filled her body. If she was still a slave, at least
she had found her true master. It did not matter that he
did not yet know she stood there, glued to his every motion.

Then she saw him cut flesh from a dead Maya warrior
and hold it to the wound of one the deer-beasts. Was it his
own form of sacrifice? Mayab and Chana were terrified.
They thought that the entire town would be sacrificed, the
dead and the living alike. The Aztecs would have spared
no one. But the handsome commander did nothing of the
kind. He did not even sacrifice the five warriors he had

taken prisoner. Instead he sent them back to the town with gifts of green beads. This Malinali understood since a black-robed man who spoke the Maya tongue later explained to the people that this god was very angry with them for not permitting him to come in peace. He would forgive them, however, under certain conditions.

These conditions Malinali learned the next day when a messenger from Taabscoob brought the news to Mayab. He told her that the people were too frightened not to accept his terms, especially after this strange god again demonstrated his power by making his great fire-sticks roar at them and his deer rear up on their hind legs and shriek with the voice of obsidian on flint. Then he had again promised to do them no harm if they would permit the destruction of their old idols, which he hated. Furthermore, he would give them a new idol to worship. This was the statue of a fine lady, a *tececiguata,* who looked exactly like a human being, and held a small babe in her arms. He told them she was not only beautiful, but gentle and kind and required no sacrifices. From now on they were to worship only the tececiguata and her little child.

After the messenger had related all this wondrous news, he revealed the real reason for his visit. In return for all this generosity, the townspeople could do no less than to offer the *teules,* as they called these conquering gods, a present of fine maidens to serve the great lady. Every wealthy family would have to make a sacrifice of this kind. And since it was well known that Mali was born a princess, Taabscoob had decreed that she be given to the teules who had spared them.

Immediately Malinali understood. Taabscoob had not dared to come himself to demand this of Mayab. Since she would not *give* him her slave, he would take her away under the guise of civic duty. Malinali was secretly filled with joy at the prospect, but for appearance's sake, she pretended grief. She embraced Mayab with sincere affection and promised even to return, if they should let her go. There was nothing that Mayab could do. She could not even appeal to Halach because he had been killed in the fighting. In one day the old woman lost both her son and the slave that she now loudly claimed was like a daughter to her. But that slave knew that her prayers to Quetzalcoatl had been answered at last. What could be more wonderful than to serve this fine lady and the god who fought for her!

That very day, she and nineteen other maidens were presented as gifts to the teules. The others were still bare-breasted, but Malinali put on the huipil that she had not used for many years and twined white ribbons into her long, black braids. She must let this great leader know that she was not born a slave, but a princess of her own people.

Marina

SEVEN

Confessions of a Priest

*T*he *twenty   maidens   were
quickly   rounded   up   and*
herded to the great square of Potonchán, where the teules,
who called themselves Spaniards, had made their camp.
Taabscoob, bowing very low and preceded by bearers of
the sweet-smelling copal incense, approached the teules
and made a fine speech about these maidens of good families whom he was now bestowing upon them. Malinali
seethed with indignation. Any fool could see that the other
maidens, shameless in their semi-nudity, did not belong to
good families, but were only slaves. The important families
were rich enough to provide slaves and thus spare their
own children.

The leader of the teules, Cortez, whose name she now
heard the black-robed interpreter pronounce, thanked
Taabscoob profusely, as if he believed every word. His
voice was strong and thick, like the honey of the nardo
blossom. She whispered his name to herself: "Coltez, Coltez." She could not pronounced the r, but she determined
to try. It was such a powerful name, like the man himself.
But she was troubled: why did he not keep his name of
Quetzalcoatl, as before?

When he had finished his magnificent speech and the
little interpreter took over in his weak, foreign-sounding

voice, she strained to hear every word, impatient with the whispering maidens around her who were too excited to listen. "Before I can accept this splendid gift," he said, "and before I can allow my men to take these women as companions, they must be purified of their former habits of worship. They must learn about our Christian religion and accept it for themselves. Our good Friar Olmedo will begin to teach them. They will not board our vessels until they become Christian ladies."

Did this mean that they were really being rejected? Would Taabscoob accept this condition? But of course, he had already consented to the felling of their idols. He had no other choice. Taabscoob instructed the women to follow the little man in black who allotted them a small corner of the plaza which was shaded by some huge silk-cotton trees. There they would be taught the ways of the lady. At the same time they were exposed to the view of Cortez's men encamped not fifty feet beyond.

In the next two days the tall, stout priest, Olmedo, spoke to them through the small one, Aguilar, about the new god called Jesus who was the son of the tececiguata and came from a very distant land in the east. This god was very poor when he lived as a man. He was not even a king. But people did his bidding because he was so good. He was a god who demanded that men love and forgive each other and certainly not kill and eat each other. In many ways he did sound like Quetzalcoatl.

While Olmedo preached, the soldiers went about their business, preparing cargo for the floating houses, which they called caravels. They drew water from the wells, built barrels, and repaired their damaged swords and armor with such a banging that some of the girls did not even try to listen to the religious instruction. When the priests had gone for the day, the men often walked very close to the women's corner and studied their future companions with obvious relish. Malinali was very thankful that she had kept her huipil and was not exposed to the lewd remarks which she sensed but could not understand.

On the day they said was "Palm Sunday," the farewell ceremony took place. Carrying palm branches which they had ordered the townspeople to cut for them, the newcomers marched around the square, bending on their knees before the large white cross which they had erected. Olmedo spoke to them, and also chanted in a new language which even some of the teules did not seem to understand. Aguilar explained to the women that it was a special religious language called Latin. After this they brought each girl to the altar. Some feared that this was the moment of sacrifice, but nothing of the sort happened. Olmedo sprinkled a few drops of water on each girl's head, congratulated her on becoming a Christian, and gave her a new name. Malinali was henceforth to be known as Marina. This name was difficult not only for her, but for all her countrymen, who began to call her Malina, and finally, Malinche or Malinchin—an ending that connoted respect when addressing a member of the Aztec nobility. The new Marina could at last cast aside the role of Mali, the slave. She would now serve only the teul king with black curls in his beard and raven black eyes like her own.

After the naming ceremony, the girls were helped into the large canoes which the men of Cintla and Potonchán had been building for the Spaniards. When at last they drew up beside the towering caravels, which rode at anchor safe from the treacherous tides of the coast, she could see many little windows. Some bristled with huge metal sticks, which Aguilar told them were cannon. From other windows people were leaning out, waving and shouting. To her surprise some of these people, on closer inspection, turned out to be women. Above her a rope ladder dangled precariously. Aguilar instructed them all to climb, although their long skirts made this a dangerous enterprise. Marina clenched as much material as she could in her teeth so that her feet would be free to make the ascent. Most of the girls were too terrified to try. Instead, screaming, they were lifted up in huge nets just like the deer and barrels of provisions. Marina at least spared herself this indignity.

After the cargo had been stored in the hold of the ship, the men again turned their attention to the native women, who now huddled together for mutual protection on the slippery deck. Voices were raised among the onlookers, and Marina saw a knife flash in the sun. A fight was about to erupt as each man tried to claim the captive he found most attractive. Suddenly the raucous shouts ceased. Swords were again sheathed. Even the grumbling stopped. In a few seconds Marina understood why. From below the deck Cortez appeared, and all eyes were turned to him. Now the girls listened with all their attention to what he said, although they could not understand a word. Aguilar told them that Cortez would assign each one to a single soldier. That man would be her champion, to protect her from all the others.

Slowly Cortez called out names: "Juan," "Pedro," "Cristóbal." At each summons a soldier stepped forward to lead away the helpless girl at whom Cortez pointed. How did he choose the girls? How did he choose the soldiers? No one knew. Soon all had been taken except Marina. She could hardly breathe. Cortez examined her closely as if she were one of the precious beasts the Spaniards called horses. Why did he not simply say, "The princess will be mine"? But he did not. To her disbelief he called out another name: "Portocarrero." She saw a tall, very fine-looking soldier approach her, and she felt him take her arm. Cortez had given her to someone else! Although the daughter of a chieftain, she was not worthy of the leading teul. He had taken no one for himself. There was some consolation in that.

By comparison to Halach, Portocarrero was affectionate and gentle with Marina, but there was nothing to talk about since they did not have a common language. She shared a corner of a tiny cabin with him which he in turn shared with several other captains and their new companions. Privacy was an unknown luxury. And when Portocarrero and his cabin mates were off exploring the coastline for Cortez, there was no protection from the other soldiers but their fear of revenge.

Four days passed like this. When their protectors were gone, the girls remained on deck in public so that no one would dare to accost them. Still, the women who had come from Cuba often jeered at them and made unflattering remarks. This Marina knew without a precise understanding. Only one of the women seemed to treat her kindly. She was tall and dark, like Marina, but had short hair, like a man's. Marina could tell that she inspired fear in her sisters aboard ship because she carried a dagger, and when she spoke, they would scurry out of sight. Using sign language, the woman showed Marina how she could obtain some privacy for matters of personal hygiene and where on shipboard she could wash and dry her one garment without having to go naked in public. She told Marina that she was called Maria de Estrada. Though they shared no common tongue, Marina wondered if she was a woman of her own world — of perhaps a different race of native peoples—or of Cortez's world. There was only one way to find out.

She searched out the priest, Jerónimo de Aguilar. She found him hiding behind a huge coiled rope on the ship's stern. He was crouched on the deck, picking up little white squares with black dots on them. He was all alone and seemed upset to find her suddenly staring down at him.

"Father, may I ask you a question?" she began timidly in the Chontal Maya language.

"You may ask, but I do not promise to answer," he replied, getting up from his knees slowly.

"I merely wish to know whether the one who calls herself Maria de Estrada is a woman like myself of this land. She has been so kind to me."

He half laughed as he put the white objects into a pocket of his black robe. "Well, it is good to hear that this hellion is kind to someone. No, she is not of your world, as you suggest, but of our own. She comes from Castile, like many of our soldiers. But unlike them, she is a gypsy. She is Maria of the Road, one of the thieving race of wanderers. Although I was not present when she came aboard, I have been told that she persuaded one of the soldiers to take her with him and then she deserted him for another! Now I think she has no one. Certainly she needs no protector on this ship, since both men and women fear her. But I understand she is a brave fighter. She insisted on going ashore at Potonchán. They say that Cortez was most impressed with her courage at the Battle of Cintla."

Marina felt her heart plunge. "Is she then the companion of Cortez?"

"Methinks you ask many questions, my child. But I can tell you she is no man's companion. Unlike the other wenches who came to your world looking for rich husbands, she came to win the treasures here by herself. She acts and thinks like a man. The old witch must have many sins on her soul, but she never comes to confession."

"Perhaps, Father, it is because she has nothing to confess."

"Well, you are a contrary girl, and a proud one, aren't

you! You should come to me yourself and confess your sins of pride."

"I did not know that pride was a sin, father. If so, I admit it. But I had thought to confess to something far worse."

Aguilar leaned forward intently. "Then do not hesitate. Wipe your soul clean at once, my child. What is it you wish to tell me?"

"My thoughts have been evil, Father. I have wished for the death of Portocarrero, although he is a good man. I have hoped he might be killed in a skirmish along the shore so that Cortez would take me for himself. There! I have told you, so you may now punish me! If you give me a broom, I will sweep for as long as you say."

This time Aguilar laughed in a high whinney, almost like a horse. "I shall have to think of a penance for you, my girl. You certainly do suffer from inflated pride. But first I will tell you how stupid is your wish. Portocarrero hails from a noble family. He is related to counts and dukes, great men! Cortez honored you by giving you to this man. He himself is of common birth. His father was only a poor soldier. Cortez is an excellent leader, and I do not wish to say ill of him, but perhaps he believes himself unworthy of a princess."

"Unworthy of me? Oh no, you do me too much honor, my father! You do not understand. Cortez walks and speaks like a ruler of men, like one who knows he is destined for great and noble deeds. I recognize this in others, because I have also felt it, though now you tell me it is a sin. But even so, I cannot put out this fire inside me that burns for him. At first I thought it was because he was my lord, Quetzalcoatl. Now I see that it does not matter. I still would rather belong to him than to any ruler in the world."

Aguilar looked at her kindly and sighed. "Such passion is a terrible thing, Marina. You should pray our true Lord,

Jesus Christ, to rid you of it. It is a vice, like pride, that you must strive to overcome."

Marina's eyes grew large with a flood of tears that she would not release. Her voice became brittle. "Please, sir, do not talk to me about this vice. You, someone like you, do not, cannot, understand. You call it vice, but it gives me life. If I lose it, I die! What can you, a priest, know about such things?" She turned away from him.

Aguilar reached up to put his arm around her shoulders. The plight of the poor slave-princess touched him deeply. He knew he could help her if he could show that he was no stranger to passion. He spoke, almost to himself.

"Marina, again you are blinded by pride. But so you will see that I, too, know the meaning of passion, I shall tell you something that I have revealed to no one else on this ship. I shall tell you this because I know that you will keep my secret."

Marina turned to face him again with disbelief. How could a priest dare to reveal himself as a human being? How very strange these Spanish people were, with women soldiers and priests who tried to be like everyone else! Fascinated, she forgot about both Portocarrero and Cortez.

Aguilar was reaching into his robes again and took out the small white speckled cubes. "Do you know what these are, my child?"

She shook her head silently.

"Then I shall tell you. They are dice, little ivory squares that we use for making wagers. But my passion for these objects is so great that I wager with *myself*. That was what you found me doing a few minutes ago. I cannot overcome my weakness for the vice of gambling. As you say, it gives me life, it is the spice of my life. If not for my wagering, I probably would have never come to the new world in the first place. But that story will remain untold. You will hear from the others that I was shipwrecked and afterwards enslaved by the Chontal Mayas for eight long years. Then Cortez's men found me only a short time ago and brought me back to my countrymen on this ship. As former slaves in this land you and I have much in common."

Marina was dumbfounded. Why had she never asked herself how a Spaniard came to know the Maya tongue!

"But I suspect that your life as a slave was far different from my own," he mused, without waiting for comment. "Well then, after the wreck, we swam to the beach, clinging to timber from the ship, and we were captured by many warriors. We almost wished we had drowned at sea. They put us all in wooden cages to fatten and then to be sacrificed and eaten. Only I and a sailor named Guerrero escaped. We were the last, the thinnest. We did not eat what they gave us and finally we slipped through the bars of our prisons. Then, almost dead of starvation, we were found by servants of the chieftain of Xamanzana, called Aquincuz. We were lucky to be taken as slaves by this learned ruler who saw that I, at least, would be useless for drawing water or tilling the fields. He also observed that I had no relations with the female slaves of his household. You see, sinner that I am, I have always kept my vows of chastity. So he placed me in charge of his well-populated harem. There I assisted the ladies and gave him no cause for concern.

"When I had mastered the Maya tongue sufficiently, I discovered that this man knew all about the civilization here in bygone days, his people's study of the stars, their construction of observatories and of causeways across the swamps and jungle. As a slave I dared not tell him of our own religion or of our modest accomplishments. I prayed the Lord to make me less of a coward. But instead of preaching to Aquincuz, I joined him in his great vice. This was the national sport of *pok-ta-pok*. Since you dwelt only as a slave among the Maya, I presume you have never seen one of their games?"

"No, father, I had not that opportunity."

" 'Tis a pity, my child, because then you might understand how it came to obsess me, just as it obsessed my master. It is an ancient game among them. In their bible, the *Popol Vuh*, it was played by men against the gods of hell. My master allowed me to sit next to him in a seat of honor above the court where we had an excellent view of the action. If I close my eyes, I can still picture the players in their feathers, each team of a different color, struggling to keep the tiny ball in movement. It was the first rubber ball I had ever seen, so perhaps you can understand my fascination with its liveliness. The point of the game is not to capture the ball but never to let it stop. They could touch it only with their knees, shoulders, head or buttocks, never with hands or feet. But the way to drive the crowd wild was to pass the ball through a small stone ring in the enemy's court. It was almost a miracle when this happened.

"As you can imagine this was the devil's own game, for many players, in spite of their leather harnesses, died of accidents or of their great exertions. They would gallop through the court like monkeys, trying to catch the ball on their bottoms or screaming and dropping dead when they were struck in a vital organ. But the game did not stop even while bodies were removed. And even worse were the spectators. They roared and howled like animals when someone scored a pass through the ring. They wagered everything they had on winning; their houses, their slaves, their wives and children, even themselves. Free men could leave the court as slaves because of the wrong wager. Yet I never uttered a word against it. I would even have bet my freedom on this game if I were not already a slave.

"But I have wandered in my story. Let me return to my duties as harem keeper. From an older, rejected wife, I learned that one of the younger women had a lover and was planning to drug my master's cup of pulque and then escape. I therefore duly informed Aquincuz of this plot. The drug was discovered and proved to be a dose so high that it might have been lethal. In short, I had saved my master's life. But in doing so, I was responsible for the sacrifice of his young wife, which I shall regret to my dying day. If I had not so enjoyed my position as gambling companion, I would not have disclosed the plot. In all events, after this he gave me my freedom. But there was no place to go with it until I received the letter from Cortez. It was not until then that I realized all the Indians of these parts knew my story. Surely it was our heavenly father who made them repeat it to Cortez and helped him to understand what they said. The rest of my adventures you know."

"No," she replied, "not all of them. You never told me what happened to the other survivor, the one called Guerrero."

"Oh," he said, smiling. "I had almost forgotten. I brought him the letter from Cortez, but he refused to return with me. He had married a daughter of Nachancan, lord of Chetumal, and was now a chieftain himself. He had tattooed his whole body, had many little children and a wife he did not want to leave. He said that he would be nobody, or worse still, a curiosity, if he returned to Spain. He was happier here among his adopted people. So he stayed. And of course this was wise because he had led the fight against the Spaniards at Champoton. If this were discovered, he would hang as a traitor."

"Would you have revealed this to Cortez?" Immediately she realized that the question was too painful. She should not have asked, but she could not retract her words.

Aguilar looked out to the sea. "I thank our good Lord that I did not have to make that decision." Then he sighed and smiled at her again. "So now you know that even a priest understands passion. But let us say no more about this. Even though the soldiers do not understand our words, I have a feeling that someone is listening."

Suddenly a young soldier appeared only a few feet away, writing in a small book. "Do you mean that one?" she whispered. "He often follows me, but he is very shy. And he is very proper in his manners."

"Indeed, he is the person I refer to. I do not trust that fellow."

"But I often see him with Cortez; they seem to be close friends."

"My child, things are not always what they seem to be. He is a relative of Velasquez and is probably spying on all of us."

"Velasquez?" she repeated softly. "Which one is he?"

Aguilar held his finger to her mouth. "Marina, do not let others hear you mention that name. He is the governor of Cuba who has sworn to have Cortez captured and brought back to him in chains."

EIGHT

Preparing for Conquest—
Cintla to Cempoala

*A*t this very moment the sailor in the crow's nest cried out loudly, and Cortez emerged from below deck. He headed directly toward them, his brow wrinkled. Something was troubling him. But on noticing the young soldier, he clasped the fellow on the shoulder with great bonhommie.

"*Hola*, Bernal. How goes it? When are you going to show me your literary endeavors? You know I spent two years at the University of Salamanca. Or are these poems to be seen only by a lady?"

The soldier blushed. "No, sir, but they are not worthy of your attention." Cortez smiled graciously and immediately proceeded to address Aguilar.

He pointed to the crow's nest and then to the distant shore. Marina saw that the small boats of the exploration party were rowing toward them at great speed. Portocarrero was coming back.

Her musing lasted only a minute. Both Cortez and Aguilar now turned to her while Aguilar, in the Maya tongue, explained the situation. The sailor on the lookout had observed many canoes gathering on the shore and had seen smoke signals arising from points in the distance. Did this mean, the captain wanted to know, that the natives were preparing an attack?

Marina had not seen the signals and did not know, but if there were no war drums, they were in no imminent danger. She was afraid to look at Cortez, but she could feel his eyes upon her. She spoke only to Aguilar. "Tell him, Father, that since we have passed the Coatzacoalcos River, which the rebel chief Tuchintecla now controls, the warriors on the shore are Aztecs, loyal to Moctezuma. The smoke signals are to inform the next town of our position. They will be expecting us wherever we land."

Cortez grasped her hand to thank her, and she felt as if she had been struck by lightning. She could not meet his gaze. Quickly and with relief she turned away and stepped up to the railing to greet Portocarrero whose shouts she could hear already.

She did not see Cortez again until the flagship dropped anchor at San Juan de Ulua. No sooner had the Spaniards arrived than two large pirogues with many rowers approached them at full speed. But the natives were not wearing war paint or beating drums. It was clear that they wished to be invited aboard.

Marina watched as ladders were lowered and many important-looking officials quickly ascended. One of them she recognized: Tletelpotomki, the Aztec ambassador who had interrogated her at Potonchán. Aguilar and Cortez stepped forward to greet them. Aguilar bowed respectfully and spoke in the Chontal Maya language, but these officials did not understand a word he said. Aguilar, dismayed, shook his head as he confessed his inadequacy to Cortez and smiled helplessly at the delegation. Tletelpotomki, his gaze sweeping the deck, recognized Marina. Leaving the others, he went over to speak to her.

"For a slave, you travel much, my girl. Here again there seems to be no one else who speaks our language. Tell me who the tlatoani is for we have been sent by the great Moctezuma to question him."

"He is the one who stands beside the little man in the black robe."

"Him? He is dressed no different from the others! Are you certain that this is the real tlatoani?"

She could see that this man doubted everything she said. "Why should I not tell you the truth?" she answered disdainfully.

When Marina looked around her, she realized that everyone was listening in awe to this conversation. Cortez had approached them. He was beaming with pleasure that communication was really possible now with Moctezuma. What a lucky accident that he had acquired the slave-princess! Then he remembered that he had given her away. Well, no matter. The good Portocarrero would surely lend her back again to serve as his tongue.

The procedure was clumsy, but effective. Marina translated the ambassador's words from Nahuatl to Chontal Maya, and Aguilar then repeated them in Castilian Spanish. When Cortez spoke, Aguilar repeated his words to her in the Maya tongue and she transformed them into Nahuatl. Quickly she saw that her role was a dangerous one. For although Cortez was delighted with the valuable gifts from Moctezuma—necklaces and bracelets of gold, silver and precious stones—his words of thanks were greeted with dismay by Tletelpotomki. When he heard that Cortez had come to trade and to meet with Moctezuma, he said to her proudly, "Your master has just arrived in this land and already he dares to ask for an audience with Moctezuma. Men have waited all their lives to come near the great one! Tell him to accept our gifts graciously and ask for nothing more than the provisions which we have been ordered to give you."

Marina could see that Cortez did not yet understand that the great Moctezuma was unapproachable and that he, Cortez, would have to be as patient and cunning as her own people to ever be admitted into the monarch's presence. The Aztecs were masters of the twin arts of diplomacy and deceit. It was clear that Tletelpotomki suspected Cortez of desiring more than the sight of Moctezuma. If Cortez were really Quetzalcoatl, he would also demand the return of a usurped empire. The ambassadors had come not only to greet him but to spy on him.

"Tell Cortez to beware of their smiles," she told Aguilar. "They have brought scribes to record all that they can about us. Moctezuma does not regard him as friend, but as enemy." Cortez listened intently to Aguilar. Then she received his reply. "Tell Marina that I already know this and will make sure that they see what we wish them to see. Give her my warm thanks for her advice and her loyalty. I understand by her words that she is in our camp now and not that of her own people. I shall not forget." Then Cortez ordered the cannon shot so close to the ambassador that Tletelpotomki covered his ears to protect them from the thunder and looked fearfully at the sky.

The next day was Good Friday, and the Spaniards set up camp on the sand dunes of the mainland opposite the island where they were anchored. There was a carnival-like atmosphere as fresh fruit and fowl were carried in by porters from the surrounding villages and people came to trade golden jewelry for the worthless green beads they called *chalchihuites* and which they believed were emeralds. All the Spanish soldiers turned into merchants, and everyone was smiling.

On Easter Sunday the trading stopped. Two new ambassadors, Tendile and Pitalpitoque, arrived with a small army of scribes and recorded in picture-writing the events in the Spaniards' camp. They sketched the cross that had been erected and all the soldiers kneeling before it. Tendile asked Marina if this cross was dedicated to the rain god Tlaloc, which was the custom in other villages. When

Cortez understood the question, his eyes glistened. He seized the moment to fulfill his religious mission. Without waiting for Father Olmedo, he preached a sermon to the Mexican ambassadors about Jesus, brotherly love, and the great difference between Christianity and their own religion with its abominable human sacrifices. Marina faithfully translated his words, trembling. She could see the indignation and rage in Pitalpitoque's face. He had stopped smiling. Both he and Tendile left without another word as soon as she had finished speaking.

Father Olmedo, who had hurried in at the end of Cortez's impromptu sermon, took his leader to task. Cortez, unused to such reproof, looked bewildered and hesitant. After pondering a moment, again, through Aguilar, he addressed Marina. "Princess, Father Olmedo tells me that I should not have spoken, that they were not ready to receive the truth of our faith. Woe is me! I know he is right. But words cannot be unspoken. So I must ask you a great favor. When I err again in this manner—and I wager that it will happen more than once—I wish you to help me. Please smooth over what I say. Tell them rather what it is best for them to hear. I trust your experience and judgment in these matters more than my own."

Aguilar translated haltingly, in amazement. He was obviously disturbed and resentful. Why should so great a power be given to Marina? Like him, she was only a tongue. But now Cortez was authorizing her to censor his words, even to change them as she saw fit! It was through Marina, then, that the Indians of Mexico would know Cortez. She would invent Cortez for her own people. And he was giving such power not to a fellow Spaniard and a clergyman like Aguilar himself, but to a native person, to a slave he had known only a week! Had Cortez already sensed her passionate devotion to him? Only that would explain such trust, for, as Aguilar knew, Cortez was a shrewd judge of character. He did not place his confidence in others with the same rash abandon that he showed in matters of religion. Aguilar waited for her reply. Like his own translation, it came slowly: "Tell my lord that I shall do as he commands and that I will pray to be worthy of his trust."

The delicate moment passed, but not before Marina, too, realized something: she must eliminate Aguilar's role from her communication with Cortez. Her heart swelled with joy at Cortez's confidence in her, but she did not feel the same with respect to Aguilar. The vice of gambling might not be his only passion. Jealousy, she suspected, could be another one. Marina determined to listen closely to his translations in order to acquire the Castilian language for herself. She would also ask Portocarrero or that other young man, Bernal, to teach her.

With the departure of Moctezuma's ambassadors all the men had too much on their minds to play the schoolmaster. After a few days there were no further deliveries of food or provisions, and while the natives of the area shunned them, the mosquitoes paid them constant visits. It became clear that no invitation to the capital city was to be expected. The men grumbled constantly about oppressive heat, their slim rations, and the wounds from which many still suffered. Stories of Aztec cannibalism circulated freely through the camp. It was clear that most of them much preferred to return to Cuba than to risk winding up on their enemies' dinner plates.

As the quarreling worsened, Cortez ordered a handsome blond cavalry lieutenant, Pedro de Alvarado, to explore the coast northward to find a more hospitable area for settlement. Marina clearly understood now that her countrymen's suspicions were well founded. Cortez did not desire simply to meet Moctezuma. His true objective was the conquest of Tenochtitlan, and to undertake this, he needed a secure base.

Cortez did not consult her again until five strange Indians appeared at camp, smiling and kissing the ground before him. They did not look like Aztecs or dress like them. They had large holes in their lips, ears, and nostrils decorated with golden rings encrusted with turquoise. These adornments were so heavy that their lower lips were pulled down over their chins, exposing gums and teeth. Their appearance was grotesque. Worse, however, they did not understand Marina when she spoke. But she knew they were Totonacs, unwilling subjects of the Aztecs, and she told Cortez that they were inviting him to visit their land. She did not mention that she had once been promised to a Totonac prince in marriage.

Assured of the Totonacs' hatred for Moctezuma, Cortez eagerly accepted the invitation to enter their capital at Cempoala. He and the other Spaniards were delighted by the freshly white-washed houses that glistened in the sun as if they were made of silver, but the delight was short-lived. He soon discovered inside their temples the same remains of human sacrifice that he had found elsewhere. Cortez's orders went out abruptly: no one was to let down his guard. Each man slept wearing his cotton armor and with his sword by his side. Portocarrero was too exhausted by his day-long scouting missions to even notice Marina at night, though she lay on her petatl beside him. She was free to dream about Cortez. And again she knew she could help him. She had met some traders in the city who, like traders everywhere, spoke the Nahuatl tongue as well as their own. She drew them into service the very next day.

It started as a day of reunion for the Totonac prince and his even more corpulent father, Catoxcan, who was borne into town on a litter by many weary nobles. Together they greeted Cortez and complained bitterly to him about the enormous tribute Moctezuma exacted from them, including their own sons and daughters, sent to him for sacrifice. Through the mediation of the traders their words were passed from Marina to Aguilar and then to Cortez.

As Cortez listened gravely, two Totonac messengers rushed in without ceremony, bringing terrible news. Five of Moctezuma's tax collectors had just arrived! These individuals, richly attired in feathers and gold, now appeared. Trailing behind came a retinue of servants carrying great cones of roses, whose scent was reserved only for their masters, and fans to dispel flies and other insects from their presence. The tax collectors ignored Cortez and his company. They strode directly to the two Totonac princes and demanded the sacrifice of twenty youths and maidens in retribution for entertaining the Spaniards against Moctezuma's instructions.

Because they spoke in Nahuatl, Marina understood their fearful message instantly. Thanks to her, Cortez knew what had been said even as it was being translated. Immediately he told Marina that he wished to speak with both rulers the moment the tax collectors left. By the time the Aztecs were shown to their quarters, the king and his son were so nervous that they could hardly listen.

Marina tried to calm their terror by adopting Cortez's own soothing tones and smiling cheerfully. Then, as he had instructed, she faithfully repeated Cortez's words of assurance. "Do not fear these messengers of a cruel despot. No longer will they rob you of your beloved children. We are here to protect you. But first you must seize them and we shall imprison them ourselves. You never again need pay tribute. You will become vassals of our own emperor of Spain, who is kind and generous to his people." By the startled expressions on her listeners' faces it was clear that the Totonac traders had accurately translated Marina's words.

The young prince was the first to recover his voice. In spite of his bulk, the voice was hardly above a whisper.

"What you ask of us is impossible. If we dare to do such a thing to his officers, Moctezuma will come down on us with his great host of warriors. They will sacrifice every one of us. No, we cannot even consider such foolhardy action."

Cortez did not require a translation. The desperate, reedy voice and flutter of the fat man's hands gave him away. Cortez addressed himself now only to Catoxcan, the father. "Fear not, your excellency. With us as your allies, Moctezuma will not dare to attack you. I shall inform him that you are under our protection. He already knows how so few of us defeated the mighty hosts of the Tabascans. Surely you do not wish to keep sending him the flower of your youth forever? If you fail to act now, there will be no second chance."

At this the young prince wavered. He knew that he would be the first victim demanded by Moctezuma. Within very few minutes both rulers agreed to a plan architected by Cortez. In short order, several dozen of their Totonac bodyguards stormed the elegant quarters where the tax collectors lounged, disarmed them, bound their wrists, and fastened them to long poles by collars around their necks. The prince called for their immediate sacrifice so that no word of this would reach Moctezuma, but Cortez intervened. He insisted that the Aztecs be left in his care. Several Spanish soldiers were posted to guard them.

It was past midnight when something awakened Marina from her sleep. Rubbing her eyes, she saw what at first seemed like an apparition in the moonlight. There was Cortez standing above her in the little house that she shared with Portocarrero. The soldier was still sound asleep, breathing peacefully. Cortez put his finger to his lips and motioned her to follow him. Without a second thought she threw a blanket over her shoulders and followed Cortez across the moonlit square into the large house that he occupied. There in the darkness, she heard the familiar voice of Aguilar, already waiting. Her heart sank. Cortez did not wish to see her alone. Again she was to be his tongue, not his companion.

At first no one spoke. She could almost hear the beat of her heart. Then Cortez gravely placed his hands on her shoulders. Beneath the blanket, she shivered. Cortez and the priest exchanged some words. Then Aguilar explained that Cortez wanted a favor of her—a favor so important that their cause depended on it, yet so perilous that her life would be at risk. Would she do this for him? Would she act as his agent in secret dealings with the Aztec prisoners?

Hoarsely she whispered, "I will do as you command, sir. I do not fear danger."

He had been sure of that. She could see his white teeth flash in the moonlight as he spoke to Aguilar, who grinningly described her task as if there were nothing to it. She was to sneak past the guards into the quarters of the tax collectors, and assure them that Cortez played no role in their imprisonment. She was to say that the Totonacs had treated them unjustly, but that he, Cortez, was their friend and it was he who had arranged for their escape.

Marina was perplexed. She did not understand why Cortez had urged their imprisonment if now he plotted their release. But she would do exactly as she was bid. She tiptoed past the Spanish guards, half-drugged by all the wine Cortez had plied them with at supper, and slipped into the room where the indignant Aztecs lay bound and humiliated. In whispers she explained all that Cortez had instructed. She insisted that the Spaniards were the friends of the Aztecs and that they should make this known to Moctezuma as soon as they reached Tenochtitlan. At first the tax collectors snarled at her in disbelief: they trusted neither her nor Cortez. With a small knife she cut the ropes that bound them and led them silently into the forest. When they had fled, she returned to Cortez.

Aguilar was still with him. In the darkness she heard the priest wearily translate her account of what had happened, and she could feel Cortez's approval. Perhaps he could not permit Aguilar to change his Castilian words and rob them of all intimacy, Marina thought. Cortez acknowledged the success of her mission by only a squeeze of the hand, as he might have done with any soldier. But her hand began to tremble at his touch. Moonlight lit his face again, and it glowed, but she did not dare look at him directly. She bowed her head, avoiding his eyes. The warm pressure of his fingers told her unmistakably that he had felt the same small shiver. How would he have acted if Aguilar had not been there?

Marina walked slowly back to her own house, still tingling with excitement and savoring the cold night air and the dazzling stars above her head. As she walked she wondered: what would have happened if she had been caught by either the Spaniards or the Totonacs? Would she have confessed that she was sent by Cortez? They would have demanded that she be punished as an Aztec spy, and the Totonacs punished spies the same way her own people did—immediate sacrifice, or worse. Would Cortez have saved her? Yes, of course! If he did not yet love her, he knew that he needed her. This was at least a beginning.

Portocarrero stirred when she again lay down on her petatl. Marina hardly looked at him. At last she was beginning to understand Cortez. He was as wily as any of her people. In one move he had assured himself of the eternal allegiance of the Totonacs who, having incurred the wrath of Moctezuma, would have no recourse but to be his allies forever. And at the same time he had mended fences with the Aztec emperor by demonstrating his own friendship through his rescue of the tax collectors. Perhaps the Spaniards, after all, might be allowed to enter the great city of Tenochtitlan.

The Totonacs were now more nervous than ever about Moctezuma. To cement their alliance with Cortez they offered seven young women as wives for himself and his highest officers. The girls came complete with golden necklaces and a retinue of servants. Marina suffered silently as she related the old prince's gift. Would Cortez actually marry one of these noblewomen and so extinguish her own hopes? She was consoled when the Totonacs proudly brought forth the proposed brides. Their jewelry dangled from their lips, noses, and ears. She could see that none of the Spaniards found them attractive.

Cortez, furthermore, made the same stipulations for the new women that he had established at Cintla. "Tell them we can be their brothers or their husbands only when they all put an end to the abomination of eating human flesh and sacrificing to the devils they keep in their temples." And he winked at Marina. "Don't trouble yourself too much about their sensibilities. They have no choice; they are already dependent upon us."

Marina now went about the business of interpreting with more gusto than ever. She told the unhappy Totonacs how in Cintla the idols had been thrown down from their altars and had crashed into a thousand pieces. "They were only of stone and mud, objects which we ourselves had made. They were powerless either to help us or to harm us. Yours are just as useless. Do you not prefer the protection and good will of my master and his almighty God to these worthless statues?"

Forced to choose between the wrath of Moctezuma or the vengeance of their idols, the Totonac rulers sensibly allowed Cortez to topple the dragon effigies from their pedestals. They came crashing down in a huge dust of plaster and bricks, and the skies did not loose on the Totonac heads oceans of rain or bolts of lightning. Cortez then obliged them by marrying the Totonac women to seven reluctant soldiers, who had hoped for less exotic brides.

For several more weeks the Spaniards remained with the Totonacs, making peace among their various rival cities and beginning construction of their own base for conquest, the little port town of Vera Cruz. But Marina saw that the many priests who had tended the fallen idols were secretly soliciting the Totonac warriors with demands for revenge. Cortez was not especially disturbed at this news. He merely ordered the scheming priests to appear before him after they had first cut off their blood-clotted hair and bathed away their stench of rotted flesh. Then he announced that he wanted to pay them honor; he was leaving the statue of the virgin lady named Maria in their keeping. They were to give her the same devotion that they had lavished on their worthless idols. Through Marina, Father Olmedo then lectured about Christian love and charity. The old sacrificial temple was whitewashed and adorned with flowers. And so the disgruntled clergymen were passed from one religious world to another, with no loss of employment or prestige.

In a final consolidating stroke, Cortez ordered Portocarrero to depart for Spain with the king's share of the treasure they had already received from Moctezuma. With Velasquez, the governor of Cuba, sworn against him, Cortez had to assure the support of his monarch, and such a treasure was very convincing. Without the king's sanction, his intended conquest of Mexico could be viewed at court as an act of insubordination, almost of piracy. Of course Cortez said nothing about what was to become of Marina. They all knew she would remain.

With Portocarrero gone, Marina's situation became very unclear. She now had no protector. Was she still a slave, or free to leave the camp and go where she pleased? The thought of leaving did not enter her mind. There was nowhere she belonged now except beside Cortez, whom she served without question. But she knew there were men in camp who had no loyalty to him and who had often eyed her lustfully. Even Cortez might not always be protection enough. She thought again about Maria de Estrada.

By now Marina's command of Castilian was adequate for basic communication on her own. She joined Maria and the other soldiers in carrying earth and stones to build the foundation of the fort and in fetching water for making bricks. Marina also proposed that they join the other women in grinding corn and preparing tortillas. Maria refused. "Do not perform women's work or they will treat you only as a woman," she warned. "Stay with me and win their respect. You are almost as strong as I am. It would be wiser for you to learn how to handle a sword."

Marina understood everything the gypsy woman said because she spoke slowly. For the gypsies too, Castilian was an acquired language. Or perhaps it was because, as Maria said, they were distantly related. Her grandmother had told her that all the gypsies had migrated from India. And did not the Spaniards call these people of the New World "Indians?" Who knew but that their ancestors came from the same land?

As they hauled water from a well, Marina haltingly asked her friend about Spain, the land where Cortez was born. She felt it must be a glorious place. She did not understand when Maria spat on the ground. "That is what I think of Spain," the gypsy muttered. "They have hounded my people and burned many others there because they said we were not good Christians."

"Then why do you fight for Spain and Christian religion?"

"Hah, you make me laugh! I don't fight for Spain. I fight only for myself. I will make my fortune and stay here, living like a queen. Maybe I will send for my grandmother."

"But, Maria, Cortez is not like those other Spaniards. He speaks to me with respect. Cortez is good man and kind."

The gypsy woman looked at her with pity. "Cortez is probably better than the rest. Certainly better than the false priest Aguilar whom you talk to so much. But as for kindness, you will see. They are all just as bad as I am."

Marina did not have to wait long to understand what her new friend meant. Shortly after the departure of the treasure vessel, the followers of Velasquez in camp tried to commandeer one of the caravels and sail back to Cuba. There they planned to alert the governor so that he could intercept the treasure before it reached Seville and the king. Cortez's punishment of this treason was swift and terrible. He ordered two of the conspirators hanged and the feet cut off the pilot of the ship. This was a kind of cruelty Marina had never before seen in the white men. In the Aztec world, self-mutilation was a penance. As punishment she thought it was kinder to remove a victim's heart than his feet, so he would not have to endure a lifetime of being planted, like a tree, dependent on others for every bodily need. Even so, she would not admit the truth of Maria's words. Mere humans like herself could not question the agent of a divine power. Whether he was called Quetzalcoatl or Cortez, how could she dare to censor his actions?

Soon Cortez's fearful sentence was followed by another even more disturbing to his followers. Aware that the temptation to desert might be irresistible as long as their ships

were close at hand, Cortez, with the consent of his most
devoted captains, seized upon a daring tactic. First he dispersed his soldiers on new exploratory missions into the
Totonac lands. Then he had the sailors bring on shore
everything movable from their vessels. Besides nails, tar,
spars, rigging, and sails, they tugged the immense iron an-
chors onto land and stashed everything away in the new
fort.

The next part of his plan was more delicate. Cortez
knew that none of his men could bear the onus of laying
hand to the ships. Even though he himself owned a good
part of the fleet, having exchanged all his property in
Cuba to purchase it, others who had also invested in the
expedition might later sue him in Cuban courts for the
destruction he was about to wreak. He sent for Marina. She
was with her gypsy friend when a sailor brought her the
message. "Ah, so the master calls again. You had better
leap to service, my dear," Maria laughed with derision as
Marina hurried to the beach where Cortez was directing
traffic.

He put his arm around her shoulder when she came
up to him. He knew she understood him now. Aguilar was
not always necessary. Pointing to the emptied ships, he explained to her what he had in mind. He saw again that he
could count on her. Yes, indeed, she would invite the Totonacs to a ship-smashing party! There was nothing they
would enjoy more. What the Spaniards would have done
with tears in their eyes—if they could bring themselves to
do it at all—the Indians would do with the greatest of relish.

The invitation spread throughout Cempoala and the
neighboring villages. Scores of Indian warriors arrived,
and with axes and clubs they set about destroying the huge
floating houses, sinking some and running others to the
ground. They whistled and beat drums. Now, they knew,

Cortez could not sail away. The Spaniards would stay among them and protect them from the wrath of Moctezuma.

When the soldiers returned, there was a huge outcry, first of disbelief, then of anger. Of the entire fleet of eleven ships only one was left! Marina marvelled as she listened to Cortez turn the fury of his men into cheers of support. He told them that the fleet had become unseaworthy and was therefore of no use for escape. But if any man were so cowardly as to fear the great adventure of conquering the Mexican empire, there was still one leaky ship left. Let him sail it back to Cuba! Then he waited with a smile of triumph. No one stepped forward. No one dared. And so with the addition of one hundred sailors to their ranks, the Spaniards prepared themselves for the long, perilous march that was to lead them to the treasure-laden city of Tenochtitlan.

NINE

Hostile Friends and Friendly Enemies—Tlaxcala and Cholula

For all their good intentions, the Totonacs did Cortez no favor when they advised him to take the route to Tenochtitlan that led through Tlaxcala. They claimed it was the least perilous of all. The fat young prince, ever fearful of the day when Moctezuma's legions would swoop down on his city, knew that his life depended on the success of his new allies. The fate of this small band of four hundred men and women was now intricately bound up with his own.

"You should go first to the Tlaxcalans," he said. "There is no real tlatoani among them, only four tecuhtlis who make decisions on war or peace together. They are enemies of Moctezuma and have been fighting Tenochtitlan for as long as my ancestors remember. If only we dared to do as they do! They pay no tribute to Moctezuma, but no other state of the empire is allowed to trade with them. They have no cotton or salt. They are the poorest people in this land."

As Cortez listened to the prince's words, his eyes sparkled. "They sound like Extremeños, people of my own land," he told Marina. "Yes, we will go first to Tlaxcala. They should make excellent allies." But Marina was troubled by his decision. In her student days at Tenochtitlan she remembered tales of the ferocious Tlaxcalans who fought like mad dogs against the Aztecs. How could she, a woman of the enemy people, and a princess as well, ever succeed in persuading them that Cortez was their friend? Would they even give her a chance to try? She was too embarrassed to express her concerns. Cortez would consider her cowardly, like any woman. So she said nothing.

The little party set out in the middle of a hot, rainy August, accompanied by forty Totonac nobles and two hundred porters to bring the artillery over the mountains. Cortez and the cavalry rode in the advance column. Marina took her place in the rear with the throng of foot soldiers and women, both Indian and Spanish. There was jostling and cursing from all sides and sweat streaming from those who carried the heaviest loads. Slowly they made their way from the sweltering coastal plains to the forested hills and then to the passes through the forbidding mountains which encircle the central plateau of Mexico. Here the trail took them into a blanket of clouds so thick that they could hardly distinguish who went before them, much less a lurking enemy or the edge of the pathway that dropped off into the precipice. Marina had crossed this ghostly world before, so it did not hold the same terror for her as for many of the others. Those who suffered most were the Totonacs.

Accustomed to the heat of the tropics, the Totonacs shuddered with the cold and the sleet they now felt for the first time. The Spanish soldiers in their cotton armor were better protected, but even they trembled as they wound across the rim of a volcano where the sheer drop into the extinct cone made each step for man and beast a wager with death. No one dared to look down.

As they began the descent into the plateau, a remarkable spectacle spread before them. The sleet and snow gave way to rain, and then the rain stopped. At their very feet a rainbow stretched out like a pastel bridge into the flat green valley below. Many took it as a sign that God would bless their enterprise. Cortez and the other Spaniards kneeled down and crossed themselves in prayer. Marina did the same. Then they inched their way down the slippery basaltic rocks as the men cursed and the horses neighed in fear.

Marina never uttered a word of complaint. It was not her custom to complain. She knew that many eyes were upon her, that someone would tell Cortez of everything she did. Her stoic comportment put most of the other women to shame. She heard their comments as they trudged behind her, and she pretended not to understand.

"Why did I ever leave my soft bed in Cuba and follow this crazy man of mine?" one rough voice lamented.

"I'll tell you," her companion answered. "Because you want to marry into a big estate with lots of slaves so you can take it easy!"

"Well, look who's speaking! But hush up, one of them is right in front of us."

"And what of that? She doesn't understand a word. She's like all the others. They don't feel heat or pain or anything. Even the church is not sure whether they're human or not. So no wonder she doesn't suffer or complain. She's as bad as the gypsy. They're both infidels! I don't understand what Cortez sees in either of them!"

Marina quickened her step to reach her gypsy friend, who was marching with the soldiers. She had not totally understood what she had overheard, but decided it was better to tell Maria nothing or there would be a fight. Maria had a temper as quick as the dagger in her belt. Besides, there was something else that Marina wished to discover. She planned her question carefully.

"You say before that Aguilar is false priest. What you

mean, false? I not understand word false. It means not real? Is he not like Father Olmedo?"

Maria was rubbing her ears to adjust them to the sudden drop in altitude and at first did not hear. When Marina repeated her question, she laughed boisterously. "No, Father Olmedo's a real priest, but what difference does it make? One priest is as bad as another. Or maybe Aguilar is worse because he tries harder to act like one. Fact is, like Cortez, he never finished his studies. He's only half a priest just as Cortez is half a lawyer. That's why Cortez always speaks of the university and boasts of knowing Latin."

Marina bristled with indignation. "How you know all this?"

"Oh, you don't believe me, eh? You also think that gypsies lie? Well, let me tell you, I lived in Hispaniola before going to Cuba, just as Cortez did. It's a small world we had on that island. Nobody could hide anything."

"Aguilar tells me many things," Marina began defensively.

"Probably lies. He confesses to little sins so that no one suspects the big ones, the ones that the little man keeps to himself."

"And Cortez, what does he hide?"

"That's for me to know and for you to guess, my girl." And with a grin the soldier left Marina's side and scrambled behind a huge rock, to attend to a personal necessity.

At that moment Pedro de Alvarado galloped by Marina, raising a huge cloud of dust. Then he stopped to joke with one of the Cuban women. But again, as many times before, she felt his eyes upon her. Although all of the women were thrilled when the handsome blond captain paid attention to them, Marina felt uneasy and almost afraid. Cortez had ordered the soldiers not to molest her.

Pedro had the reputation of being rash and unruly. More than once he had defied Cortez.

Clearly Marina needed protection. She also needed a friend she could understand and trust completely. This friend turned out to be a greyhound bitch called Galga. The creature was tall and muscular, unlike any dog Marina had ever seen before, and although the animal terrified the Indians—since the Spaniards used greyhounds as attack dogs—she began to nuzzle Marina playfully. Marina even shared her rations with Galga, but the dog was constantly begging for more food. In spite of the animal's advanced pregnancy, she was so thin her rib cage was painfully visible. Marina always felt much safer with the greyhound by her side, but Galga was an independent beast who often ran off to hunt on her own. At such times Maria would seek out Bernal Díaz del Castillo, Cortez's trusted young friend, and ask him politely for lessons in Spanish. Bernal was delighted with the role of teacher.

As they trudged along he taught her the names for everything they saw. At first she reciprocated by trying to teach him Nahuatl, but Bernal was not a talented student of languages. He persisted in calling the *teocallis*, prayer-houses in her tongue, either *cues*, as they were called in the Caribbean lands, or *mesquitas*, the name the Spaniards used for houses of worship in the Mohammedan religion, the only other non-Christian form of worship they knew. She came to understand that the conquest of the new world, her world, was for Bernal only a continuation of an older struggle with a people called the Moors, which his forefathers had waged for hundreds of years. Eventually Bernal gave up on Nahuatl, but continued his lessons to her in Castilian.

As Marina's friendship with Bernal ripened, her relationship with Aguilar soured. He no longer revealed anything about himself to her. He shadowed her whenever he was not with Cortez, spying on her conversations with Bernal and often whispering to himself the words she spoke in Nahuatl. She knew he was unhappy with her spectacular progress in acquiring his own tongue. He must have guessed that soon she could replace him altogether as translator. To protect his position, he was becoming as intent upon learning Nahuatl as she was determined to learn Castilian.

Until they reached the frontiers of Tlaxcala the only event of importance to Marina was Galga's giving birth to a small litter of puppies. No one else paid any attention to the event. Bernal had told her that Galga was simply the Spanish word for greyhound. In fact, her poor canine friend had no individual name at all and was not treated by any of the soldiers with the same loving attention that they lavished on their mounts. Since their own lives often depended on their horses, they treated them better than they would even a human being. The Spaniards would have left the bitch at their campsite to give birth alone and catch up with the army when she and the pups were able. As these dogs ran as swiftly as hares, Bernal explained, they would have no trouble reaching them in a few days. Besides, Galga had been left on an island during one of their earlier voyages and found again in excellent shape a year later when they returned.

When Marina saw the tiny legs and paws of the two puppies, unable to stand much less to run, she understood that for Galga to rejoin them soon she would have to abandon her offspring. No mother would do this. The poor dog would then remain behind. The puppies would be at the mercy of any dog-hungry Indian, who regarded roasted puppies as a delicacy. Marina did not hesitate. A few hours after the birth, she scooped the puppies up in her shawl, which became a cradle, and resumed the march. Galga followed her like a shadow.

The word of this little incident reached Cortez, and it afforded him and the other horsemen no end of amusement. It was the last agreeable news they would receive for a long time. By now they had crossed the eastern frontier into Tlaxcalan territory. They saw no Indians, only a few farmhouses, but no one came out to greet them. Every dwelling looked abandoned. Even the air was thin and hostile. To signal his peaceful intentions, Cortez sent the wary Tlaxcalans a message through four leading Totonac nobles who had assured him they were recognized friends of this war-like people. To give the message a personal touch, he asked them to deliver a letter in Spanish, which everyone knew the Tlaxcalans could not read. Marina could have written one for him using Aztec picture writing, but no one asked her to do so.

A few days later they found out that the messengers had been seized immediately and prepared for sacrifice. The grand council called by the four Tlaxcalan chieftains had debated whether the strange white men could be trusted. The aged and blind tecuhtli known to the Spaniards as Xicotenga persuaded the others that the newcomers were allies of the Aztec emperor, attempting still another subjugation of his people. Since their Totonac friends were vassals of Moctezuma and the Spaniards themselves had accepted the Aztec emperor's gifts, Xicotenga's council of war prevailed. His son, Xicotenga the younger, led the attack.

Accompanied by thousands of his best warriors, Xicotenga silently waited in ambush, hidden inside the apparently deserted houses and behind the thorn-studded, living fences of nopal cactus. When the mounted advance party of Spanish scouts came into view, they attacked with the sudden fury of a tornado, their flint-tipped arrows and fire-hardened darts clouding the bright sky, their screams and whistles sounding like the furious voice of the wind.

With their two-handed swords bristling with flint encrustations, and their long lances, they threw themselves on the Spaniards time and time again, defying the horses and cannon that were desperately marshalled against them. Heedless of their peril, they tore lances from the white soldiers' own hands and deftly turned them against their owners. They clubbed and stabbed with a fury Cortez had not seen before.

Only at nightfall did the attack cease. Since the Spaniards had no oil, they dressed their wounds with the fat of a fallen Indian, and slept by the bed of a stream, weary but battle-ready in their cotton armor. Bernal, who had been wounded in the thigh, dragged himself along the sandy bank to where Marina, Maria, and some of the Cuban women were tending the injured.

Like many of the other wounded soldiers, Bernal was lucky. He had seen several of his comrades pulled from their horses and led away for sacrifice by whooping, screaming warriors. Marina had only heard the battle—the drums, conch trumpets, and incessant, deafening whistles. She had been too far behind to see exactly what was happening and begged him now to tell her. The arrow wound in his left thigh was not so serious that talk would be painful. The young soldier even seemed exalted by the momentous nature of all he had witnessed. Marina tried to imagine it as she struggled to understand the new words Bernal was using.

"Marina, I am not ashamed to say that it was a terrifying sight. They carried on poles the severed heads of two of our horses and also of their riders, Juan and Pedro. Did you know them? Poor fellows! Those heads were horrible to behold. You are lucky not to have seen them. And there were so many of the enemy, all screaming and throwing out threats we did not understand along with arrows, stones from their slings, and darts tipped with copper.

The darts glistened in the sun as they flew at us. They filled the entire plain, and everywhere, each minute, more and more warriors were coming, more drums, and banners of different colors. I could even see their leader with his mask and feathers, standard flying, his obsidian-studded sword raised high above his head, always in the midst of the fighting, like our Cortez. With an enemy like this one, there will be many more dead or wounded and sacrificed before all this will end." He pulled out a small book from his breeches and handed it to her.

"What is this you give me?" Marina asked. It was the book she had seen him scribbling in.

"These are notes I have been writing of all I have seen, my child." He liked to call her thus, although, by his own reckoning, he was only eight years older than she. "If I should not return from the fighting tomorrow or another day, I would like you to save this book. You may not understand it now, but some day you shall. If you do not care for it, pray give it to Olmedo. There are such untruths that have been said and will be said about all that is happening to us. Some day my words may serve to give the lie to the stories that will be told."

She did not deny the reality of his fears. But her modesty protested. "No, no, Bernal. Marina never understand this writing. Here no pictures to guide me."

He replaced the book in his pocket. "No matter, Marina. You will learn, I am sure. Already you are speaking Castilian as well as some of our own people. So promise me this. Each time, before I go to battle, I will leave the book with you."

"If you wish. I guard it for you. But now I go to see Cortez. I not like color in his cheeks. He has bad look in eyes. I fear the marsh fever."

Marina's worst fears proved accurate. Cortez did have marsh fever, an infected wound, and digestive problems.

But for three weeks he outmaneuvered the Tlaxcalans, inflicting great losses on them, although hardly a man in his own forces was not wounded. He was standing among the soldiers at the battlefront when Marina noticed a swirl of excitement around him. Aguilar met her, panting and out of breath. "We were just coming to get you, Marina. The Tlaxcalans have sent a delegation, we think to sue for peace. Cortez needs you to question them!"

Forty Tlaxcalan warriors stood defiantly in a group together with four old women as dirty and ugly as witches. Why would they send such people as their messengers? Marina wondered. It was certainly not the reply of an army that had been beaten. She was sure that they had come for another purpose. She turned to Aguilar to tell him so, but he was held back by the milling crowd. Cortez was shouting at her, impatient to know what the Tlaxcalans intended. But how he laughed when he heard her translate the speech of this strange delegation! "Sir, they say they give us corn to eat, if we be only men, or these women to sacrifice and eat, if we real teules. But these old women not worth much. Such gift is insult." The women were smiling broadly, showing their naked gums. They seemed indifferent to their fate and soon settled down to being useful by grinding the gift of corn. Cortez told Marina to speak with them and report later what she could find out.

Bernal and two of the other soldiers were appointed to observe the warriors in the delegation. They followed them from a distance, and saw how they strolled around the camp, studying the wounded and counting their numbers on fingers and toes. Cortez then asked Marina her opinion. Everyone around him was listening. She knew that the fate of these Tlaxcalans, the old enemies of the Aztecs, was in her hands. If only her father could see her now, deciding such matters of life and death! She knew exactly what she should say, but in her excitement in speaking publicly before Cortez, her fluency in the new language deserted her. "These not messengers of peace. They count wounded. Then they report. They say we too few to fight. Only thirteen horses left now. They spies, sir, except for old women. They forced to come. Old women not lie."

Cortez nodded, then commanded that the Tlaxcalans be separated. One by one, Marina questioned them. To each she said that the others had already confessed, until many of them revealed the true motive of their coming. It was as the old women had said. They also disclosed that their leader Xicotenga was planning a night attack, still believing their wizards, the *tacalnaguas,* that the Spaniards lost their magical powers when the sun was not shining.

Having defeated them once at night, Cortez was angered that Xicotenga persisted in his stubborn beliefs. The veins on his neck and forehead were bulging, and his face was flushed with irritation and fever. He had been barely able to sit in his saddle and was now resting on the ground. Still he stood up to give his orders. All who had not confessed to their spying mission were to have their hands or thumbs cut off and be sent back to their commander. This was Cortez's warning that he would do the same or worse to them all if they dared to attack once more by day or by night.

Again, as at Vera Cruz, Marina did not condemn Cortez for the cruel punishment. Nor did she unduly regret her own role in bringing it about. The fate of spies was never a happy one. They always took their chances at being sacrificed on the flimsiest of evidence. But then, so did everyone else. And in war time, there was little place for pity. She knew that Xicotenga himself had repeatedly threatened to butcher them all and eat them with a hot chili spice, since their white flesh was so tasteless.

Xicotenga was discouraged by the fate of his spies and

by the council of elders, who reversed their earlier decision and commanded him to sue for peace. Even his captains were threatening desertion if he did not follow orders, so the fiery chieftain relented at last. In a few hours he himself, humbled but still standing tall and haughty, appeared in Cortez's camp together with fifty of his plumed and painted lieutenants. Magnanimously, he insisted on accepting full responsibility for the misunderstanding between the Spaniards and his people. He asked Cortez to pardon his aged father and all the other leaders. And so the fighting ended after more than three bloody weeks. To the Spaniards it had seemed like an eternity. But their defeat of the Tlaxcalans in so very short a period was a dreadful omen to the Aztecs. In a few days Moctezuma, now filled with apprehension, sent ambassadors to Cortez to congratulate him on his stunning victory over the Tlaxcalans.

The war was over, but Marina's role as nurse continued. Cortez, so weakened by fever and wounds that he could barely walk, allowed her to nurse him with whatever medicines she knew of. In this way he did not have to confess his malady to his fellow Spaniards. With them as with everyone else, he contrived to appear strong and invulnerable. For the Indians, especially, he had to live up to the role of a returning god if he wished to assure himself of their continued support.

Only to Marina, his devoted servant, did he reveal his weaknesses. Did he know that in so doing he could shatter the illusion of himself as the reincarnation of Quetzalcoatl? Did a god take ill and shake with fever? Yet if a god could also be a man, as her father had told Marina long ago, even this was possible. Whether Cortez were god or man no longer mattered to her. She would serve him because she knew that this was her fate. It had been foretold in her infancy that she would rule an empire. Marina now realized that it was to be *his* empire, which with all her strength and skill she would help him conquer. She wanted nothing else but to fulfill the role decreed for her at the hour of her birth.

The Tlaxcalans, who stood in awe of her, supplied all the herbs she requested, especially *tlacopatli*, which caused Cortez to sweat profusely. Always strong, Marina managed to hold up his head as she applied the root to his neck. She felt the weight of his body on her breast and rejoiced in her own powers. Although this man had treated her as a child, she was now treating him as a mother would. The reversal in roles was not lost on Cortez, sick as he was. When he recovered there was a new intimacy between them. It had been so long in coming, but at last it was acknowledged in his whispered conversation and in every look he gave her. Now, when Marina interpreted the elder Xicotenga's offer of two beautiful daughters in marriage, she did not fear that Cortez would accept. She felt, without his having to say a word, that she had nothing to fear from any other woman.

As before, Cortez insisted that the Tlaxcalans become Christians if they wished to be brothers to the Spaniards. But unlike the Totonacs, these staunch people refused to allow the desecration of their idols and temples. Old Xicotenga explained that his subjects would kill him for such a betrayal. With the approval of Father Olmedo, Cortez arranged a compromise. All but one of the temples remained as they were—but this one temple was cleaned out for the Virgin. The Tlaxcalans themselves scrubbed and swept away the blood and gore. Then the place was whitewashed and decorated with roses. Here Olmedo baptized the daughters of Xicotenga and five other principal women. And here, at Cortez's request, Xicotenga gave his newly christened daughter, Luisa, to Pedro de Alvarado, the man Cortez called his brother.

Marina breathed a sigh of relief on two accounts. She could forget her worries about the attention paid by this "brother" of Cortez whose blond hair shone so the Indians called him *Tonatio,* or Sun God. And she could also feel confident that from now on Cortez would regard her as something more than merely his mouthpiece. He understood at last that she was also a woman. She knew that he admired her regal bearing, her long limbs, her slender body and quick mind. Other women of her race had by the age of nineteen already been disfigured by childbirth. But by his gaze which lingered on her for long moments, she sensed that he found her beautiful. When he was fully recovered, she had little doubt, the relationship between them would ripen to that of man and wife. With Galga and the two puppies she would be taken into the captain's quarters. Then there would then be a period of peace, both within the Spanish camp and between them and the surrounding peoples. Little did she guess how events at Cholula were to shatter this beautiful dream.

From the very first mention of the plan, the new Tlaxcalan allies were against it. "You must never trust this deceitful people," Xicotenga told Cortez. "On no account should you go to their city on the way to Tenochtitlan. They invite you only to carry out the orders of Moctezuma. He will have you surrounded there and put to death."

To Cortez and most of his captains the risk of Cholula was worth taking. Sooner or later they would have to expose themselves to the 300,000 warriors that Moctezuma was said to be capable of putting into the field. Only if they could persuade him of their good intentions might he allow them to enter that city—and leave—peacefully. If they could not risk Cholula, only a small ally of Moctezuma, how could they undertake to enter the capital itself?

Besides, Cholula was the wonderful city of hundreds of pyramids, one for each day of the year. They had seen it from afar, since Tlaxcala was only a three hour march away. It was beautiful and wealthy beyond anything they had beheld so far in the new world. The Spaniards were already dreaming of its treasure houses, filled with gold. Even Marina was excited at the thought of returning. It had been eight years since her brief nocturnal visit with Xochi to the shrine of Quetzalcoatl.

Shaking their heads sadly, the four elders of Tlaxcala walked part of the way with the Spaniards, insisting that they at least take an escort of 1,000 Tlaxcalan warriors to help if trouble should arise. This Cortez agreed to, but he was forced to command the Tlaxcalans to camp outside the city of Cholula so that their new hosts would have nothing to fear.

Their reception seemed to go smoothly. The leading warriors and priests came forth from Cholula in welcome, explaining to Marina that they had hung back before because of the Tlaxcalans, whom they considered warlike maniacs and liars. They begged Cortez not to believe any slander he had heard about them from his Tlaxcalan friends. They tendered rich gifts of embroidered cloth and jewels to the teules and lodged them in spacious rooms facing a great, walled courtyard.

Here it was that Cortez in his usual unbridled fashion harangued his new hosts about the worship of devils and their sins of cannibalism and other sensitive matters. Although Marina tried to make him sound less menacing, she could immediately feel the enthusiasm for his visit drop away. As before, the black-robed high priests left before she had even finished her translation. She saw them rush away to register their indignation with Moctezuma's representatives who were preparing to set out for the capital. They gesticulated to each other and stared angrily at Cortez.

Marina's uneasiness was soon justified. After the first few days of abundant maize cakes, fowl, and fresh fruit, all supplies stopped, except for the firewood which they needed for cooking and warmth in the chilly October nights. Cortez instructed her to complain to the leading officials, but they were nowhere to be found. A Cholulan messenger told her unceremoniously that they were ill and that the city had no more food to spare. Undaunted, Cortez sent Marina in search of any person of importance who might prove more friendly. She welcomed the opportunity to leave the restive Spaniards for the sanctuary of Quetzalcoatl, which she well remembered. There, she hoped, she might find a more benign official or at least get information from the old priestess who had counselled her so long ago.

It was already nightfall. The temple was a great distance from the Spanish quarters, and Marina feared that she would lose her way in spite of the full moon. But she remembered that the main temple to Quetzalcoatl was atop the highest pyramid of them all. At last she saw it, round and shining like the moon itself, towering above the 120 steps of the pyramid-platform that the bright sky illuminated. Almost out of breath from the steep climb, she entered the temple through a door carved in the form of a serpent's mouth with fangs and teeth exposed. She was not frightened. Total darkness gave way to the faint light of smoking torches and an altar. Suddenly she felt the presence of another person. Could it be the same priestess still there after all these years? As she breathed the heavy incense of copal, tears came to her eyes.

Marina crouched down, bowed her head low, and touching her hand to the stone floor, she said her prayers. They were not to Quetzalcoatl now, or were they still?

Quetzalcoatl or Jesus, what did it really matter? They were to the one real God. She raised her eyes slowly, hoping to see that familiar face, but even in the flickering torchlight she realized that it was not a woman. A tall priest stood before her in the shadows. He addressed her with great kindness and respect.

"Malinche, I see that you have not forsaken your loyalty to the great Quetzalcoatl. That is good. We have been waiting for you to come."

"We?"

"Yes, myself and another. But tell me first, why is it that you come to us? Is it to pray again to our lord or do you have some message to deliver?"

"It is both, great sir. Are you now the high priest of this temple?"

"It is as you say."

"Then, pray help me. My master Cortez, whom you also call Malinche, is greatly troubled that your people do not bring us food. In fact, they bring us nothing but rudeness and suspicion. We have done you no harm. We came only to rest a little before continuing to Tenochtitlan. Can you find for my master some responsible officials who will explain the reasons for this discourteous behavior?"

He did not answer at first, but seemed to be waiting for some signal, perhaps from the god himself. They both stood in deep silence. Then he laid his hand upon her shoulder and urged her to leave. "Tell your master I shall come when the sun again conquers the forces of darkness, and I shall bring others with me."

The priest was true to his word. At the first rays of dawn he appeared before Cortez with a second priest who wore the wind mask of Quetzalcoatl and did not speak. Behind them came many of the leading people of Cholula, so many, in fact, that they could not all fit inside the room. Again talking through Marina, Cortez repeated his grievances. He could see that many of these pompous individuals looked embarrassed. At first no one spoke. Finally the one who appeared to be the leading tecuhtli stepped forward. In apologetic tones he explained that they were merely carrying out the orders of Moctezuma. The great emperor had again changed his mind about the teules' visit. He did not want them to be supplied any more. They were to be asked to go back to their own land.

"Very well, if you wish to be relieved of our presence, we shall depart tomorrow," said Cortez. "But we require an escort of a thousand warriors and porters for our cannon, those thunder weapons which you call tepuzques."

The delegation quickly dispersed, delighted that the unwanted guests had agreed to leave on such easy terms. Only a few of their number remained in the courtyard. Yet Cortez was deeply concerned. By mid-afternoon Tlaxcalan messengers had secretly entered the Spanish quarters and advised them to be vigilant: Cholulan women and children were leaving the city. Thousands of warriors from Tenochtitlan were arriving, many hiding in the ravines along the road beyond Cholula. Once more Cortez approached Marina for help.

"Marina, go again and find me those two good priests of yours. The Tlaxcalans have brought me vexing news, but it is not enough. I need to know much more." He was interrupted by an agitated Father Olmedo, who had come to insist that Cortez could not punish the Cholulans on hearsay evidence alone.

"Whatever happens in Cholula must be justified by many witnesses," Olmedo declared. "We cannot simply slaughter them because they don't want us here, Hernando. In the name of God I don't know what you're thinking, but I forbid you to take punitive action without reading them the royal decree . . ."

"Which they will not understand," Cortez interjected.

"Then the girl will translate it for them. Remember, my son, that you have many critics at court, and many clergymen will censure you."

"Yes, how well I know . . . the reproof of courtiers who never lay their own lives on the line." So saying, he pushed Marina out of the door.

As she hurried across the courtyard a servant intercepted her. There were two people waiting to talk with her, an old woman and a young man. "There is no time now," Marina started to say, but the words froze on her lips. There in the courtyard, standing uncomfortably among the Spanish soldiers and their heaped-up belongings, were the two people from her past who were the dearest to her in the world. She would know them anywhere. Yet at first she thought they might be a mirage formed by the blinding sunlight. Could these really be Ciuacoatl and Xochi?

She had the servant usher them to her own room immediately. She examined the old woman's face, which had not really changed very much from her school days. The priestess had reached a stage in life where time seemed to stand still in its ravages. But she was much stouter than before. Ciuacoatl noticed Marina's puzzled glance at her voluminous skirts. As if in answer, Ciuacoatl began to unwrap an outer skirt, revealing beneath it the priestly wind mask that Marina had seen only a few hours before.

The two women laughed with a great release of emotion. So the second priest was really Ciuacoatl! But Xochi, where had he come from? Surely he must have entered the courtyard with the Cholulan delegation and remained behind when they left. Since the three friends could have been seen by anyone who came and went through Marina's quarters, Xochi did not embrace her. He merely gave her his hand, squeezing her own until she might have cried out with pain and joy. Her questions poured forth in a torrent, and Xochi answered them in very few words.

"I am a scribe now and came here with our mother to help her on the journey from Tenochtitlan. We arrived only last night, shortly before you at the temple. I knew that you would come."

"But how did you know it was I, Malinali? What made you come to Cholula? It is so long a trip for my poor mother! I don't understand. Did you come only to see me? How did you know I would be here?" She had completely forgotten all the other questions that Cortez needed answered. She almost forgot where she was. She knew only that she was among friends, family, her own people. She waited impatiently for Ciuacoatl to speak, and her teacher's words came haltingly.

"Malinali, my child, I cannot answer all of this at once. Besides, I have a question of my own. But first I must tell you that all our people are speaking of the great teul, your master. Some swear that he is the real Quetzalcoatl who has returned to rescue us from the the dark forces spawned by our evil god Tezcatlipoca. Others claim he is an imposter. Moctezuma knows not what to believe. He is consumed by curiosity as to the real nature of his adversary. If he is a god, Moctezuma dares not oppose him, though the priests of Tezcatlipoca and the bloody Huitzilopochtli assure him that even a god can be tricked as he was before. I do not know whose advice Moctezuma will follow. He is a feather in the wind. One day he plans to welcome the teul, the next day he claims he will sacrifice and eat him, together with his followers. It all depends on the last priest he consults. But I suspected from many reports that the woman they call his tongue might be you. This gave me hope that you were alive and that the prophecy of Quetzalcoatl's return would be fulfilled. This is why I came here. So now you must tell me, child. Is he really Quetzalcoatl? I thought to learn this for myself when I stood so close beside you both this morning. But I dared not touch him. Is he made of flesh? Is he man or god?"

Marina again embraced the old woman, but she was unable to answer. She began simply. "Mother, I do not know. It is possible. But. . . ." She wished to say that she was now a Christian, like this man, but she feared that her conversion to a different belief might break the old woman's heart.

"But what? Malinali, surely you know him well enough to answer my question!"

"No, Ciuacoatl, my dear teacher. I cannot help you. Do you remember our conversations about the first Quetzalcoatl? Like him, my master appears to be of flesh and bone. But does this mean that he is not a god? Even though he himself worships a different god, cannot one god worship another, a greater one than himself? You see, even I ask myself your questions. So how can I give you an answer?"

Xochi put his arm around the old woman and broke into the conversation. "Malinali, let us not bother you further with this matter. We have more urgent things to discuss. Ciuacoatl and I have come to save you, dear friend. I only regret we could not do this before, when you were so cruelly sold into slavery. Then we despaired of knowing where you were or what had become of you. Your mother, Cimatl, lamented that you had been killed by a wild beast. She even buried some poor child in your place. But now you are in danger again, and this time we can help."

Suddenly Marina remembered what Cortez had needed her to do. Yes indeed, these friends could be relied upon to tell them the truth about the Cholulans. Although they were strangers to the city, the high priest of Quetzalcoatl surely had told them what was afoot. She turned to Xochi, still so handsome and tall—far taller, in fact, than Cortez. She realized now that she felt only sisterly love for him, something quite different from the passionate excitement of being with Cortez. She listened carefully, already mentally translating Xochi's words for her master. He was telling her about the trap that the Cholulans had laid for them. "They have pits concealed under the plaza, where spears will rip open the bellies of your beasts when they fall into them. The city roofs are fortified by warriors with stones and javelins. Those who escape from here will be ambushed on the way to Tenochtitlan. They mean to kill you all, saving twenty for themselves to sacrifice to Tezcatlipoca and a like number to be sent to Moctezuma. They say that Tezcatlipoca rages for Spanish blood."

"Yes, my dear, that is the main reason we have come," Ciuacoatl murmured. "We knew that you would be here even before we found out that you were our own Malinali."

Marina ached to give this new intelligence to Cortez, but Xochi held her arm. "Do not fear, Malinali. We will not let you perish. Ciuacoatl and I will hide you in the temple and when it is safe to travel, you shall return with us to the Calmecac. Moctezuma will never dare to look for you there."

"Then I am to spend the rest of my life hidden in the Calmecac, always fearful of Moctezuma?"

Ciuacoatl hastened to reassure her. "No, my child. When it is safer, Xochi will take you back with him to Texcoco, and you will be his bride."

Marina looked up again at Xochi's grave face. He had been too shy to make the proposal himself. Eight years ago in her girlhood she would have happily taken him for a husband. Now everything had changed.

"And my master, Cortez, what will become of him?"

Here Ciuacoatl intervened. "If he is the god Quetzalcoatl, as we hope, our unworthy monarch will surrender to him and he will ride triumphant into our city. If he is an imposter, he will perish in the attempt. But at least we will have saved our own child."

Marina yearned to flee immediately to Cortez, but something stronger than her will held her back. She heard herself say, "Mother, perhaps I do not choose to leave my master, whether he be god or man. What then is my fate?"

Ciuacoatl took Marina's hands, but did not look into her eyes. She seemed to be staring at something far beyond her. "This is as I had feared. Yet I had hoped that I did not fully understand what the stars foretold. The night sky is like a huipil of many patterns. What one sees often depends upon where one stands. And the earth is like the sea now. It is constantly changing beneath our feet."

"Mother, time is running short. I am strong enough to hear your words. Speak now, what is the secret truth that you are keeping from me?"

Ciuacoatl's voice was hoarse. "Alas, my child, if you do not save yourself now and return with us, we shall all share the fate of Moctezuma. Tenochtitlan will disappear and all those within it. I again consulted the heavens last night from the great temple of Quetzalcoatl. The message I received is this. You, Malinali, will rule over many people, but you will never rule over your own heart. You will know great victories and defeats, and you will be the downfall of us all. Death and destruction will always follow in your wake. Again I beg you, come with us, my child. I have revealed to you this prophecy so that it may not come to pass."

Marina hugged Ciuacoatl as if she felt this would be their last farewell. "I must go," she almost whispered to the old woman. "Thank you, mother, for trusting me to hear your words. And raise up your spirits. The prophecy will not come to pass. As you yourself say, perhaps you did not see the stars clearly last night. Cortez, or Malinche as our people call him, will not destroy us. He has come to liberate

us from the abomination of sacrificing human beings and
eating their flesh. He loves our people and will rule them
as a father. My duty is now to him. But even though I cannot go with you, you must not yet depart. It is much too
unsafe. Wait here until the moment when you can leave
without danger. I will let you know myself, or I will send a
trusted friend. She will say she comes from Malinali. No
one else here knows that is my name. So Quetzalcoatl be
with you. And pray him to grant us that we meet again in
Tenochtitlan."

TEN

The Forbidden City
of Tenochtitlan

Marina brushed Ciuacoatl's grim augury of her own fate from her mind like a cobweb. Her thoughts were only for the safety of Cortez. She rushed out to warn him of the impending attack, leaving Xochi in stone silence and the old priestess wringing her hands.

Cortez was in animated conference with Sandoval, Alvarado and several other of his most trusted lieutenants when she found him. All were gesticulating and trying to shout each other down. When they saw her in the doorway, Cortez stepped anxiously forward. "What is it, Marina? Your eyes tell me that you have learned something from those Indians in your chamber." He took her by the hand.

"Yes, my lord. I have learned much. Tlaxcalans were right. Cholulans plan to attack us at dawn tomorrow." And then in a jumble of Spanish she disclosed all the details that Xochi had told her of the intended treachery.

Cortez's expression hardened. "Who are these people that they have such privileged information?"

She had not yet decided how much she would tell him about Ciuacoatl and Xochi. They were Aztec, like herself. He would want to interrogate them further, perhaps mutilate them as spies. Her two loyalties rose in conflict as she cast about for words to protect them. "They are good people. I know them. Long friends. They tell truth."

"Why did they come to you, Marina. Was it to warn us?"

"Yes, my lord. And now she smiled, hoping to change the subject. "Also the old woman want to marry me to her son!"

Cortez chuckled with laughter. "By my oath, she certainly knows how to pick a wedding date! But whether we question them or no, they cannot leave here. The Cholulans could find out that we are on to them. Alvarado, put a guard on them. I will not have them escape."

"Have no fear, sir. No escape. They wait. You tell them when it safe to go. Only promise Marina that you do not harm them."

"Very well," he consented. "But they must remain until this business is finished. The Cholulans must continue to think that we know nothing about their treacherous plans." Then he turned to Olmedo. "Well then, Father, do you now agree that we have proof enough? You may not trust the Tlaxcalans, but do you doubt Marina's word?"

The priest studied her thoughtfully. "No, it is clear that they are plotting to destroy us. But can we not tell them that we know of their evil design and ask them to forswear it?"

Cortez laughed bitterly. "You speak as your sacred order decrees, and so we accord you our respect, Father. But here we are outnumbered a hundred to one. Do you think we can shame them into Christian behavior? Only speed and ruthlessness can save us now. If our holy mission is to succeed, we must survive in order to carry it out."

The priest bowed his head in assent. "Very well, Hernando, but still I must insist that before we beat them in this bloody game, we inform them of the reasons for our action. That is what our monarch expects."

The morning of the massacre at Cholula Xochi and Ciuacoatl were kept under guard in Marina's chamber, where they could overhear the interrogation of the Cholulan warriors. First they heard Marina translate Cortez's accusations, then the Cholulans' admission of their own treachery, and finally their protest that everything had been done by order of Moctezuma. Then the two visitors shuddered at the roar of the black metal tepuzques that shot out lightning, killing a terrible number of Cholulan warriors. All those who appeared in the square thinking to make short work of the Spaniards were felled either by cannon or sword.

From Marina's dark chamber Xochi tried to count the dead until he could count no longer. Ciuacoatl was frozen with terror, but Xochi reminded her that these were the very people who had already prepared their cooking pots with chili to receive the teules. Still, he had not expected such slaughter. It became far worse when the Tlaxcalan allies entered the square, whooping and killing any Cholulans they could find. Even Cortez, who had ordered the massacre, seemed sickened by their vengeance and tried to stop them. But the frenzied Tlaxcalans would not obey. Cortez had to order them out of the city at gunpoint. He allowed no one to desecrate the temples of Quetzalcoatl or any of the other fine public buildings. He had made an example of the Cholulan warriors. That was enough.

Ciuacoatl and Xochi did not see Marina when the killing was over. She feared that she might arouse Cortez's suspicions if she tried to speak to them again. Instead she begged him to let Maria de Estrada escort them out of the now silent city. "They will be less afraid of a woman," she suggested.

"But not of that one," he laughed in relief now that the peril was over. "By my oath, she is the most bloodthirsty

soldier in my army! But do as you will. You and your Mexican friends have saved us. Let's give them a good escort
out of the city. I'll have Alvarado warn the Tlaxcalans to
give them safe passage."

She found Maria in the square, removing golden ear-
rings from the body of a fallen warrior. The woman did
not interrupt her treasure-gathering even as Marina stood
before her, trying not to look at the carnage all around.
"Cortez wants you to take those Indians who wait there to
city gates. Please not to frighten them. They are my
friends."

Maria gave up her plundering with reluctance. "Then
you can finish this job for me. Forget the feathers. I want
only his gold. Sorry, my love, if this offends your delicate
taste."

With the mocking figure of Maria before her, one
bloody hand on her sword, the other heavy with Cholulan
gold, something that Aguilar had said flashed before her.
Her friend was a convicted murderess! The Spanish king
had released her from a Castilian dungeon on condition
that she embark for the new world, and she had come on
the same ship as Cortez. The crown would stop at nothing
to send Spanish women to the conquered lands, Aguilar
told her, because without them, the soldiers' lust always led
to trouble with the Indians. Marina wavered. She wished
she had entrusted her friends to Bernal. But it was too late.
Only at the last moment did she remember the proof of
safe passage she had promised Xochi and Ciuacoatl. She
rushed after Maria and thrust a stone, on which she had
written "Malinali" in Nahuatl, into the gypsy's hand.

After a few days the dead were all cleared from the
plaza and the intended sacrificial victims of the Cholulans
were released from the wooden cages where they were being fattened. At Cortez's instructions, the priests of Quetzalcoatl brought all those who were hiding in the hills back

to the city, and life went on. With Marina at his side, Cortez again attempted the conversion of the populace. But the slaughter of his recent enemies, though it had saved the Spaniards' lives, did nothing to promote their religion. How could the Cholulans reconcile Christian love with the bloodbath Cortez had visited upon them? As before, Olmedo warned him that the people were not yet ready to receive the new faith. There was nothing further to be done. His men had collected their golden trinkets and were now rested. Cortez could begin preparation for the last and most dangerous lap of the voyage, the entry into Tenochtitlan.

Against the warnings of the Tlaxcalan elders, the Totonac allies and many of his own soldiers, Cortez and the small band of Spaniards now began the final march through the mountain passes that led to the central valley. The Totonacs refused to continue, but some Tlaxcalan warriors went with them. Again, all suffered from terrible snow and cold winds. But this time Marina rode with Cortez, and the warmth of his body against hers turned her discomfort to delight. Galga and her two greyhound pups, now grown and fast enough to race Cortez's mare, kept close behind them.

At every village along the way they heard rumors of the ambushes that Moctezuma had laid for them. People everywhere complained of the cruel demands from Tenochtitlan for sacrificial victims and enormous tribute, and they willingly allied themselves with the army that had come to liberate them. Cortez listened carefully to these new friends and never took the roads that were well swept and most inviting. Such roads, he was told, led to traps where the Mexicans hoped to destroy him. Instead the Spaniards followed the paths that had been blocked with trees, removing the fallen trunks as they went. Discouraged neither by Moctezuma's bribes of gold and jewels to turn back, nor his attempts to destroy them, the Spaniards finally reached that very same causeway through Iztapalapa by which Marina had entered Tenochtitlan many years before.

But how different was the reception! The great emperor Moctezuma—borne on his litter of gold, emeralds, and pearls, with its canopy of green feathers, and carried by his leading nobles—came himself to welcome them. Before him other important officials swept the ground on which he was to tread. No one dared to look at his face. But this time they were not thinking of Moctezuma. Everyone strained to catch a glimpse of the man they thought was the returning god-king, Quetzalcoatl.

Marina stood beside Cortez as he leapt from his horse and stretched out his right hand to shake that of the Aztec ruler. As she was explaining to Cortez that it was absolutely forbidden to touch the Great Tlatoani, she could not help but see Moctezuma's face, and she knew that Cortez had seen it as she had. Although his chin was slightly bearded, he had the look of an aging Aztec priest, not a soldier. The corners of his mouth ended in jowls, and his brow was deeply furrowed beneath the heavy gold headdress which clearly taxed his endurance. Ordinary sweat glistened around his eyes. His was a tired and joyless face trying to wear a mask of hospitality and grace.

For his part, Moctezuma's narrow eyes were glued to Cortez, the enigmatic stranger. Was this man a divinity? Had he come to reclaim a throne that had been usurped five hundred years before? Perhaps he had come only for a visit. He was young and strong-looking, but he did not seem vengeful. He might be propitiated by a generous reception. Moctezuma carefully did not take offense at Cortez's ignorance of court protocol. They bowed to each other, and he smiled at Cortez. "For many suns I have waited to see you, Malinche. You do us great honor to come so far. But now you must be tired. We shall visit with each other in the evening. Now I beg you to rest and refresh yourselves in my father's palace."

Cheerfully Cortez accepted the invitation. He did not discover until some time later that King Axayacatl's palace was also the storehouse of the royal treasures, the very gold and jewels for which most of these adventurers had already risked their lives.

During the next few days Moctezuma and Cortez paid each other courteous visits. Each tried to outdo the other in lavish compliments and gifts, although when it came to gifts, Moctezuma was clearly the winner. Marina had by now become an expert in refining and polishing Cortez's often blunt speech so that Moctezuma must have imagined his guest was a poet of the caliber of Nezahualcoyotl. But it took all her skill at diplomacy to undo the damage of Cortez's rash observations the day he decided to visit the great pyramid and temple of Huitzilopochtli. Cortez's curiosity was not religious, but strategic. "From this great height, my dear," he had told Marina, "I can study the entire city and choose our route of escape—if this should become necessary. Remember the warnings of the Tlaxcalans and the Totonacs! If this Moctezuma of ours receives counsel from a new host of priests or wizards, he could change in a second," he said, snapping his fingers. Then he asked, "Do you think they will let us go up to see it?"

Marina advised that they carefully follow protocol, first requesting permission to visit the sight. To their discomfort, Moctezuma insisted upon accompanying them. The tired monarch was then supported by servants who almost carried him up the one hundred and fourteen steep steps of the pyramid. When the same assistance was offered to Cortez, he refused, insisting that Spaniards never tired.

Marina saw that this boasting was a mistake. His display of such physical superiority to the proud Moctezuma, who required that anyone entering his presence be barefoot and dressed in rags, would not be well received. She dreaded what would come next.

Cortez then asked to visit the two temples where the sacrifices took place, and again Moctezuma assented. Marina herself nearly retched at the sight of the severed heads and limbs from a recent sacrifice strung on pikes, and the smell of blood and guts decaying in the hot sun. Even the idols themselves, richly adorned as they were, had a foul stench, for they were made of seeds glued together by blood. She knew that Cortez would lose control in his disgust at such an abomination. And of course she was right.

"I cannot understand how so great a prince as you can worship these idols, who are not gods but only devils and very evil," Cortez, almost beside himself in revulsion, began his sermon to Moctezuma. With Marina cringing as he spoke, he attempted to convince Moctezuma of the vileness of the Aztecs' religion and the superiority of the Lady whom he wished them to worship. "Even the Tlaxcalans have given her a shrine," he concluded, hoping that Moctezuma would not wish to be outdone by his old enemies. Cortez conveniently forgot to mention that the Virgin given the Tlaxcalans had been installed only *after* the Spanish victory, not *before* it.

Silently Marina studied the expressions of great hatred on the faces of the priests around Moctezuma, realizing that they might all find themselves on a sacrificial stone in the very near future. But Cortez seemed oblivious of the situation. He had become more enthusiastic as he went along, preaching hellfire and damnation to all devil worshippers. Did Moctezuma suspect what Cortez had said?

Marina smiled sweetly at the monarch and delivered

her translation. "Although I am deeply saddened to see these rites of human sacrifice, I realize that they have served you and your people well for many years. So that we may worship too, while we are among you, I beg leave to add a small cross to the platform and also erect a statue of our Lady, who has always given us victory."

But the damage was done. Her diplomatic words were received with cold stares. Cortez, finally realizing that he should not have spoken at all, begged permission to leave. Moctezuma remained behind to atone to his gods for his mistake in permitting the blasphemous visit. The Spaniards could see that he was ordering new human sacrifices, igniting their fears that the hospitable climate in Tenochtitlan was about to change.

After this incident there were no more of the sumptuous forty course feasts served on fine Cholula ware with napkins and fingerbowls that had delighted them during the first few days. They were lucky now to get a few tortillas, and their horses received no fodder at all. Slaves no longer came to their chambers, while groups of sullen warriors strutted back and forth outside the palace. Moctezuma denied Cortez's petition for an audience, feigning illness, and the cold winter nights on the high Mexican plateau rang with the piercing screams of sacrifice. It was the same pattern of hostility they had noted at Cholula. And then came the disquieting news that Aztec warriors had attacked and killed several of the Spaniards whom Cortez had left garrisoned in Vera Cruz. The Mexicans would not have dared do this without explicit instructions from Moctezuma. Cortez could see that he had to make his move quickly or all would be lost.

"But we are in the lion's den," Cristóbal de Olid protested. "If we try to escape, the drawbridges over the canals will be raised. We'll be trapped."

"By my oath, do you think I don't know that?" Cortez

snapped back. "If one is in the lion's den, the only thing to do is capture the lion."

"You mean take Moctezuma prisoner, there in his own castle?" Now the wise Gonzalo de Sandoval interrupted. "But Cortez, we are only a few pawns!"

Cortez smiled at his illusion to chess. "But you forget, old man, that this is an end game, and a pawn can become a knight or even a queen when he reaches the enemy's camp. This is our only chance. Sleep now and prepare yourselves for tomorrow."

That night he tossed in the broad feather bed where once the emperor Axayacatl had slept, and Marina, by his side, felt his anguish.

Gently she stroked his brow. "What is it, my lord, what troubles you?"

He rubbed his eyes and kissed her forehead. "My child, I had thought to spare you this until tomorrow."

"Tell me now, and then you sleep better."

He kissed her again. "You are always right, Marina. Very well, you may as well know. We are planning to capture Moctezuma tomorrow and take him here as hostage. It is for our own safety. No one less than he will do. We *must* do it, Marina, don't you agree?"

She sat up in bed, eyes closed for a minute. Then she lay down again, turning to him. "It is well. Tonight I saw clouds hiding the great jaguar of the night sky, Tezcatlipoca. He sleeps now. It is our chance to act."

Cortez laughed. "Well then, we shall use the jaguar to capture the lion." In a few minutes he, too, fell promptly asleep.

The next morning Cortez, with six fully armed men and Marina, unannounced, reached Moctezuma in his own chamber and complained bitterly of the attack on the Spaniards at Vera Cruz. He demanded punishment of the guilty. Although Moctezuma agreed, Cortez gently informed him that as guarantee of his word, he would have to come to the Spanish quarters. The astonished monarch at first refused, and a long argument ensued. Moctezuma offered instead two of his legitimate children to serve as hostages. After a half-hour of listening to Cortez's legalistic speeches and Marina's translations of Moctezuma's replies, several of Cortez's men lost patience. One of them, Juan Velasquez, turned to Cortez angrily. "What is the use of all these words? Either we take him or we knife him. If we do not look after ourselves, we shall all be dead men."

Moctezuma quickly asked Marina to translate. She seized the opportunity. " Oh great Moctezuma," she replied, "my master's men will kill you if you do not agree. Do as Cortez has asked and you will be treated with all the honor you deserve. Tell your captains that Huitzilopochtli himself has ordered you to stay with the teules and all will be well."

Half-believing that he dealt with gods, the emperor of all Mexico was made prisoner by only six men. To make matters worse, the chieftains charged with the death of the Spaniards confessed to their crime and implicated their monarch. Cortez then ordered Moctezuma chained, and forced him to watch the punishment. The guilty were lashed to posts and tinder piled high about their legs. At a signal from Cortez, soldiers torched the grasses until flames sprung up around the victims. Moctezuma tried to hide his eyes. But the acrid odor of burning flesh and the screams of the dying men made the nightmare scene a reality.

Cortez and Marina stood beside the trembling tlatoani. Suddenly the great Moctezuma seemed to Marina like nothing more than a frightened child. Her heart went out to him in his bewilderment. Cortez, sensing her sympathy, whispered, "Steel yourself to this, Marina. We must strike terror in the heart of any of the Mexican captains who might rise up in Moctezuma's defense. I like this no better than you do." She looked at him quizzically and thought of Cholula. Was there a part of Cortez that shared the agony of his victims? Could she be sure of his words?

At least one thing was certain. Cortez was a master politician. Having achieved the desired effect, he kneeled down and personally removed the fetters from Moctezuma's feet, swearing that he had suffered from the chains even more than the tlatoani himself. Watching the hopeful expression on Moctezuma's face, Marina was amazed at how much he seemed to believe. How could someone who was not an Indian lie so convincingly as her master? How much of what he told her at night in their chamber could she believe herself? Cortez was now calling the emperor his honored guest and ordering all the Spaniards to treat him with the greatest of kindness. Moctezuma resumed all the outward forms of ruling his empire, receiving ambassadors and giving orders to local authorities. But Cortez was never far from his side.

With time they became good friends, or so it seemed to Marina. Occasionally the two men would dine together. In order to please his host, Moctezuma even agreed to excluding human limbs from among the delicacies prepared for his consumption. They particularly enjoyed gambling together in a way that delighted all the Spaniards. According to the rules of Moctezuma's game, the winner's reward was to give valuable gifts to the loser. She noted that Cortez very seldom won. In order to amuse Moctezuma, Cortez also had a small vessel built so they could sail together on the lake. On such occasions they engaged in philosophical conversations which Marina's earlier training in rhetoric made possible. One day she was particularly intrigued by Moctezuma's words, but did not dare to question him.

"You know, Malinche," he said to Cortez, "I have long

wondered whether you are man or god. My own wizards
have told me so many different tales. I do not think they
know. Many moons ago I decided to send a spy to your
camp, someone of great honor whom I could trust to report to me truly. I chose an old woman, a high priestess of
Quetzalcoatl. She came to you when you were in Cholula.
Do you remember her?"

"No, I do not," said Cortez, for he had seen only two
priests.

"Perhaps you were too busy to take notice. But she
swore she had seen you."

"And what did she tell you about me? Am I god or
man?" He laughed, almost winking at Moctezuma.

"She said that you appeared to be of flesh, but your
strength and voice bespoke the deity. She said that you had
different forms of sacrifice from our own, but that you
could see through men's minds and could punish betrayal
with more cruelty than mere men can do."

"Then she spoke wisely, this old priestess."

"Perhaps," said Moctezuma slowly. "But I wonder that
you do not remember her."

So Ciuacoatl had spied for Moctezuma! Marina was
dumbfounded. Is this why she had come to Cholula? Was
it not to rescue her, Malinali, as she had said? Or had Moctezuma knowingly planted this story only to discredit poor
Ciuacoatl? If only she could get to the Calmecac and beg
for an explanation! But it was too dangerous to leave their
quarters now, except in company of the king. Like him,
they too were hostages. Surely the warriors outside the palace would seize her to bargain for Moctezuma. All of Tenochtitlan knew how precious she was to Cortez. She had
finally been recognized by her own people.

Moctezuma was the equal of Cortez in his ingratiating
speech and easy manner, and he cultivated friendship with
the Spaniards who guarded him. Frequently he gave them

beautiful gold jewelry. Other times, he gave them women. He tried to use all the subtle weapons in his possession to escape from his gilded cage. Bernal Díaz himself could not say enough flattering words about the king. Moctezuma had promised him a beautiful maiden from his own harem, a girl he selected personally and presented with great ceremony. When the concubine was brought to the throne room, Marina was so surprised that she stuttered in her translations. Although she had not seen her for eight years, she knew this plump young woman was her cousin Metzli! Did old Moctezuma also know that they were almost sisters? If so, he said nothing about it. Metzli eyed Marina in mute astonishment, but they did not speak to each other until safely out of his presence. Marina completely forgot her duties as Bernal's interpreter. The two girls ignored him as they embraced.

Chattering at once, each demanded to know how the other had come to the palace of Moctezuma. Perhaps the surprise of Metzli was the greater, since she had believed her father's report that Malinali was dead. She had even witnessed her burial!

"After your 'death,'" she told Marina, "your mother devoted all her attention to the new baby and to my father, of course. She paid no heed to my spinning or sweeping or anything else. I might as well have been dead, too. We hardly spoke. But everything was peaceful at home. That is, until Cimatl discovered that my father had other women friends. Of course all of Painala knew about this before she did. I would have liked to tell her, but I knew my father would kill me! Anyway, she found out by herself. Then they fought every night. I heard her accuse him of lying about you, blaming him for everything that had happened to you. If he did not control our warriors, I am sure she would have had him sacrificed!

"And then to make matters worse, a messenger came

from Moctezuma. It seems the mighty one"—Metzli giggled—"wanted you brought back to Tenochtitlan so that he
could determine what kind of tecuhtli you'd make—or so
he said. I'll bet that all he wanted was to look you over for
his harem. But anyhow he did not know of your death."

"Was this messenger called Xochi, by any chance?"

"Yes, that was his name. Oh, he was very tall and handsome, that one, but he only wanted to talk about you and
your days at the Calmecac. Too bad."

Metzli paused to flash a smile at Bernal. "So both Cimatl and my father were very worried that Moctezuma would
find out about all they had done. At the time even I didn't
know, so I could not betray them. Then your mother—she
was always a sly one—thought to appease Moctezuma by
sending me as a concubine for his harem. I suppose this
way she achieved a kind of revenge against my father.
Since he had taken away her daughter, she would now do
the same to him."

"And then . . . ?"

"The rest of the story you already know. I have been
here at the palace since then. Although Moctezuma is an
old man who is not to my taste at all, I am well treated. I
get plenty to eat, as you can see. You know he has about
two thousand women here. No one has ever really counted
us. The worst part is that we all have to work, to spin, em-
broider, even to sweep. Not very different from before, except when he chooses one of us for a visit. But this is very
rare. Often he gives us away as rewards to those he favors,
or just forgets all about us."

Marina personally took charge of Metzli's required
conversion to Christianity, and although she was now baptized Francisca, the two women continued to call each
other by their old names. A second woman bestowed upon
the Spaniards by Moctezuma did not please Marina nearly
so well. This was his daughter, who was promptly named

Doña Ana. Moctezuma gave Ana specifically to Cortez, and there was no way he could refuse the offer.

The gift of a new and attractive companion for Cortez was only one of the many misfortunes Marina had now to contend with. Another, and more serious one for them all, was the arrival of the army of Narváez, sent by Cortez's old enemy, the governor of Cuba, to wrest control of Mexico from Cortez and to bring him back in chains. Now the tiny band was threatened not only by the chieftains of Moctezuma, in open rebellion against their captive king, but also by their fellow Spaniards. As usual, Cortez defended himself by going on the attack. With a small force he slipped out of Tenochtitlan to confront Narváez at Vera Cruz.

For this exploit Cortez did not really need the services of Marina. This was to be Spaniard against Spaniard. Besides, Aguilar was now almost proficient in the Nahuatl tongue. Yet Cortez could not bear to be without her. In short order his boldness again rewarded him with success. Through both his political and military skills he won over most of Narváez's army of adventurers and brought them back to Tenochtitlan to bolster the tiny garrison of Spaniards he had left to watch over Moctezuma. But it had been a strategic mistake to take Marina with him. She was his conduit to the minds of the Aztecs as surely as she was his mouthpiece. Her place was in Tenochtitlan.

Without Marina to span the great gulf between the Indians and the Spaniards, all their accomplishments were put in jeopardy by the rash Pedro de Alvarado. In Cortez's absence he attacked the Aztecs during a celebration at the altar of Huitzilopochtli, a celebration for which he had earlier given his approval. The unarmed dancers and drummers were butchered by the Spaniards before they could flee from the pyramid. But when Cortez angrily confronted Alvarado, the arrogant officer explained that the "innocent" Indians had been working up to full-scale murder and had planned to sacrifice all the Spaniards to their god. "Just as at Cholula," he smiled, staring Cortez in the eye. "I have merely turned the tables." But the reasons for the massacre no longer mattered. The results were painfully evident to Cortez. All of Tenochtitlan was up in arms. Although they numbered 1,300 now, including most of Narváez's men, and nearly one hundred horsemen, the Spaniards were no match for the countless thousands of Indian warriors arrayed against them.

The struggle of the Spaniards to fight their way out of the watery trap of Tenochtitlan lasted more than three weeks, from Midsummer Day to the 14th of July, 1520. Bernal Díaz was too busy fighting to record every day in his diary. Like all the others he was wounded repeatedly. Marina, Metzli, the Tlaxcalan princess Doña Luisa, and even Moctezuma's daughter cared for him and all the other wounded soldiers when they retreated each night into the relative safety of their compound. Maria de Estrada did double duty, fighting by day and tending wounded comrades by night. But she cursed and swore under her breath.

Worst of all, there was no respite, no sleep for any of them. When not attacking the palace or trying to burn it down, their enemies kept them awake with taunts, whistles, and drums. Daily they paraded in front of the palace with the severed heads of the Spaniards and their horses who had fallen in battle. Only once did Cortez and his men manage to leave their quarters long enough to fight their way up to the great temple of Huitzilopochtli and hurl the idol down the steps of the pyramid, taking some priests as prisoners.

The only pause in the fighting came when Cristóbal de Olid, who had been particularly friendly with Moctezuma, persuaded the fearful monarch to make a last attempt to pacify his people. Moctezuma, in despair, at first refused. "What does Malinche want with me?" he cried. "I wish neither to live nor to listen to his words!" But at last he agreed to face his people. With Spanish soldiers as bodyguards, he was lifted up to the battlement of the palace roof, and from there attempted to address the human sea of warriors below. There was a chilling silence. At first they tried to listen. He begged them to stop their attack, saying that the Spaniards would leave peacefully, and that he would be free. His loyal chieftains wept to see him. But soon the restless multitude of warriors turned away from his pleas. As he had foreseen, his effort was useless. They had already chosen another tlatoani in his place. A shower of stones and darts burst from the crowd. Perhaps they were meant for the Spaniards around Moctezuma, but three of these stones found a target in the emperor. He sank to his knees and was caught by Olid. The Great Tlatoani had been killed by his own people.

Marina exhorted the prisoner priests who were to carry his body out for burial, reiterating Moctezuma's desire for an end to hostilities. But the assembled chieftains again rejected the offer of peace. They claimed that the Spaniards were completely responsible for Moctezuma's death and would pay for it with their lives. After this the attackers grew even bolder, and each Spanish attempt to break out of their stronghold was repulsed with terrible losses.

With food and water almost gone and their ranks decimated, even Cortez was at last convinced that their only hope lay in retreat. Because of the lakes and canals with their movable bridges, and the flat-roofed houses where their Aztec attackers waited, his horsemen and artillery were almost useless. They would have to steal away under cover of darkness. All the Indian women were asked if they wished to go. Marina would always be with Cortez. But oth-

ers too, especially the Tlaxcalan maidens, feared that anyone who stayed behind would be sacrificed. Even Metzli decided to go with her friends, and so did Moctezuma's
daughter, Doña Ana.

They departed at night, as quietly as was possible, taking advantage of fog and drizzle. They carried with them
a wooden bridge they had constructed to replace the ones
sure to be removed from the causeway. Cortez and Sandoval were in the advance guard. Each man was allowed to
take all the gold or jewels he wished to carry, and the men
of Narváez's army loaded themselves and their horses with
all they could scoop up from the king's treasury. This
greed was to be their undoing. As Cortez had feared, the
bridges were quickly destroyed by the enemy. The heavily
laden men and beasts, surrounded by swarms of warriors
ahead and behind, could not swim across the canals which
were crowded with war canoes. In the frightful gloom most
of them drowned, and their bodies then created a hideous
platform for those who followed. By stepping across the
bodies many saved their own lives. One of these was Pedro
de Alvarado.

Of the Spanish and Cuban women who fled with the
army on this *Noche Triste*, as it was later called, only one
survived: Maria de Estrada. She fought desperately, trying
to protect Marina, Metzli and Doña Luisa, the Tlaxcalan
princess, when a bridge they were crossing was pulled
from under their feet. The attacking Aztecs would have
quickly shot them all full of arrows, or carried them off for
sacrifice, if not for their rescue by a group of Tlaxcalan
warriors, who arrived at just that moment. As the women
foundered in the dark waters of the canal, Marina
shouted, "Swim! It is only a few strokes to the other side!"
She did not know that Metzli had never learned to swim.
And when they scrambled up the opposite bank, there was
no time to look back. Their enemies were in hot pursuit,
screaming and whistling.

ELEVEN

The End of an Empire

B^{*y*} *the time the little band reached Tlaxcalan territory* they had lost nearly a thousand Spaniards—two-thirds of their entire army—and as many Indian warriors. Metzli and Doña Ana were missing, and so was Doña Elvira, one of the Tlaxcalan princesses. Cortez worried about the reception awaiting them. He had learned that many of the natives were friendly when he was powerful, but hostile when his fortunes ebbed. To his relief the chieftain Xicotenga, who was now called by his Christian name of Don Lorenzo de Vargas, forgave the Spaniards the loss of one child and rejoiced that at least his Doña Luisa was safe. Together they prayed for the souls of relatives and friends.

Those who returned were so covered with wounds and so ill from exhaustion that they could do nothing but rest. But while Cortez tossed on his mat, tended again by Marina, his mind was fixed on revenge against the Mexicans. He would stare at the wall for long periods for time, his face flushed with ire and with fever. He did not even seem to be aware of Marina. While he was in one of these terrible moods, she left his side and walked into the little garden outside their house. There she found the gypsy Maria, sitting under an avocado tree and repairing her cotton armor.

"What's happened, Marina?" she asked, immediately rising to her feet. "There is a cloud over your face. Is Cortez worse?"

Marina looked at the other woman with suspicion. Did she also love Cortez? It did not matter. She had nothing to fear now on that score. She remembered Cortez referring to Maria as "that old Amazon." Maria was around thirty-four, almost the same age as Cortez himself. She was a most unlikely rival. "He is not worse, Maria, but different now," Marina replied thoughtfully. "He burns with anger more than fever. I think that he hates all my people . . . I almost fear him sometimes. I begin to wonder if he is good Christian."

Maria laughed loudly. "A good Christian? Of course he's a good Christian, just as I am, when it suits us. But let me remind you of something, dearie. Even you have seen the flayed faces of our soldiers' heads on hooks in their temples. Not a pretty sight, eh? They're attacking us on the road and sending our men to Tenochtitlan to have their hearts ripped out. And the lying swines promised to be our allies! Who wouldn't want revenge?"

"But we brand them with hot irons! It is so cruel. Many are women and children. I could be one of them."

"Well it's too bad, your majesty," and Maria bowed in mockery, "but try to understand. We must make an example of them, or all the other Indians will be at us, now that they know how weak we are."

"Maria, you sound like him—only worse," replied Marina, shaking her head.

"Well, of course I'm like him. We share the same dangers. Aren't we both soldiers?"

Marina could not endure such presumption from her friend—even if the gypsy carried a dagger in her belt. She burst out suddenly. "How dare you compare yourself to *him*! I know about *you*. You are a common murderer!"

She turned quickly to leave, but Maria swung her around and held her shoulders in an iron grip. Her coal-black eyes were flashing with anger. "Who told you that story? The hussies feeding the fish in the big Aztec ditch or that gossip, Aguilar? Well, who cares! You know why they call me a murderess? I stabbed the soldier who raped me when I was only sixteen! They would have hung me, a despised gypsy, but in court I lied and said I was pregnant. Then to be released from jail, I let them ship me to the colonies. They were so desperate to satisfy their soldiers' lust that they would take any woman, even one of us."

Marina bowed her head in shame when she heard these words. If she had used her spear on her stepfather, surely she too would have been sentenced to death. She hated herself for having spoken. After a moment's hesitation, she threw her arms around Maria and begged forgiveness. Why had she ever believed Aguilar! Maria might be wild, but she had always been kind. Like Ciuacoatl, Maria had never failed to protect her. If only she herself could be more like this strange woman, strong, courageous, and wise!

Sadly she returned to Cortez. He was now sitting up and looked surprised that she had left. When she squatted beside him, he pulled her down with his old strength. "Marina, why did you desert me just now? I must talk to you. I have decided on everything." His eyes had suddenly become alive again. "Now I know how we can take Tenochtitlan!"

He seemed delirious, like a mad man, hardly able to walk but believing he could capture the impregnable city from which they had barely escaped with their lives. But she let him hold her there and she listened. At times she thought he was talking to himself.

"Yes, my darling, now I see it all clearly. We must build a naval armada so that we can attack the city by water as well as by land. There is no other way to take it. We can use all the materials that we salvaged from the ships to construct the new fleet. You remember how we packed them into the fortress at Vera Cruz? I still have some able-bodied men. Olid, Alvarez, maybe even Maria. None of them are in bad shape. I will send them to Vera Cruz to organize the transport."

She thought he was raving, but within a few weeks, sails, rigging, cables, blacksmiths, and carpenters arrived in camp. Then came a supply of gunpowder and fresh horses. These had been sent from the governors of Cuba and Jamaica to support Narváez, who was now Cortez's prisoner. The ship captains in charge had readily transferred everything to Cortez's men in exchange for gold ingots.

By Christmas of 1520, Cortez felt sufficiently recuperated and prepared to begin the campaign for the recapture of Tenochtitlan. In addition to his own reinforced army, he now had thousands of Tlaxcalan warriors supplied by Don Lorenzo. All were thirsting for revenge against the Mexicans. Marina was invited to the war council as Cortez and his captains debated which route to take. They could make their base either in Texcoco or Ayotzingo. There the sloops would be assembled and launched in the creeks that ran into the great salt lake. But which of the two cities to choose? Finally Cortez asked Marina's opinion. By now everyone was confident of her fidelity and wisdom. Still she hesitated to give advice. So much could go wrong. "I am not sure," she said finally, "but I think Texcoco is better. There are many in that city who hate the men of Tenochtitlan."

Their welcome was far from certain, even in Texcoco. At first they were warmly greeted by a chieftain and a delegation of warriors bearing a golden banner and an invitation to enter their city. But once inside, they noticed that there were few people in the streets. Marina climbed with Cortez the highest pyramid of the city. From there they could see long lines of women and children, heading either for canoes in the lake or the hills beyond.

"I do not like the look of this, Marina," he said, remembering how the Cholulans had evacuated the women before their attack.

"No, my lord," she murmured. It had been her advice to enter this city.

Cortez made no recrimination, however. He simply commanded, "Have them bring me that chieftain who met us with the golden banner. I will force an explanation from him."

But that chieftain too had left the city.

Cortez stared at Marina in a way she had not seen before. Did he doubt her loyalty or her judgment? Even if he said nothing, she could not bear that strange, critical expression.

"My lord, it does not matter that he has fled. There are still important men left in this city who will help us. Let me seek them out."

"Very well, I shall provide you with an escort."

"Do as you will," she whispered, and set out with a sagging heart for the temple of Quetzalcoatl. If there was anyone in Texcoco who could help her, that again would be the place to look.

Much to her relief, there were many priests gathered at the temple along with other leading officials. Marina realized that some sort of meeting was going on and suddenly feared she would be taken for a spy. The Spanish soldiers following close behind her only made matters worse, but the priests greeted her warmly.

"Malinche! Malinche!" one of them called out. "We thank great Quetzalcoatl that you have come! Here we have gathered to go all together to your master. We of this holy temple have long opposed those cowards who fled the city. The treacherous dog who gave you that gold banner had no right to be our ruler. He is a spider, a criminal, the murderer of his eldest brother! We are lucky to be rid of him. But there is a young man, a good man, whom we wish to propose to your leader as the new tecuhtli."

Greatly relieved, Marina led them all to the empty house where Cortez had taken up lodging. Then in the respectful silence of these local dignitaries, she explained to him all that they had told her, and he seemed pleased with her again. In the past months he had himself chosen the chieftains for many of the subject towns, so that he could build up trustworthy allies. This task had been made easier because of smallpox, which was spreading like wildfire throughout the land. Many of the old tecuhtlis had succumbed to this plague, and since the Spaniards seemed immune to it and did not die, the remaining Indians were all the more certain that they were real teules.

Now once again Cortez was being given the chance to choose a new ruler, and nothing could please him more. He addressed the priest who seemed to be the spokeman for the group. "You must bring me this young man you speak of so that I may see if he is worthy to rule your great city."

"Oh, Malinche, he is more than worthy to rule. He is a son of the great Nezahualpilli and a most learned man. Look now. He enters your chamber this very moment!"

All eyes turned to the door. There was a rustle of feathers. They could see a tall, dark figure approaching, carrying a staff in one hand and a scroll in the other. Marina wondered if she should dare look at the man's face, since Moctezuma and most of his leading officials had forbidden this. But curiosity overcame her. When the newcomer reached Cortez, she looked up timidly, trying not to meet his eyes. Within a second she forgot every precaution. Her wavering gaze was met by another, smiling and self-confident. She could not believe it. "Xochi!" she cried, without realizing that she had spoken.

Cortez examined him critically, surprised and perhaps disturbed that the newcomer was known to Marina. Then he scowled at her. "You seem to know this young man. Have I not also seen him before?"

"Yes, your eyes speak truly. He came with the old woman who warned us at Cholula."

"What a strange coincidence! So this is the man whom she proposed that you marry?"

"Yes, my lord. . . ."

"Well, by my oath, girl, if I decide to make him king of Texcoco, you can be the queen! Would you like that, Marina?"

"My lord, I will do as you command. But I prefer to remain . . . with you." Even as she spoke, Marina wondered if Cortez was serious. Would he really marry her off to Xochi?

He patted her gently on the back as if she were a small child. "That is well, Marina. Because I am not yet ready to give you away to this fellow. But let us question him a bit before we crown him. There are some matters that he must answer for."

Marina then explained to the assemblage that Cortez desired to talk privately with Xochi, and the three walked out of the crowded room into the morning sunlight.

"Interrogate this princeling about his role at Cholula," commanded Cortez. "Do you recall what Moctezuma said about the spy he sent to our camp? What does your Xochi know of this?"

As Cortez spoke, Marina wondered how much of Xochi's answer she would translate for him. If indeed Xochi or Ciuacoatl were spies, would she betray her old friends, or would she lie to this man she loved? She knew that Xochi would tell her the truth. But now she would again have to choose where to place her loyalty.

Xochi's words, however, made deceit unnecessary. The story he told was so patently true that Cortez could hold no suspicions about him. "Yes," he admitted, "I acted as a spy for Ciuacoatl several times, as you yourself knew, Malinali. And Moctezuma did not lie. He sent Ciuacoatl to Cholula to find out whether Malinche was man or god. Oddly enough, he trusted her more than any of his ambassadors. He knew that as the daughter of Nezahualcoyotl, she would tell the truth. She could not refuse this mission. I helped by carrying her on my shoulders most of the way. As you now know, Ciuacoatl is my aunt, the sister of my father, Nezahualpilli. No woman her age could walk and climb for so many days without help. She asked to have me with her, and Moctezuma agreed. At that moment he had not yet made up his mind to destroy you. But while we proceeded slowly over the mountains, we saw many warriors racing on past us. We did not yet suspect that the priests of Huitzilopochtli had won him over.

"Only when we were in Cholula did we learn of the treachery planned against you. Seeing you, Malinali, there at the temple of Quetzalcoatl, we realized to our great joy that you were alive. We also then understood that you were the famous 'Malinche,' the companion of Quetzalcoatl. We could not let you perish. It was better to risk the wrath of Moctezuma. And so we betrayed our original mission and warned you about your danger. Of course, when we returned to Tenochtitlan, Ciuacoatl reported nothing of our discovery to Moctezuma. He was then trembling with fear after your victory in Cholula. She advised him only to welcome you as a messenger of the departed god."

As Marina knew, Cortez had forgiven far greater transgressions on the part of his Indian allies than that of spying for Moctezuma. If he could pardon the Tlaxcalans and the Cholulans, he could certainly forgive Xochi. And true to form, he embraced the young man and thanked him for having saved their lives. He then immediately announced his approval of Xochi as the new tecuhtli and instructed Marina to teach Xochi about Christianity so that he could be baptized before being crowned. By now she had listened to Olmedo so often that she knew all he had to say. It was not the first time that Cortez had delegated this task to her.

It took Marina no time to explain to Xochi that Jesus and Quetzalcoatl were the same person. "They had trouble saying his name when he went to Castile," she said, "so they called him 'Jesus.' But his commands were the same: that men should be humble, kind, generous, and forgiving, and that human sacrifice was not to be tolerated."

"But the cross these Christians worship. Does it not belong to Tlaloc, our rain god?" Xochi asked.

She smiled and took his hand. "No, dear brother, it is to show that Jesus sacrificed himself so that men should be sacrificed no longer. This was the way he proved that he was also Quetzalcoatl."

Neither Olmedo nor Cortez knew what Marina said in making her conversions, but her fame as a preacher to the Indians soon spread throughout the camp. Xochi was only one among her many converts, but he was the best known. Much to Cortez's embarrassment, upon his baptism Xochi, whose full name was Ixtlilxochitl, insisted that he now be called Don Hernando Cortez. Cortez's enemies, as everyone knew, would ridicule him for naming this prince after himself. But for Marina and all of Cortez's friends, the name was only a source of amusement. Since the original bearer of the name had always insisted upon being known simply as "Cortez," democratically refusing to be called "Don Hernando," this honorific form of address was reserved for Xochi.

The newly baptized Don Hernando proved a worthy match for his namesake. He persuaded other lake towns to make peace with the Spaniards and then joined them with many of his relatives in the campaign against Tenochtitlan. One by one, and at great cost, Cortez and his allies from Tlaxcala and Texcoco subdued the remaining towns bordering the lakes so that Tenochtitlan was finally encircled by enemies. In the few peaceful moments between campaigns around the lake shores Marina and Don Hernando caught up on each other's lives. He knew nothing of the fate of Metzli, but Ciuacoatl remained at the Calmecac. Now that he controlled Texcoco, he had sent messengers to urge her to escape to the city of her birth. "The climate in Tenochtitlan has become very dangerous for her. The new emperor Cuauhtemoc is completely in the hands of the priests of Huitzilopochtli. Since I have become your ally, they may seize her at any time."

Marina approached Cortez with her fear for Ciuacoatl's safety. Could some horsemen be spared to stage a rapid rescue mission to the Calmecac, she wondered? Cortez offered no encouragement.

"Upon my word, girl, your idea belongs in a novel of chivalry! In the real world it is impossible. Horsemen are useless there, as you well know. The minute they approach, all the drawbridges will be opened. The only way to enter that city is to destroy every house along the causeways so that they cannot attack us from the roofs, and then use the debris to fill in the canals under the bridges. We will rescue your priestess in due time. Trust me. But first we must take every causeway, cut off their aqueducts and blockade them with our navy so that their canoes can no longer bring in food. Surely you have explained this often enough to our allies to understand it yourself?"

Marina did understand and said no more about Ciuacoatl. The final attempt to capture Tenochtitlan was about

to begin. Revenge was now at hand. The thirteen brigantines were launched, and the causeways became the scene
of constant bloody fighting between the Spanish forces and
the stubborn defenders of the city. But the siege of Tenochtitlan would take three months, and each day of it Marina worried about the old woman. Cuauhtemoc, advised
by the priests of Huitzilopochtli, repeatedly refused to surrender, although he knew the city was dying of hunger,
thirst, and plague. Always in the camp of Cortez, Marina
stayed awake at nights listening to the terrible shrieks and
whistles from the war canoes and the deafening drum that
sounded from the temple of the war god whenever a new
heart was ripped from the chest of a captive or a head
severed from its body. Could one of these victims be Ciuacoatl?

Even worse were her fears for Cortez. He was the prime
target of the Mexican warriors, and so he was always at the
point of greatest danger. At the moment when he was actually seized at the great square of Tlatelolco she felt a
sudden tremor in her heart, although she did not see his
struggle with her own eyes. But when the din from the
Aztec warriors crescendoed, she knew that something terrible was happening. And then she saw him, blood streaming from one leg as he and two others were carried into
the courtyard where she was tending the injured.

At first she had eyes only for Cortez, and saw with relief that his wounds were not serious. Then she looked
quickly at the others. To her great dismay one of them was
Xochi! His chest was covered with blood and his right arm
dangled uselessly. They said he had struggled with the
warriors who were pulling Cortez from his horse and received most of the blows intended for his captain.

Cortez now pushed the other soldiers away and limped
over to Xochi. "You are making a habit of saving my life,
your majesty," he grinned at him, "I cannot be so indebted

to any one man. So, although you are the tecuhtli, I am ordering you to return to Texcoco. There you can have your wounds properly attended." Xochi was too weak to protest. They carried him to one of their canoes as Marina watched sadly, wondering if he could survive the loss of so much blood.

A second time that Cortez was pulled from his horse and nearly led to sacrifice, it was Cristóbal de Olea who saved him. This brave soldier paid for his heroism with his own life. Still, there were others to take his place. Nothing ever seemed to stop Cortez, not for long. He survived all attempts to capture him in battle or to destroy him by treachery. There was treason on the part of his Tlaxcalan ally, Xicotenga the younger, who tried to desert him for the Aztecs. And in his own camp one of Narváez's men hatched a plot to murder him. Both traitors he ordered hanged, without a moment's hesitation.

Cortez was invincible, Marina thought, as only a teul would be. How else could she explain the taking of the great city of Tenochtitlan by a mere handful of Spaniards? At the very beginning of the siege there were only eighty-four horsemen, 650 soldiers with sword and shield and 194 crossbowmen and musketeers. At the end there were far fewer, and although Cortez had many Indian allies, most of these deserted when he seemed on the edge of defeat. Countless thousands of Aztecs were arrayed against them. Furthermore, the warriors of Cuauhtemoc often used the Spanish arms—lances and swords which they had captured—and planted sharp stakes in the water to ensnare and impale their brigantines.

Perhaps worst of all, by shrieking and howling day and night, they allowed no rest for the weary Spanish army. Even the wounded were obliged to fight; nearly every man had suffered some injury. Day after day the Aztecs threw the severed heads of captured prisoners at the attacking army, and each man knew that the next day one of these heads might be his own. Once they threw the head of a woman at Marina. She dared not look closely for fear it might be Metzli or Ciuacoatl. Like her friend Maria, she pretended indifference. And to add to all the other miseries, it was always raining.

The war ended when Cuauhtemoc was captured in his elaborate war canoe as he and his family were escaping from the city. That night there was constant thunder and lightning, with worse rain than usual. But the next day all the noise stopped, the shouting, the drums, the trumpets, the whistles, even the thunder. Suddenly they were all swallowed by silence, a silence so sudden that it was almost deafening. It was the 13th of August, just a year and a month since the terrible *Noche Triste* when the Spaniards themselves had fled from Tenochtitlan. Now the splendid metropolis of the Aztec people was burnt and in ruins, the streets and causeways choked with the victims of famine, disease, and battle. But the silence was of short duration. Among the Indian allies of Cortez, all the lake peoples who had borne the fearful yoke of the Aztecs, and especially the Tlaxcalans, their traditional enemies, wild jubilation broke out. The hated oppressor was no more. And then the beating of drums began again.

Yet Marina, who stood atop the great pyramid of the Tlatelolco market with Cortez and watched the capture of Cuauhtemoc, almost wept when he was brought before them and she translated his words of surrender. She had never seen the young Aztec king before, but in chains he looked delicate, and still very noble. He was the nephew and son-in-law of Moctezuma, but he bowed before them. "Take your dagger," he said to Cortez, "and put an end to my life. I have listened to the wrong gods. It is because of me that my city has been destroyed. Let me die with it."

Cortez refused. Very soon Marina would learn why the Aztec king was spared.

Now she begged leave to enter the main square where the Calmecac had been to search for Ciuacoatl. Cortez denied her request. "It is of no use, Marina. The Calmecac is gone. Do not blame me. They burned it themselves. But I cannot let you wander through the city. By my oath, you would be overcome by the stench of rotting flesh. Every house is full of corpses, vermin, and disease. This is not the moment to enter the city, but to leave it." Even as he spoke she saw long lines of emaciated women and children making their way out along the ruined causeways, some silent as corpses themselves, some moaning in despair. They had had no water or food for so long that they could hardly walk. Cortez grabbed her wrists and forced her to descend the pyramid with him. Then he pushed her into a brigantine which brought them to the lake town of Coyoacán. This was now the Spanish camp. It was safely beyond the putrid air of the city.

Within little more than a week Cortez had organized a great celebration. He took over the palace of the leading chieftain, and this was where the victory party was held. Wine arrived from Vera Cruz, as did a musician and his lute, some suckling pigs, and even a few Cuban women. There was singing, dancing, drinking, and brawling because there were not enough chairs or women for all of the men. Those soldiers lucky enough to have captured pretty Indian girls tried to teach them Spanish dances. Some of the horses that were brought into the patio and decked out with straw flowers were made to prance to the music. Father Olmedo discreetly absented himself from the celebration.

Marina left the great salon as Cortez laughed and joked with an admiring circle of Cuban women. He did not notice that she was gone. She hoped to talk to Maria, but the gypsy was being toasted and embraced by dozens of Spanish soldiers. Her daring exploits had made her one of the heroes of the conquest. Marina turned away. She thought of Ciuacoatl, who was probably dead, and of Xochi, who was himself between life and death. Where did she belong now? She made her way down a dimly lit hall, where a single torch flickered, past another patio and then to the palace entrance. There was no one to guard it. Every man among them was drinking and dancing. The danger was over. The great Tenochtitlan was theirs.

She walked out unobserved into the dark, muddy streets of Coyoacán. Again the skies began to pour down. This time she welcomed the beating of rain and the claps of thunder; they drowned out the raucous noise of the celebration. Yet no storm, no matter how fierce, could silence old Ciuacoatl's words that drummed now in her mind: "You will know great victories and defeats and you will be the downfall of us all. Death and destruction will always follow in your wake." Ciuacoatl was dead, but her words were alive, louder than the music and laughter, louder than the storm itself. She would hear Ciuacoatl's words as long as she lived.

TWELVE

The Loss of Friends—
and Enemies

*F*or the first few months after the surrender of Tenochtitlan, the palace at Coyoacán was the most important place in all of Mexico. It was here that Cortez lived and here also that the members of the new city council, the *ayuntamiento,* met. The palace served too as the prison for Cuauhtemoc and all the other leading chieftains, who were interrogated about the gold that had been lost on the *Noche Triste.*

Through Marina Cortez spoke kindly to his defeated rival, hoping that he would reveal where the treasure was hidden. When Cortez could not get the information demanded by the officers of the royal treasury, Narváez's men whispered that he was conspiring with Cuauhtemoc to keep all the gold for the two of them.

At first Marina could not believe that Cortez was powerless to prevent what was happening. "Do you know that they torture him, that they burn the feet of Cuauhtemoc with oil, and they tell me to help them? How do you permit this? *You* are king now, is it not true?"

Cortez, exasperated, seized her accusing hand. "Marina, there is only one king, and he is very far away. These men who torture Cuauhtemoc are agents of my enemies. They are very powerful in court. If I stop them, it will look as if their charges are true. I can do nothing to help

Cuauhtemoc, though as God is my witness, his suffering grieves me as much as it does you."

"But why do you not write this king yourself and tell him the truth?" She looked at him quizzically.

Cortez sighed as he pointed to the parchment spread on his writing table. "My dear, this is exactly what I am now doing, but they have the support of the Bishop of Burgos, and he is related to my enemy, the governor of Cuba."

"Bishop? What does this word mean?"

"Well, he is something like the high priest of Huitzilopochtli. He is the one the king listens to, at least most of the time."

"I do not like this bishop. And I am not sure I like your king, even if I must swear to obey him. He sounds like old Moctezuma. At least *Marina* shall not serve these friends of bishop. They will have to find someone else to help them torture noble Cuauhtemoc!" At that she made for the door. What she did not express to Cortez was her amazement that all the Spaniards, including himself, could quarrel so over the division of gold. Why did they value it so? And even more surprising was that they gave so much of the treasure many had died for to a distant ruler who had risked nothing.

Cortez, caught off guard by the sudden surge of independence in Marina, commanded her to stop. "Marina! You are beginning to talk like your gypsy friend! Where are you going in such haste?"

She faced him again from the doorway. "Must Marina still beg leave to retire?"

"No, no," his voice became mellow. "We have long since settled that. You are not my slave now; I will not make you serve these thugs. But pray tell me, my dear, why you flee from my presence? What is it you conceal?"

"I do not conceal. I try only to spare you worry. But since you ask, I received message that Xochi is much worse. So I now hurry to Texcoco with his young brother, Carlos. He awaits me."

"Stay, I will accompany you. I owe Don Hernando my life." Cortez buckled on his sword and threw a large velvet cape around his shoulder. They had hardly reached the courtyard when a messenger, arriving at a full gallop and splattering them all with mud, cried out to Cortez that he bore important news. Cortez's face clouded while he read the scroll which was thrust at him."Tell him I will come as soon as I can," he instructed the messenger. "Marina, Don Carlos, forgive me. I must attend to this matter immediately. I am informed that the Inspector-General of Santo Domingo has just arrived in Vera Cruz, by order of the king, to take over command of this entire country!"

Marina immediately guessed that Cortez was again in a perilous situation and would certainly have to fight this new Spaniard, just as he had fought Narváez. Would his countrymen never cease trying to destroy him? she wondered. But now Xochi needed her more than Cortez did. Without further words she and Don Carlos headed for the canoe that would bring them across the lake to Xochi's palace.

She found Xochi lying flat on his petatl on the wooden shelf that was his bed. His simple life style was still that of the Calmecac student she had known so long ago. There were two cotton blankets over his body, but he was shivering with cold. The wound that he had taken for Cortez in the battle at Tenochtitlan was finally claiming his life. It took all Marina's strength to hold back tears as she squatted beside him. He gazed at her with a serene expression. He had passed beyond pain. She bent over and held her face close to his to better catch the words he directed to her with feeble breath.

"Malinali, I am glad that you have come. I have been thinking of a plan for you. It is not too late to become my wife. I have always wished for this. If you marry me, Cortez will certainly appoint you ruler of Texcoco after my death. Do not fear my brother Carlos. He is a good man, and he has agreed to accept this decision."

She looked up at the younger brother who stood at a respectful distance from them. Don Carlos would not challenge Xochi's wish. He nodded in agreement. Still, she remained silent, not knowing what to say.

Xochi raised his head with great effort. "Malinali, Mother Ciuacoatl wished for us to marry. You remember her foretelling that someday you would be the ruler of many subjects? She meant it to be here in Texcoco, not in Painala."

Painala. She had not heard the word for many years. All that was so long ago. Before she met Cortez, before she became Marina. She tried to find words to explain this to him. But she could not. Finally she replied, "Xochi, I will gladly marry you, but you forget that we both are now Christians. We will need a priest to marry us."

"Then tell Carlos to return to Coyoacán and find one. Is there not one there with *him*?"

Carlos had heard and left the room immediately. Xochi and Marina waited, clasping hands, waiting for marriage or for death. The afternoon sun disappeared quickly as it does in late December, and now Marina felt the cold and dampness of the room. Finally she realized that there was no more pressure on her hand. In the shadows she looked down at Xochi. He still stared up at her face, smiling, but he did not speak. He had already gone. Was it to a Christian heaven, she wondered, or to the afterlife of the hummingbird warriors? It did not matter. He had gone to a place better than this one.

She kneeled at his side until Carlos returned. Father Olmedo and Cortez were with him. She was pleased that Cortez had come despite his new emergency. Candles were lighted, and all kneeled to pray over Xochi's body. Later he was buried with much ceremony, and Cortez named Don Carlos the new king.

Marina felt now that all her family, her people, were gone: her father; her grandmother and teacher; frivolous Metzli; and finally, the loyal, brave Xochi. Maria de Estrada and Bernal were the last friends she had left, but both were away on missions of exploration and conquest. Apart from her greyhounds, Marina had only Cortez, and he was so busy fighting the plots hatched by other Spaniards that she scarcely saw him. Her loneliness was intense. She withdrew into her quarters, brooding on the years of strife that had extinguished the world she once knew, and wondering if the new world that she was helping to make would be a better one. She swept her room many times each night and prayed, not knowing if it was Jesus who would hear her, or Quetzalcoatl.

A few months passed before her loneliness faded. It was early in 1522 that joy and strength returned to her life. She was with child! She would no longer be without kin in this world. Her child would be the son of the mighty warrior who had conquered the Aztec empire. He would be tall and strong like herself, graceful like her people, with her father's intense eyes and dark curls, and his authority. . . . But she hesitated. How would Cortez receive this news? Would he want a child? It would be a disturbance in his campaigns to pacify the country. Would he love a child with Aztec blood in its veins?

To her great happiness, Cortez seemed highly pleased at the prospect of becoming a father. He was in an excellent mood. The Inspector-General who had thought to wrest control of his domain had been sent back to Santo Domingo in disgrace. No military operation had been necessary. Luck was now on his side. He embraced her with greater passion than usual and insisted that she remain in

Coyoacán for the period of her pregnancy. Even more surprising, he offered to remain with her.

"We shall both stay here now and look to the rebuilding of Tenochtitlan, Marina. Is that not what you wish?"

Her joy was so great that she could not speak. But he understood. He cradled her on his lap and began to spell out his dream for her. "But the new city will not be Tenochtitlan. We will call it the City of Mexico in the province of New Spain. My friends at court write me that soon the king will appoint me governor."

"You are not governor now? Not king? What are you, Cortez?"

"I am still only a captain, my dear. I am just commander of the army. I rule only in military matters. But soon this country will be at peace. So you see, Marina, I *must* become governor. I have earned it, by my oath! How can the king not reward me in this way after all the lands and riches I have given him?

"And as soon as I am governor, I shall stay here to govern. I can let my good friends have the glory of discovering the unknown lands. Sandoval I shall send to colonize the northern provinces, and Alvarado will explore Oaxaca and Guatemala to the south. Then I will build a fleet of ships on the great South Sea so that we can find the riches of Cathay and the Spice Islands. This is something that all the others have dreamed of, from Columbus to my old enemy, Velasquez. But *I* am the one who will do it. If we are lucky, we shall even find the hidden strait that connects the Atlantic with the South Sea. Just wait, Marina, this son of ours will be so rich that someday he will marry the daughter of a king!"

"And which king do you mean?" she asked mischievously. "Cuauhtemoc?"

Cortez stiffened. "Marina, there is only one king in the world for me, and that is the King of Spain."

In the months that followed, Cortez's energy knew no bounds. He sent out parties to explore not only for gold, but also for tin, copper, lead, sulphur—all the minerals they needed to make their own arms and ammunition. The Bishop of Burgos had prevented outside supplies from reaching them, but news of Cortez's success had traveled throughout the West Indies, and now many adventurers were arriving to seek their fortunes by offering Cortez their services.

The new arrivals were often greedier than the original conquistadors and badly mistreated the peaceful Indians. Marina loathed them for their cruelty, but Cortez would do nothing about punishing them. Again they began to quarrel. Cortez found that he always had to defend himself against her accusations.

"I can do nothing to punish them because we need their services," he told her harshly. "This is a huge country to subdue and colonize. I cannot be too fastidious about those who choose to come. On my oath, I like them no better than you do. But the king provides me with no money to pay them. All I can offer is land and the labor of the natives who live on it." His tone was defensive, but laced with anger.

"So you enslave my people to please lazy Spaniards and a greedy king! Why do you not cast him off? He does nothing for you, only sends spies and overseers who come to steal gold. They are no better than the tax collectors of Moctezuma. My people died to be rid of them, not to have instead bearded vultures who eat us while we are still alive!"

Cortez placed his hand firmly over her mouth. "Marina, let no one hear you say such words! They would accuse you of treason."

Cortez avoided her recriminations by throwing himself

into the immediate task of rebuilding the city, and he did
not return to Coyoacán until late every night. Since he was
now accompanied by Aguilar, who had learned Nahuatl,
he insisted that Marina rest in the Coyoacán palace. The
construction, he said, was a danger for both her and the
child she carried. Many of the workers were killed by falling beams and rocks. It was dangerous for anyone, even
Cortez, to move through those avenues, choked with
stones and mortar and thick with dust. There were no
beasts of burden, and everything was brought into the city
on the backs of the enslaved Mexicans, or pulled and
dragged in with heavy ropes. Thousands of laborers were
involved in simultaneously pulling down what was left of
the old structures and building the new. Often the old materials—pillars and posts, parts of temples and pyramids—
were reassembled in new shapes. Supervised by Spanish
carpenters and masons, the Mexicans labored day and
night. Sometimes they sang, but more often they wept.
First they built an impregnable fortress to protect the city,
and when this was finished, they began work on lavish palaces for Cortez and the other Spaniards. They also built a
hospital and started construction of the Great Cathedral
of Mexico City.

Unlike all the other conquistadors, Cortez was determined to colonize the new land. He would not have it plun-
dered and abandoned, as the Spaniards were wont to do in
the islands of the Indies. He had to anchor his men in New
Spain, and so in addition to giving them title to hundreds
of acres of land together with the free labor of the inhabitants, he decreed that they must bring their wives from
abroad. But for himself, Cortez's policy backfired. Shortly
after the decree reached Cuba, he received notice that Catalina Xuarez, the women he had been forced to marry by
the governor of Cuba, was on her way to join him in Mex-

ico. He saw that Velasquez was plotting to put him in chains again—the chains of unwanted matrimony.

Although Cortez was one of the bravest men alive when it came to fighting Indians or other Spaniards, it was almost impossible for him to engage in open warfare with women. He knew that when Catalina found a pregnant Marina living at his palace, the scandal would reach even the Spanish court. He turned to his constant companion, Aguilar, for advice. It was easier for Cortez to discuss these matters with the worldy-wise Aguilar than the angelic Father Olmedo. His eyes brimming with sympathy, Aguilar listened to Cortez's admission of his unwilling marriage to Catalina, who also had powerful connections at court. Aguilar had heard this story many times before from others, but it pleased his vanity to hear it now from Cortez's own lips. He shook his head sadly and intoned, "There is no way out for you, my son. You must quickly rid yourself of this Indian girl."

"But, Father Jerónimo, how can I do this? She is carrying my son!"

"Are you sure it is yours? These Indian women do not have the same code of morals as our Spanish ladies."

Cortez said nothing, but looked offended. Aguilar quickly continued. "Be that as it may, she must leave the palace before your wife's arrival. You might easily get young Bernal Díaz to persuade Marina that the palace is not healthy for her child. So much bustle! So many strange people! She needs quiet. She would be more comfortable elsewhere. Let's see . . . Juan Jaramillo's quarters are far too large for a bachelor, and discreetly out of the way. I am sure he would be happy to share them."

Cortez's face brightened. "That is a capital idea, Father!" he cried. "Bernal has just returned with Gonzalo Sandoval. I shall send Gonzalo to greet Catalina at Vera Cruz and arrange for so many celebrations that her arrival here will be delayed enough to get Marina safely out of the palace and settled in with Jaramillo."

Jerónimo de Aguilar then scurried home to enjoy in solitary splendor the large bottle of sherry he had been saving for this occasion. He had at last put his Indian rival in her place!

Bernal, on the other hand, was far from happy with his assigned role. He could not defy his commander. That was far too dangerous. After several visits to Marina and many false starts, he finally suggested the new living arrangement as tactfully as he could.

"Then why does he not tell me this himself?" asked Marina suspiciously. Although Bernal was still her loyal friend, she knew that he obeyed Cortez in all matters.

"Oh, he will surely speak to you about this, but he is so busy with the restoration of Moctezuma's palace he thought I might discuss this with you first." Bernal pulled a loose thread on his sleeve. "He feels that larger and quieter quarters will be necessary for you and the baby. And you know the constable, Juan Jaramillo? Well, he lives alone—he does not need so much space. He will be delighted to have you stay with him. He says you can have all the high sunny rooms of his second story. From there you can even see the volcanoes. . . ." Bernal trailed off when he realized she was not listening and tried to steady his nerves with the exotic tobacco he had been given by Moctezuma.

A heavy, sweet smell from his pipe invaded the dark room. Marina, to all appearances busy in the corner with her embroidery, tried to ponder the true meaning of Bernal's message. Their silence was interrupted by the hurried footsteps of a messenger who burst into the room. Without seeing Marina, the newcomer blurted out to Bernal: "Sir, Señora Cortez has arrived and is waiting at the main gate! Shall we show her in?" Bernal was still lost in a cloud of euphoria induced by his pipe. At first he thought that the messenger was a phantasm. What he said was impossible! Catalina Xuarez was not due for several days. Sandoval could not have arrived so quickly. He turned his back and hoped the messenger would disappear. But the fellow tugged at his shoulder. "Sir, what shall I do with the señora? Cortez is still in the city and cannot be found." The rough hand of the young fellow brought Bernal back to his senses. Something had indeed gone wrong. Cortez would be furious. Now the whole shady matter was out in the open.

Bernal struggled to his feet and looked at Marina sheepishly. "Well, you now see the plain truth of the matter. I have got to get you out of here as fast as I can, I'm afraid. So please gather up your belongings and come with me."

She regarded him bitterly. "Yes, I see. I am now like Moctezuma. You imprison me in the quarters of the town constable. Or will I be like Cuauhtemoc and also have my feet burned?"

Bernal groaned and swayed on his feet. He would have fought a thousand Indians rather than face this righteous indignation. He had always cared for Marina and respected her intelligence and courage. But he was a soldier, under orders. His only dismal task now was to bundle her out a back door so that Catalina would not see her. He lurched toward her.

Marina had exceptional physical strength for a woman. She pushed him from her, abandoning everything, even the small garment she had been embroidering. "No, I will not leave by the rear entrance, like a slave. I will look upon the face of this new wife who banishes me from my home, and"—her gaze cut Bernal like obsidian—"this new wife will see Marina's face."

Bernal followed helplessly into the courtyard as Marina threw out her huge belly, making her condition thoroughly evident to the slim young woman waiting there with Sandoval. Their eyes caught as they examined each other with evident interest. Blond Catalina in her tight corset and her hooped skirts of grey velvet, her face framed with lace, was totally unlike anyone Marina had ever seen. The Spanish women with the conquistadors dressed in simple skirts or the same cotton armor as the soldiers. Marina had never seen a costume so preposterous and uncomfortable-looking as that worn by Catalina. And her face was so pale she seemed on the verge of death. "Well, *she* will not last long here," Marina thought with some comfort. Then she deigned to let Bernal fetch a litter and four Indians, who bore her to the mansion of Jaramillo. Purposefully she left the delicately embroidered garments for her infant behind.

Cortez did not dare to appear before her. He confined himself to sending messages which Bernal dutifully delivered. Cortez begged forgiveness and hoped that she would understand his situation. Also, under his commander's instructions, Bernal related to her the whole story of Cortez's enforced marriage in Cuba and how little he desired the presence of this official wife. He promised to visit her as soon as he was able.

Could she believe this story? With all her heart she wished she could. Cortez was her entire world, now that Xochi, Ciuacoatl, and all the others were gone. The Indians who served her regarded her as a Spanish woman, the consort of Cortez—and they feared her. The Spaniards still looked upon her as an Indian. Only in Cortez's eyes could she recognize herself as a whole person. But what if those eyes deceived her? She had seen how expertly he had lied to the Totonacs, to Moctezuma, and even to her. Could she ever fully believe him again?

The good Jaramillo turned out to be a perfect host. He often took his meals with Marina, and in a few weeks she was looking forward to their times together. Since Jaramillo had been the captain of a brigantine and fought in the siege of Tenochtitlan, they had many common memories. He was the only person to whom she talked, except for Bernal, who had never overcome his shame as Cortez's errand boy, and therefore stayed away more and more. So she clung to the presence of Jaramillo. He was a brave soldier, and he treated her with great affection, but she was still his prisoner. Perhaps Cortez confined her there for her own protection, or perhaps it was as punishment for flaunting herself before Catalina. She did not know.

Important officials came daily to discuss matters with the constable, and Marina often overheard the conversations. Catalina had protested, she gathered, that the household servants did not obey her. Jaramillo could not possibly remedy this since all Catalina's servants took their final orders from Cortez. Señora Cortez was always complaining; a daily stream of problems came to Jaramillo's attention but none like the one that rocked Coyoacán three months later. Marina, heavy and sluggish with child, awoke abruptly one morning to news of a scandal so shocking that it reached the Spanish court. The charges were against Cortez himself. The supposed crime had taken place on a rainy, windy All Soul's night after Cortez and Catalina had hosted a great celebration at his palace. Certain guests, all members of the Velasquez faction, reported that Cortez and his wife were quarreling openly and that she had retired early with a headache. In the morning she was found dead! Some said they saw marks of strangulation on her neck. Others claimed to have heard her scream. Still others said it was only the wind howling. But there were no witnesses who said they had actually seen Cortez murder her.

Neither Marina nor Jaramillo believed the charges. For Jaramillo, it was discretion not to believe them. As for Marina, she remembered her impression of Catalina on their first and only meeting. Even then she had looked on the doorstep of death.

It was at this very turbulent time that the child inside Marina chose to make his entry into the world. Juan quickly summoned a midwife and sent for Cortez. Still draped in his black cloak and the plumed hat that he was wearing for Catalina's funeral procession, Cortez came immediately after the burial. And how delighted he was to turn from mourning to the jubilation of a new life! The child was a boy, as he was sure it would be. Marina wished to call her son Hernando, for both Cortez and Xochi, but he insisted on Martín, to honor his beloved father. Jaramillo offered to be godfather.

After this it only remained for Marina to move back into Cortez's palace—or so she imagined. When she brought this up to Cortez, he turned very grave. "It is much too soon, Marina. It would only add to the scandal of Catalina's death." He looked to Juan for support. "You know she had what they call 'mother's sickness', a kind of epilepsy. Several of her relatives have also died of it. It often comes on with a headache."

Juan hastily agreed with this diagnosis. "I am sure it is as you say, Cortez. And you are right that Marina should not return to your palace. She is welcome to stay here with Martín as long as she likes."

"Thank you, my good friend, but she can remain only a short time. I fear she must leave soon because of the disturbances in Panuco."

"Is Velasquez behind this too?" Jaramillo inquired.

"Yes," Cortez sighed and stroked his beard. "He and Garay, the governor of Jamaica, and also Diego Colombus in Hispaniola, are preparing an expedition to conquer Panuco. They have already been busy stirring up the natives. Marina will be more needed than ever."

"But Cortez, what are you talking about? Leave now? What of our son?" Marina burst in at last. She was unable to contain herself any longer. "He is only a day old!"

Cortez finally acknowledged her, smiling and stroking the head of the newborn. "Martín will be well cared for. My servants will find him a wet nurse. Jaramillo will look after him. Besides, my dear, you will have a few days with Martín before we go."

THIRTEEN

Till Marriage and Death Do Us Part

*T**he Panuco campaign was as fierce and as bloody as any* that went before it. As usual, Cortez emerged victorious. By the time Garay reached the Panuco River in July of 1523, the province that royal decree had authorized him to conquer and control had already been settled by Cortez.

Marina would never cease to wonder how this man could pursue his plans for creating an empire far greater than that of the Aztecs and at the same time attend to so many details of the rebuilding of the land. Even during the campaign he ordered a new palace started for himself in Cuernavaca and another in Coyoacán. Nor did he forget his debts to old friends. While he was still fighting in Panuco, he ordered the civil authorities in Mexico to bestow upon Juan Jaramillo a large *encomienda,* a land grant together with the Indians who inhabited it. And when Marina returned from the expedition, she found she had a fine house in that part of Mexico City reserved for Spaniards.

For a few months she seemed to have all she could ever want. Although Cortez did not permit her to visit him in his palace, he frequently came to her with all the pomp and ceremony of a king, wearing his favorite black silk tunic and hose and his fine gold cross, his retinue of servants waiting outside her door. He pampered and fondled the infant; he threw him up in the air and caught him at the last minute so that he should learn courage. Yet not once could she turn their conversation to the subject of marriage. He had no wife now, but he did have a son. Why did he not speak the obvious words?

It was through Juan Jaramillo that she finally learned to face the hopelessness of her desire. Juan, quite unlike himself, was complaining loudly that because of Cortez's decree, he must now find himself a wife.

"And there is no one whom you would like to marry?" Marina asked boldly.

"That my lady will discover in due time."

"Oh, I see. It is secret. Then I will ask another question. Why does Cortez not obey his own decree and choose a wife himself?"

Juan smiled and said nothing. Was he sincerely her friend, she wondered, or like Bernal only the obedient functionary of Cortez? When he finally spoke, she thought she knew the answer.

"Marina, Cortez is not a man like the rest of us. Surely you already know that. But let me tell you more. All his enemies, like Velasquez, owe their power to influence at court, and this influence they enjoy because of birth or marriage. So far, Cortez has no such influence. He is of a good Christian family, but it is poor and not noble. If he is to win the ear of the king, he must marry into one of these powerful families. So you see, he cannot please himself by marrying the woman of his choice. He must make an alliance as well as a marriage."

"Ah, I begin to see." Her eyes burned from holding back tears. "I thank you, Juan. You are a friend indeed."

"Marina, I should like to be more than a friend." Jaramillo brought her hand to his lips.

Suddenly she laughed. "You are the constable, Juan.

No one will arrest you even if you have no wife. Cortez will not have *you* thrown into jail!"

By summer's end she briefly took hope that Juan might be wrong and that the Spanish king would reward Cortez, even if he were not married to an important person. Because of the great treasure that he was now receiving from Mexico, King Carlos had finally made Cortez governor of New Spain with power to settle Panuco and anywhere else he chose. Now Cortez was no longer threatened by Garay, who soon suffered the loss of so many ships and men that he was almost powerless. Shortly before Christmas Garay invited himself to Cortez's palace. And again it was from Jaramillo that Marina learned of the meeting.

"Can you imagine, Marina, now that he has nothing to offer us, Garay proposes an alliance with Cortez based on the marriage of his son with Cortez's daughter! He is just like one of those Indian chieftains. . . ."

She was no longer listening. "Cortez's daughter! Cortez has a daughter? I thought that Catalina had no children?"

"Oh, I am sorry, Marina. I thought you knew. This is the child he had with a Cuban woman many years ago. I suppose she's about ten now. But of course Cortez humored Garay and signed the marriage contract. Maybe it was an act of charity because Garay died only two days later. They say it was pneumonia. The climate of your country is certainly not healthy for us poor Spaniards."

Marina's mind raced wildly. So Martín was not his only child! Not even his first child! Immediately she left Jaramillo and began to question her servants about rumors they heard at market, rumors she would have forbidden them to repeat a few months earlier. Some held that not only did his daughter, also named Catalina, live in the palace but her mother as well. She was a Cuban Indian woman whom he had named Leonor Pizarro. And in addition he had many Mexican women in residence, most of them given to him by chieftains he had conquered. It sounded like a veritable seraglio of Moctezuma resurrected on the sight of the dead monarch's own palace. No wonder Cortez did not wish her to visit him!

She struggled to disbelieve these stories, or at least to forget them. There was so much that was good and noble in her Cortez. He had written to the king to send him honest, humble friars to see to the conversion of the natives. The heathen priests, he wrote, in spite of all their defects, had not engaged in riotous living. Corrupt bishops and pompous prelates from Spain would make a mockery of the Indians' simple grasp of the faith. So the king, in order to humor him, sent twelve barefoot Franciscans who trudged through jungle and mountain passes for a month to make their way to Mexico City. When they finally arrived, Cortez, in his silk and velvet tunic, together with his richly clad captains, bowed to the ground and kissed their tattered robes. All the Indians were watching. It was the most moving spectacle that Marina had ever seen. Again hope rose in her breast. This man could not be judged as a mere mortal.

Yet the next day, it seemed, she was again staring at his clay feet. This time it was his wounded pride that demanded revenge when Cristóbal de Olid betrayed him at the instigation of Velasquez. Olid, whom he had sent to Honduras to explore a possible passage to the South Sea, decided to conquer the land in his own name and not under the banner of Cortez. It was exactly what Cortez himself had done to the governor of Cuba. But Cortez could not tolerate the comparison. He had worked and paid for his expedition, whereas Olid had arrogantly usurped a trust. First Cortez sent out an expedition to punish him, but when he received no word from its commander, he decided to do the job himself.

He had other reasons too for getting out of Mexico City. He could no longer bear the constant quarrels with the king's civil administration, which challenged his every edict. He hated their petty bickering. He was a soldier, used to command and used to danger which could be confronted head on with the tip of a sword. He could not engage day after day in verbal and legal squabbles with these scribblers. Although King Carlos had made him governor, he had also made it impossible to govern. Even Marina now no longer obeyed him. Worse still, she offered unsolicited advice.

"Do not undertake this voyage, Cortez. I never asked this of you before. But now I know it will be a disaster. I saw a terrible omen in the shooting star which fell to earth before my very eyes."

The veins in his forehead bulged. "What do I care for shooting stars? I am not Moctezuma. I make my own fate! What has happened to you that you so fear this trip? You are acting just like an Indian. You are not at all yourself now."

"And you, who are you? How can I know when you are yourself and when another? You are Quetzalcoatl and Huitzilopochtli, Jesus and your devil! And sometimes you are both at the same time. Though I have known you for six years, I do not know who you are."

"I am *Cortez*. That is enough. I am a free man who has no use for stars and omens and all that Indian mumbo-jumbo. Though you have the spirit to censure me, I know that you love me still, as I love you. And I need you now, so again you must come with me."

He had said it. He needed her. All the omens told her that this expedition would end badly, but it was useless to plead with him. Neither the stars nor the vulnerability of little Martín moved him. Aguilar had gone insane and was long since useless. Besides, she was his best interpreter.

She knew that her fate was sealed. So when Cortez moved out of the newly built city, taking most of his huge court with him, Marina was again by his side. Soldiers, horsemen, servants, scribes, clowns, dancers, jugglers, cooks and musicians marched along the causeway in a colorful parade. In the rearguard of the procession were Cortez's old adversaries, Cuauhtemoc and the other chieftains who had been allied to the Mexicans, together with their wives and children. This he considered a precaution against their fomenting an Indian uprising in his absence.

The vast caravan of more than three thousand people had reached only the town of Orizaba at the foot of the great volcano when Cortez made an extended halt to await a report from the capital. At previous stops, news had reached him of disturbances that broke out as soon as they had left. That part of his nature which was soldier and explorer urged Cortez to disregard these tidings and to go on. But the statesman in him feared that his old enemies were taking advantage of his absence to seize control of the government. For the moment he dared travel no further.

Marina and Cortez dined the first night near Orizaba at the large home of a local chieftain which had been given to him. She could hardly touch the succulent roast pig, prickly pears and frothy chocolate prepared by his favorite cook. "What ails you, Marina?" he addressed her at last. "You have eaten nothing. Shall I send for my doctor?"

"That is not necessary, Cortez. This time I know why I am not well. I am with child again."

His furrowed brow gave way to a broad smile. "That is wonderful news, my dear. I shall celebrate with a glass of *aguadiente*!"

"Before you celebrate, I must speak with you." She stood up, summoning all her courage. "Cortez, I have seen that García de Pilar is among your soldiers. He understands the Maya tongue, and his Nahuatl is very good —

for a Spaniard. So in truth you do not need me. I am not well, as you can see. I have decided to return with the messenger you await."

He refused to take her seriously. "Marina, stop speaking such nonsense. You know I need you with me for more than your services as my interpeter. What is it that you are really trying to tell me?"

Her voice dropped to a whisper. "Since you ask me to talk from my heart, I shall tell you. For many months I wish to tell you this. I do not want to have another . . . " she searched for the word, "bastard child! I do not want to leave my children whenever you say 'March.' I want to return to the city and to find someone who will marry me, someone who will give this child a name and make him a gentleman. I am not another of those women you can keep in your harem. I am a princess of the people you destroyed, but I am still a princess!"

He walked the length of the table to where she was standing and forced her black eyes to meet his. "Ah, so now the temper of this fine lady is released in all its fury! Yes, my princess, I understand your concerns. And do not think that I am indifferent to them. I have long considered that you should marry. I should have done this before. But now, as you say, is as good a time as any. Have you given any thought as to who the groom might be?"

"I shall choose him for myself. And because it is now *your* world, I shall choose a Spaniard." Did the thought of giving her to a fellow Spaniard cause him pangs of jealousy? If it did, Cortez revealed nothing.

"Not Jaramillo, by any chance?"

The question caught her off balance. "Well, perhaps, yes, since he has asked me to marry him. . . or at least he almost asked."

Cortez smiled broadly. Suddenly she suspected that it was he who had chosen Jaramillo for her in the first place, perhaps as long ago as Martín's birth. "Bravo! he is a clever fellow, that one! But of course, you *shall* marry Jaramillo. An excellent choice. I will give you away myself."

Maria was thunderstruck. She returned Cortez's smile with feigned enthusiasm. She did not love Jaramillo, and Cortez knew her so well that he could take comfort in that. By promoting this marriage Cortez would keep her most valuable services while avoiding responsibility for her future. It was an arrangement that suited him perfectly. Did it also suit her? Jaramillo had been kind to her. In the absence of Bernal and Maria, he had become her best friend. Certainly he would be a better husband than the fat Totonac prince chosen for her so long ago. She thought fleetingly of Xochi, and sadness overcame her.

She heard Cortez as if he were miles away. He was still exclaiming about her forthcoming wedding. "And for a dowry you will have that island that you like in the middle of the Coatzacoalcos River. It will make a good place for a honeymoon, heh? But you will have to take that later because of course you cannot leave this expedition. I shall order Jaramillo to meet us here. If he rides fast, it will take him only a few days. We will have time to prepare the wedding celebration."

As constable Jaramillo could not leave Mexico City for good until his term of office expired, but he did join them long enough for his own marriage. Upon his arrival he went immediately to see Cortez. Marina was not invited. When Cortez finally summoned her to appear, everything was arranged. Had he told Jaramillo about the expected child? The subject was so delicate she could not broach it to him herself.

The wedding feast was served to hundreds of guests, Spaniards and Indian allies, on a huge, flat slab of a rock. It was almost as majestic as the towering peak of the volcano which looked down upon the celebration. Marina hardly ate a morsel and scarcely saw Jaramillo. During the two days he spent with them, he was nearly always closeted in with Cortez. There was more trouble brewing in the city; the king's treasurer and the royal accountant were quarrelling and had once even drawn swords against each other at a council meeting. Jaramillo was told by Cortez to warn them against further misbehavior and was dispatched to the capital. He was instructed to rejoin the expedition later at the town of Espíritu Santo, their point of departure for the unmapped and totally unknown territory of Honduras.

This city—which in Moctezuma's day had been known as Coatzacoalcos, and had been wrested from his control by other Indians and then taken over by the Spaniards—was but a day's canoe trip to Painala. Here was the very same Coatzacoalcos River that Marina had loved as a child, where she had come with her father and her monkey, Chitl. It was the same treacherous river which had brought her into slavery. And here dwelt her mother, if she were still alive.

But the first familiar face that appeared in Espíritu Santo was that of old Taabscoob, the prince of Potonchán, who had given her to Cortez. Now, of course, he expected a reward for his fine deed. He bowed before Cortez and reminded him of the great favor he had done.

"Ah yes, I shall always be grateful for such favors," Cortez answered, nodding to the old chief. "But if you wish to win even more gratitude from me, what I require is a map of the entire region to the south, because that is where I am now going."

"Surely he is not thinking of traveling by foot to what you call the land of the Fig Trees?" asked Taabscoob with evident disbelief.

"Yes," Marina replied. "Malinche wishes to know the

secrets of this land, whether it is rich in gold or other minerals."

"With all respect," Taabscoob hastened to reply, "tell him that it is rich only in water and marshes. Neither our own traders nor those who inhabit this land between the two great seas ever travel by foot, only by canoe. Our best advice is that Malinche should do the same."

Cortez was not so easily discouraged. "Our horses are useless in canoes," he muttered almost to himself. "Tell him that we shall look after ourselves. But he must bring us a map."

While they waited for the map and for Jaramillo, other Indian dignitaries arrived to kneel before Cortez. One of these was a woman, who covered her face and spoke in whispers.

"I cannot hear what this woman is saying," Marina told Cortez, "but she is speaking Nahuatl."

"Then tell her to remove that cloth from her face and speak up. I don't have time for such female tricks from my vassals."

Although the woman tearfully removed her shawl and bent her head very low, Marina quickly understood. It was her mother, Cimatl, old and wrinkled beyond her forty-two years, but Cimatl without doubt. When the woman realized that her daughter recognized her, she lost all control. Bending her head down to the stone floor, she beat her forehead, wailing, "Kill me, Malinali, for what I have done. Kill me, sacrifice me, my daughter! I deserve it."

Cortez was impatient. "Make her stop this, Marina, or I shall have her lashed. Is she some sort of idiot?"

"No, Cortez," Marina sighed. "She is my mother. She weeps out of shame for what she has done to me. It was she who sold me into slavery. But I know she has repented. In truth it was all the work of her husband, my stepfather."

"Then we shall deal with him. Have him brought before me. I shall do justice for you, Marina, even if it is tardy."

Marina lifted the kneeling woman to her feet. With her hands she tried to push away the tears, as she spoke softly, so softly that no one else heard. "Mother, it is all right. Do not cry. I forgive you. You knew no better. It is all right now. See how fortunate I am. I have become a Christian, I have found the one true God. I even have a child from this great lord you see before you. I shall not punish you. No, I shall reward you, mother, instead, for now I am a wealthy woman. But it will be otherwise with your husband. You must tell me where he is."

Gradually the sobs stopped, and the poor woman in turn embraced her daughter. "If I tell you, Malinali, will my son be safe? He is a mere child, only twelve."

"Yes, mother. He is innocent. He is the same age I was when you . . . ." She did not finish her remark. "I shall not blame him for his father's sins."

"Then I owe you the truth. Atlaua instructed me to say that he was dead, but you will find my husband at the temple of Huitzilopochtli. He is hiding there with the priests. They are all afraid that Malinche will sacrifice them."

On hearing this, Cortez had Atlaua seized together with the renegade priests, and the altar of the war god destroyed. Atlaua could hardly be distinguished from the others. He had allowed his hair to grow long and matted; his robe was dirty and blood-smeared, like those of the priests. In the course of years he had grown more fond of death than of women. He cowered before them, shielding his eyes from Marina's accusing stare.

Cortez busied himself first with the priests. "These butchers are not guilty because they lived in ignorance of the true God. I shall have them bathed and shorn, and then they will be worthy to construct a new house of worship for Our Lady. Marina, you will help brother Johann," he pointed to one of the Flemish Franciscan friars, "to instruct these devils in the true faith. But as for this dog of a stepfather, what revenge do you desire, my dear, burning? Decapitation? You shall decide."

She had been pondering this matter for several hours. Now she was ready. "No, none of these. I want only for him to understand what he has done. Once this man sold me into slavery. Now I wish him the same fate. Let him serve our men and follow us in chains. Let him feel the cruel bite of insects that he cannot ward off and the sweat in his eyes that he cannot wipe away. Perhaps when he has done penance enough, he can go back to my mother, if she will have him."

Cortez was delighted with her decision. "I see you have learned much wisdom from me, my child. It will be as you say. I shall give him to Cuauhtemoc and his friends as their slave. *They* understand captivity. Since their feet are still tender, perhaps he can help to bear their litters."

Cortez himself refused to heed the advice offered by Taabscoob. Although the Maya did give him a map, it was so vague it was almost worthless. No man, not even an Indian, had crossed that treacherous land on foot before. Juan suggested it would be better to leave Marina in Espíritu Santo, with her mother and the young stepbrother, now baptized Lazarus. But again, Cortez would not hear of it. "She is the only one the Indians here understand and obey," he said with some annoyance to Jaramillo. "She must come with us."

Their voyage across the Isthmus of Tehuantepec and the Yucatan peninsula was like no other campaign waged by Cortez. Before, their enemies had been men, Spaniards or Indians, and they could endure great hardships when they struggled against others of their kind. Now there was no one to hate, only the country itself. The land, if one could call it that, was all marsh, jungle and river. Often one could neither walk over it nor swim through it. Some river beds were so thick with mud that they could not be forded. Other times swift flowing currents dashed both men and horses against rocks and tree trunks.

In such a world without firm ground, roads, or even paths, with huge trees and jungle underbrush everywhere, their only guide was Cortez's compass. The Indians came to believe that this instrument possessed magical powers and could tell him all manner of secrets. For some of them this belief had tragic consequences. One of these Indians was the defeated emperor Cuauhtemoc.

It happened at some unknown point in that wilderness that Atlaua sidled up to a Spanish-speaking Indian and confided that Cuauhtemoc and the prince of Tacuba were planning treachery. He urged him to tell Cortez immediately that the two chiefs had been encouraging the peaceful tribes around them to fall upon the Spaniards and kill them all. Once Cortez was dead, Atlaua declared, they planned to instigate a mass uprising in Tenochtitlan. Not a Spaniard was to be left alive.

It was to prevent this very thing that Cortez had kept the king prisoner and always with him. Now, more than ever, lost as they were in the jungle, he could not tolerate the least disturbance provoked by Cuauhtemoc. He turned to Marina to uncover the truth of this rumor. She had done it so often before. But to his amazement she refused to interrogate Cuauhtemoc.

"The idea is impossible. Cuauhtemoc does not even speak their language. He is not such a fool as to attempt an uprising now. It would be suicide. I will not humiliate him further with your questions."

It was the first time she had treated his orders in this high-handed fashion. He was incensed with Marina and angry with himself for not being able to find his way out of the endless labyrinth of mud and water. Turning his back to her, he ordered the inexpert Pilar to interrogate Cuauhtemoc. Knowing that the Indians believed in the powers of the compass, Pilar informed the captive king that if he lied, the compass would let Cortez know. Cuauhtemoc, who was as tired of the endless wandering as everyone else, finally confessed to everything he was accused of. Marina listened to his mournful voice with a lump in her throat.

"Do what you will to me," the unfortunate king said. "I have known for these three years and many days that I have been your prisoner that all would end thus for me. You have given me a deceitful person as a slave. The story that he told your spy is untrue, but that is of no importance. Under different circumstances, I would have gladly done the things I am charged with. Ask your compass if you do not believe this. Now kill me as you should have done in the first place."

Pilar did not do justice to the words of the noble Aztec. Jaramillo tried to restrain her, but Marina broke loose from his grasp and threw herself at Cortez's feet.

"You cannot execute Cuauhtemoc because he wishes to be free!" she cried. "It is my stepfather Atlaua who has stirred up this trouble. If only I had asked you to kill him! He wants only to curry favor with you. But I *know* he is a liar. Cuauhtemoc surely speaks the truth and has done nothing treasonable."

Cortez was not to be moved. "Treasonable desires are treason enough, my lady. I shall do as my prisoner wishes and order his execution. But first we shall have our good friar Johann make one last attempt to convert him so that he can make his confession and his peace with God. As for the other fellow, I can also see that he has lied. He will join the others in this hanging."

Marina wept bitterly, "He does not deserve to die in the noble company of Cuauhtemoc."

"Very well, my dear. I grant you this. He shall be beheaded instead."

Atlaua was put to the sword on the last day of February, 1526, the same day that Cuauhtemoc and the prince of Tacuba were hanged from a ceiba tree. In spite of what Cortez later wrote his king, they made no confession. They had steadfastly refused to become Christians. But Marina tried to comfort them as best she could. She assured them that Malinche would look after their wives and families. Little did she imagine how well he would perform this obligation. Before they reached Honduras, Cortez had taken for himself Cuauhtemoc's beautiful young wife, who was also a daughter of Moctezuma. He had her baptized Isabel.

After the execution of Cuauhtemoc, Cortez withdrew more into himself than ever before. The one person whose company he sought out was Friar Johann. With Marina he spoke no more than was necessary. Again she was only his "tongue," but she performed her duties as diligently as ever. On the surface all that had changed was that she now slept beside her husband Juan instead of Cortez. She felt she had been returned to Portocarrero. Cortez had borrowed her for seven years only.

Often days passed without food. The few villages in these forsaken parts were frequently abandoned and burned by the fearful Indians before the Spanish, slogging through endless marshes, could reach them. They subsisted on roots and berries, turtles, iguanas when they could catch them, and small snakes. Marina was almost sure that she would lose the child she was carrying, and she almost hoped that it would be so. For if it were a son, would he not continue the enslavement of her people? And if it were a daughter, would the girl's life not be almost a repetition of her own?

In spite of her hardships, Marina still suffered less than most of the other Indians. Dozens were drowned in laying bridges across the rivers and bogs. In the journal he kept for the king, Cortez never mentioned their deaths, while he lamented loudly, and recorded, the loss of every one of his horses. If a mare drowned it was a double tragedy since she would never foal again.

One injured horse was abandoned in Itza territory where the local chieftain promised to care for him. Later Cortez found out that the poor beast had refused to eat the chili and turkey stew he was offered and had finally died of starvation. Terrified of the animal's magic powers, the Itzas had a stone statue made of him and began to worship the horse in place of the Virgin. After this, not another horse was abandoned. Yet by the time the Spaniards had crossed the terrible mountains of flint before reaching Honduras, half of their horses either had fallen from precipices or died from hoof wounds inflicted by the razor-sharp outcroppings. Cortez was beside himself with grief. Although all the people were starving, he halted for three days while their two blacksmiths reshod the surviving animals. Even then, the horses almost had to be carried by the men for they could hardly walk, much less trot or gallop.

It was in an abandoned Indian village that Marina's daughter was born. Jaramillo said that the baby was premature because of Marina's weakened condition and lack of nourishment. For this reason the birth was recorded as taking place on shipboard several months later. This pious lie was needed to confirm Jaramillo as father of little Maria. The true miracle is that she survived at all. By the time Cortez finally decided to return to the city of Mexico, at least half of the Spaniards were sick or injured and both he himself and Marina were shaking with malaria.

They had at last reached the town of Naco, the camp

of Cristóbal de Olid, when Cortez found out that his entire journey had been unnecessary. The first expedition had already located Olid, taken him prisoner, judged him, and chopped off his head. There was nothing more for Cortez to do but to return home, empty-handed.

Then, with the arrival of a ship from Cuba, he received news that the officials in charge of Mexico City had announced his death and taken over control of the country. His friends were being persecuted or slain. Everything he had struggled for was at risk. It was not Cuauhtemoc he should have feared, but his own countrymen. Together with the Jaramillo family and all of those too sick or weak to march, Cortez embarked for Vera Cruz in September. There was not room for all in one small ship. The others were forced to make their way back over the watery lands they had hoped never to see again.

The ocean voyage in hurricane season was another ordeal by water. Cortez, always a soldier rather than a sailor, suffered keenly during the tempests and near-shipwrecks that befell them. Marina, more seasick than ever, could not nurse her baby and struggled to keep little Maria alive with weak sugar-water. By the time they reached Vera Cruz, they were almost unrecognizable. Cortez's complexion had turned sallow and his stomach was bloated from hunger. Marina was skeletel. Her cheekbones jutted out and her eyes were dull with fever. She felt keenly that her end was approaching. To make matters worse, when they were borne from the ship in litters, they found that all their property had been confiscated by the outlaw government.

Cortez's quest to regain the power and the recognition that he felt his vast conquests deserved was to last the rest of his life. But Marina, as she suspected, did not have long to live. Once Juan's property was restored, they both moved back into his mansion in Mexico City.

Little Maria grew to have rosy cheeks like other babies, but Marina was never able to nurse her. Sometimes Cortez would visit, bringing the handsome four-year-old Martín with him. Although Marina missed this child with all her heart, she was happy to see that Cortez, too, adored him and would not part with him. "At least everyone knows that Cortez is his father," she consoled herself. Cortez also promised her that he would have the boy legitimatized, so there would be no stigma attached to Martín's name. Since he had several other illegitimate daughters, he was less interested in Maria. And besides, she was officially Jaramillo's child.

Apart from Cortez the only other person who visited Marina was Bernal Díaz, and this happened rarely, as he was usually busy on errands of exploration or settlement. Maria de Estrada had married another conquistador, Pedro Sánchez Farfán, and Maria was now living in the Indian town she had conquered, Tetela del Volcán, where Cortez had awarded her an encomienda. Marina was too proud to ask her friend to make the journey of several days in order to pay her a farewell visit.

In the twenty-eighth and last year of her life, Marina was alone with her servants, her child, and the surviving offspring of Galga, the greyhound. Like Chitl, the old dog padded after her from room to room as if afraid to let her out of his sight. Marina was this poor beast's world, but she, who had been accustomed to life exposed to the elements in all their splendor and their cruelty, found Jaramillo's mansion oppressive and tomb-like. She was so weak from her recurrent fevers that at times she could barely even walk to the courtyard. Jaramillo was nearly always away, either exploring or celebrating with his host of friends. Although Cortez was usually too busy combatting intrigues, writing letters, or planning campaigns to linger at her bedside, still she did not feel abandoned. Nor did she berate him for the briefness of his visits. She told him that she felt the presence of God with her always and was not alone.

Without her, Cortez *was* alone. At the very end, she called for Father Olmedo. Cortez came with him and was the first to enter her chamber. He kneeled by her bedside, kissed her hand with bewildered desperation, and asked for forgiveness. "I have used you ill, my poor girl. And for me it is worse that you do not even accuse me. . . ."

Her lips parted in a thin smile. "Accuse you of what, Cortez? You have given me fame, wealth, two beautiful children. Of what should I complain?"

"But I have never given you what you wanted most. I have never given myself to you, nor to anyone else."

"No, because you saw yourself as a god, Cortez, although you would not admit this. Yet it is only gods, not men, who make their own fate. I did not expect you to love me, as I did you, I, who was only an Indian and a slave."

"But Marina, I did love you, I do love you. I will never love another woman as I have loved you. But I did not deserve you. I thought I was a crusader for God and my king, but I know now that my first loyalty was always to myself, always to Cortez. I am a poor soldier driven by false gods — love of fame, wealth, position in society. You are above all this. You are wise, pure, faultless in body and soul. You are without vice or sin. You have nothing to confess."

Her colorless lips again parted. She had just noticed the grey that shot through Cortez's beard. She placed her hand in his. "You are wrong, Cortez. I have the sin of pride, just as you do. Aguilar told me this long ago. I shamelessly wished to rule over an empire when I could not even control my own heart. It is just as Mother Ciuacoatl said. I have betrayed my people out of pride. . . ."

"No, Marina. It was they who betrayed you, who sold you into slavery. They cast you out! Everything you did at my side was done because of love."

"That is true. First I loved Quetzalcoatl. Then you. Now I love God."

"There, you see, all this cannot be a sin, Marina. This is what makes you an angel, a saint. . . . Alas for my soul! If only I too could give the gift of such love. . . ."

"My poor Cortez, poor Malinche," she whispered and closed her eyes. Cortez could not speak. His voice choked and he wept without shame. With head bent, he left the room.

Although Marina then made her confession to Father Olmedo, she refused to see any physician, so no one ever determined the exact nature of her last illness. She died with the old greyhound at her feet and her servants in silent attendance. Cortez did not record the date in his letters to the king nor where Marina was buried. She simply ceased to exist sometime before 1528, the year that the conqueror of Mexico took little Martín and set sail for Spain.

Epilogue

J *ust as Juan Jaramillo had pre-*
dicted, Cortez bolstered his po-
sition at the Spanish court by marrying the daughter of a
count and the niece of a duke. With this lady, Juana Ra-
mirez de Arellano y Zuñiga, he had six children, including
another son also named Martín. He kept his promise to
Marina and had her son legitimatized by the Pope. Marina's Martín was said to be his father's favorite child, and as
his mother had done, he accompanied Cortez nearly
everywhere. Martín married a Spanish woman and died in
Spain in 1569.

Cortez, having been made Marquess of the Valley of
Oaxaca, but, to his great disappointment, not governor of
New Spain, returned to Mexico and lived there ten more
years, from 1530 to 1540. During this period he dwelt in
Cuernavaca as a great landlord, introducing many new
breeds of plants and animals into the country. Wearying
of a sedentary life, he also embarked on voyages of discovery, exploring the Sea of Cortez in Baja California as he
continued his search for a passage between the Atlantic
and Pacific oceans.

When he had expended his fortune in projects of discovery, and already in debt, he returned to Spain to appeal
to the king for support against the civil government of
New Spain. The local authorities treated him with disre-
spect and often contempt. In Spain he received no satisfaction from King Carlos who was, in fact, discomforted by
Cortez's enormous prestige and the huge moral debt he
was owed by the country. It was the policy of the Crown

never to let any conquistador become as popular and powerful as Cortez had been.

But Cortez, never discouraged, volunteered to fight in Carlos's ill-fated expedition against Algiers. Here again Cortez nearly lost his life, but received no appreciation from his monarch. Finally, despairing of success and broken in health, he determined to return to Mexico. He died in December of 1547 at the very start of his voyage back. He directed in his will that his body be buried in the chapel of the convent for nuns which he had founded in Coyoacán.

His will provided generously for all his children, including those he had fathered out of wedlock, and also left large amounts to charities for the native inhabitants of New Spain. Included with his will was a letter to his principal heirs questioning whether the institution of the encomienda, with its implicit slavery of the Indians, was justifiable from either a moral or a legal standpoint. He asked his children to study this matter and strongly suggested that they make amends to the Indians. It is clear that Cortez, in spite of his many ruthless actions, did in fact suffer pangs of conscience.

Whether this was also true of Jaramillo we do not know. He remarried almost immediately after Marina's death, and in his will he left nearly all the lands he had obtained from Marina to his second wife. He provided an inheritance of less than the legal minimum for "his" daughter Maria. Was this revenge against Cortez for being forced into marriage with his captain's mistress? If so, the final two years of Marina's life could not have been happy ones.

As for the other principal conquistadors, Maria de Estrada (who may or may not have been a gypsy) was also awarded encomiendas by Cortez of the Indian towns of Tetela and Hueyapan that she captured after many other soldiers had failed. Maria probably lived in Tetela del Volcán (State of Morelos) during the years of her marriage to Pedro Sánchez Farfán, one of Cortez's most trusted captains. At his death in 1536, she married Alonso Martín Partidor, one of the founders of the city of Puebla. Maria is said to have died here in 1545 during an epidemic of typhus. Her story has been forgotten, even by most Mexicans. But Bernal Díaz del Castillo was to become the most famous of the conquistadors, after Cortez, because of his classic *True History of the Conquest of New Spain* which he wrote when he was a very old man, living on his estate in Guatemala.

This would seem to be the end of Marina's story, but Mexico has never been willing to let her go. People in the Coazacoalcos region talk about her as if she were still alive. The island between the branches of the river they still call "Marina's Island." She continues to live in memories which are handed down from generation to generation, and also in popular legends. According to one of these, an original conquistador reported his terror on encountering the soul of Malinche wandering one night in the square where the old temple of Huitzilopochtli had once been. Another asserted that he had seen her at a crossroads in Texcoco. After this, people would glimpse her on dark nights, draped in long white robes, and fallen to her knees, her face covered, wailing long and piteously before hurrying away again to disappear into the great salt lake. Even her daughter Maria Jaramillo may have seen this ghost because there is a record of her having paid for daily masses at the Church of the Holy Trinity for the repose of her mother's soul. This the poor woman did throughout her entire adult life.

Thus the legend of *La Llorona,* the Weeping One, continues to permeate Mexican culture. She is said to be the soul of a woman seeking her lost children at every crossroad. Many of those who are familiar with the history of

Marina believe that she is still looking for Martín, who was taken from her as an infant, and Maria, who was barely two at her death. Perhaps, they say, she is still even searching for her monkey, the Aztec god of happiness, and the other animals which were lost so long ago.

Those who are more sophisticated believe that La Llorona is far older than Marina. She goes back to the very beginning of Nahuatl legend when she was thought to be Ciuacoatl, the serpent goddess or "Snake Woman." It is said by Father Bernadino de Sahagún, one of the original missionaries sent out by the king, that ten years before the conquest this ghost-goddess, draped in her own long white hair that reached to her toes, was the first to announce the fall of the Aztec empire. She appeared at night in the streets of Tenochtitlan crying out, "My children, we must leave here now!" And other times she wept, "But where shall I take you?"

Today Ciuacoatl has returned again to the realm of myth or legend. But Malinche remains as a curious creature, half legend, half reality. History records only the seven years she spent as the companion of Cortez. But this does not diminish her enormous importance for Mexico. Cortez once declared under oath that the greatest aid he had in the conquest, after God, was Marina. Without her remarkable talent in languages, her skills in diplomacy, her love and fidelity, he never could have conquered the lands and the people of the Aztec empire.

Pronouncing Dictionary of Indian Names

Pronunciation follows 16th century usage

Gods and Goddesses

Ciuacoatl. (See-you-ah-KO-ahtl). Mother goddess of the Aztecs, Snake Woman.

Huitzilopochtli. (Weet-see-low-POCH-tlee). Aztec god of war and the sun.

Kukulcán. (Koo-kool-KAHN). Maya god of wind, agriculture, etc. Similar to Quetzalcoatl.

Quetzalcoatl. (Kayt-zahl-KOH-ahtl). Toltec and Aztec god of the arts, the wind, the morning star, twins, agriculture, etc. Known as the Feathered Serpent. Also the name of many Toltec kings.

Tezcatlipoca. (Tez-cah-tlee-POH-kah). Toltec god of war and death. Also god of the night sky, sometimes symbolized by the jaguar or the Smoking Mirror. Huitzilopochtli is the specifically Aztec version of this god.

Tlaloc. (TLAH-lohk). Ancient god of rain and vegetation, common to most Indians of Mexico.

Human Characters

Aztecs

Atlaua.* (Aht-LAU-ah). Stepfather of Malinali.

Axayacatl. (Ah-shah-YAH-kahtl). Father of Moctezuma. Ruled 1469–81.

Cimatl. (SEE-mahtl). Mother of Malinali.

Ciuacoatl.* (See-you-ah-KO-ahtl). High Priestess of the Calmecac, great-aunt and teacher of Malinali.

Cuauhtemoc. (Koo-au-TAY-mok). Last Aztec warrior king of Tenochtitlan, ruled 1520–21.

Malinali. (Mah-lee-NAH-lee). Original name of La Malinche.

Malinche or La Malinche. (Mah-LEEN-chay). The Indian name of respect for Malinali, the daughter of an Aztec chieftain, who became mistress and interpeter of Cortez. The Indians also called Cortez by this name.

Marina. (Mah-REE-nah). The Christian name given Malinali by Cortez. Also Doña Marina.

Metzli.* (MEH-tzlee). Step-sister to Malinali.

Moctezuma II. (Mok-teh-SOO-mah). Aztec ruler of Tenochtitlan, 1502–20, and Emperor, or Great Speaker, of Mexico.

Nezahualcoyotl. (Neh-sah-whoahl-COY-ohtl). Philosopher and poet-king of Texcoco. Also spelled Netzahualcoyotl.

Nezahualpilli. (Neh-sah-whoahl-PEE-lee). Son of Neza-hualcoyotl. Father of Xochi.

Pitalpitoque. (Pee-tahl-pe-TO-kay). Ambassador of Moctezuma.

Teteotcingo. (Tay-tay-ot-SEEN-go). Father of Malinali, tecuhtli (chieftain) of Painala.

Tendile. (Tehn-DEE-lay). Governor of a Mexican province and ambassador of Moctezuma.

Tlazolteotl.* (Tlah-sohl-TAY-otl). Eagle captain from Painala who escorts Malinali to Tenochtitlan.

Tletelpotomki.* (Tlay-tehl-po-TOM-kee). Aztec ambassador to the Mayas.

Quetzaltotolin.* (Kayht-sahl-TO-toh-leen). High Priest of Quetzalcoatl in Painala.

Xicotenga. (She-ko-TAYN-gah). The elder is one of four rulers of Tlaxcala. The younger Xicotenga is a war chieftain.

Xochi. (SHO-chee). Full name is Ixtlilxochitl. Student and friend of Malinali. Later becomes Don Hernando Cortez, ruler of Texcoco.

Mayas

Chac.* (Chahk). Trader from Xicalango.

Chana.* (Chah-NAH). Slave in Mayab's household.

Mayab.* (Mah-YAHB). Wife of Tabascan ruler, living in the suburb of Cintla.

Halach.* (Hah-LAHCH). Son of Mayab.

Taabscoob. (Tahb-SCOB). Ruler of Tabasco, husband of Mayab. (His name was corrupted by the Spaniards into Tabasco.)

Xul.* (Shool). Second trader from Xicalango.

------

*Indicates that this character is purely fictional.

Places

Cempoala. (Saym-PWAH-lah). Totonac capital.

Cholula. (Cho-LOO–lah). Mexican city allied to Tenochtitlan.

Coatzacoalcos. (Cwat-sah-KWAAL-kos). Great river in the Isthmus of Tehuantepec. Also name of city at its mouth on Gulf of Mexico.

Coyoacán. (Koy-yo-ah-KAHN). Headquarters of Cortez near Mexico City.

Iztapalapa. (Eez-tah-pah-LAH-pah). Town at the entrance to one of the causeways connecting Tenochtitlan with the mainland.

Potonchán. (Po-ton-CHAN). Maya city on the Gulf of Mexico, ruled by Taabscoob and conquered by Cortez.

Tenochtitlan. (Tay-noch-tee-TLAHN). Capital of the Aztec empire and home of Moctezuma. Later becomes Mexico City.

Texcoco. (Tesh-KO-ko). Lake city of Aztecs allied with Cortez.

Tlaxcala. (Tlash-KAH-lah). Enemy city of Tenochtitlan, ally of Cortez.

Xicalango. (Shee-kah-LAHN-go). Maya town on the Gulf of Mexico.

Aztec Words

Amatl. (AH-mahtl). Bark of a tree, boiled, flattened, and used for paper.

Atlatl. (AH-tlahtl). Spear-thrower. The name Atlaua comes from this, i.e., he who carries the spear-thrower (used for the taking of wild fowl).

Besucona. (bay-soo-KO-nah). A small, brown wall lizard.

Calmecac. (Kahl-may-KAHK). Monastery and school for the nobility.

Chalchihuite. (chahl-chee-WEE-tay). Emerald-like stone.

Cihuapatli. (see-you-ah-PAH-tlee). "Women's medicine." An herb (*M. tomentosa*) used to induce contractions of the uterus.

Copal. (ko-PAHL). A clear white resin used as incense.

Huachinango. (ooah-chee-NAN-go). Red snapper (fish).

Huipil.   (WE-peel). Sleeveless   blouse,   usually embroidered.

Macana (mah-KAH-na). Wooden sword edged with flint.

Maxtlatl. (MAHSH-tlahtl). Loin cloth.

Metate. (meh-TAH-tay). Stone mortar to grind corn.

Nawal. (NAH-whal). A were-tiger (tiger man) of ancient Mexican belief.

Petatl. (peh-TAHTL). Straw mat, used for sleeping.

Pochteca. (poch-TAY-kah). A trader or merchant.

Pozole. (po-SO-lay). A porridge made of corn meal, water, and brown sugar which can be served hot or cold.

Pulque. (POOL-kay). A fermented drink made from cactus.

Quachtli (koo-ACH-tlee). A length of cloth.

Quetzal (KAY-tzahl). A beautiful bird much admired for its green tail feathers.

Tacalnagua. (tah-kahl-NAH-gwah). Aztec wizard.

Tecuhtli. (te-KOO-tlee). Chieftain, leading official.

Tececiguata. (tes-es-ee-GUA-ta). Great lady. Name given by the Mayas to the statue of the Virgin.

Telpochcalli. (Tehl-poch-KAH-lee). Military school for upper classes.

Tepuzque. (teh-POOS-kay). "Iron stick" or cannon.

Teul. (tay-OOL). Deity. The Spaniards were first thought to be teules, or gods, by the natives.

Tilmatli. (teel-MAH-tlee). Elaborately decorated cloak worn by men.

Tlacopatli. (tlah-ko-PAH-tlee). An herb whose root was supposed to restore strength. Often worn on the body as a necklace.

Tlatoani. (Tlah-to-AH-nee). Chief speaker, the title of the ruler of Mexico, Moctezuma.

For More Information

A *lthough there is a considerable*
bibliography available on La
Malinche or Doña Marina, there are few primary sources.
The one in which she figures most prominently is the classic work by Bernal Díaz del Castillo, *The True History of the*
Conquest of New Spain, translated by A.P. Maudsley (London: The Hakluyt Society, 1908–16). However, there are
many editions shorter than this five-volume work. One is
the Penguin classic translated by J.M. Cohen, *The Conquest*
of New Spain, which relates the history only up to the defeat
of Tenochtitlan. This is also true of the edition edited by
B.G. Herzog as *Cortez and the Conquest of Mexico by the Span-*
iards in 1521 (Hamden, Conn.: Linnet Books, 1988). Carlos
Fuentes, the Mexican novelist, has called Díaz's work the
greatest adventure story ever told.

Bernal Díaz's first-hand account of La Malinche varies
considerably from the brief mention of her provided by
Cortez's secretary, Francisco Lopez de Gómara in his *Cor-*
tés, Life of the Conqueror (Berkeley: University of California
Press, 1964) which was first printed in 1552. Lopez de Gómara, however, did not participate in the conquest, and it
was the paid secretary's version that Bernal Díaz set out to
correct when he wrote his *True History.*

A totally different version of the conquest, from the
viewpoint of the Aztecs themselves, can be found in a work
edited by Miguel León-Portilla which is called *The Broken*
Spears in the English version and is translated by Lysander
Kemp (Boston: Beacon Press, 1962). Its Spanish version is
entitled *Visión de los vencidos.* The original translation by

Angel María Garibay was from the Nahuatl language. Finally there is Cortez himself, who mentions Malinche briefly in his letters to King Carlos I. These are reproduced with copious notes in *Hernán Cortés, Letters from Mexico,* translated and edited by A.R. Pagden (New York: Grossman, 1971).

Further commentaries about Malinche can be found in carefully documented secondary sources such as *The Rise of Fernando Cortés* by Henry Wagner (Berkeley, Calif.: Cortés Society, 1944). There are also entire volumes about her, one by a descendant, Federico Gomez de Orozco, *Doña Marina, la Dama de la Conquista* (Mexico: Ediciones Xochitl, 1942). Like this latter work, most of the secondary studies devoted entirely to La Malinche have not been translated from the Spanish. However, the classic secondary source for the overall picture is still the nineteenth-century historian, W.H. Prescott. A convenient modern edition of his two-volume work, *The Conquest of Mexico,* is published by J.M. Dent & Sons (London, 1957).

For those interested in the anthropological material of the time of the conquest there are numerous sources. One succinct source is *Mexico Before Cortez,* translated by Willis Barnstone from the work of the Mexican anthopologist Ignacio Bernál (New York: Doubleday, 1963).

As for the Mayas, the National Geographic Society has published considerable well-illustrated material. The October 1989 issue of *National Geographic* magazine, with its leading article, "La Ruta Maya," brings the civilization up to date. The Maya civilization at the time of the conquest is dealt with in the primary account of Bishop Diego de Landa, edited by A. R. Pagden as *The Maya* (Chicago: J. Philip O'Hara, 1975).

For the Aztecs, the most comprehensive work in English is probably Jacques Soustelle's *Daily Life of the Aztecs,* translated by Patrick O'Brian (Stanford, Calif.: Stanford

University Press, 1961). This includes a good index and pronouncing dictionary. Some simpler texts and beautifully illustrated are *The Aztecs, Gods and Fate in Ancient Mexico* by Cottie Burland and Werner Forman, (Racine, Wi.: Golden Press, 1985) and *The Mighty Aztecs* by Gene S. Stuart (Washington, D.C.: National Geographic Society, 1981).

For those who can read Spanish there is a nicely illustrated book, full of Aztec poetry, translated by Miguel León-Portilla. It is called *Los antiguos mexicanos a través de sus crónicas y cantares,* last published by Mexico's Fondo de Cultura in 1988. There are also the large art volumes called *Historia de la Ciudad de México* by Fernando Benítez (Mexico, D.F.: Salvat, 1984).

Finally there are specialized studies of possible interest to some readers. One of them is *Aztec Medicine, Health and Nutrition* by Bernard Ortiz de Montellano (New Brunswick, N.J.: Rutgers University Press, 1990). For military historians there is *Aztec Warfare* by Ross Hassig (Norman, Okla.: University of Oklahoma Press, 1988). Another such study for Spanish readers interested in the role of women of the period is Anna-Britt Hellbom's *La participación cultural de las mujeres en el México precortesiano y postrevolucionario* (Stockholm: The Ethnographic Museum, 1967).

A number of general audience or juvenile books on the conquest of Mexico, Cortez, or the Aztecs and other Indian peoples can be found by checking the holdings of any library.

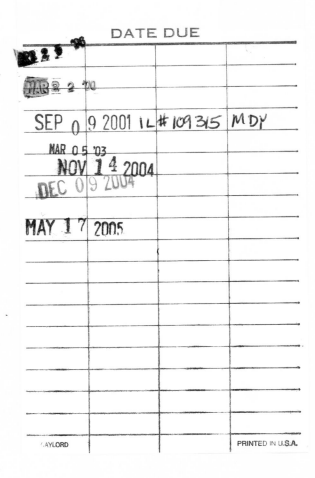